Caffei

All or Nothing

Garry Bushell

With

Craig Brackenridge

Fiction aimed at the heart
and the head..

Published by Caffeine Nights Publishing 2019

Published in Great Britain by
Caffeine Nights Publishing
4 Eton Close
Walderslade
Chatham
Kent
ME5 9AT
www. caffeinenights com

Also available as an eBook

British Library Cataloguing in Publication Data.
A CIP catalogue record for this book is available from the British Library

ISBN: 978-1-910720-94-3

Everything else by
Default, Luck and Accident

For Wilf, who opened the door

Acknowledgements

Garry Bushell: Thanks to Darren Laws and Caffeine Nights for believing in this book, and to Tania and Kate for their constant support. Cheers to absent friends, lost too soon, and to Whaley, Terry H and the Hoppers crew for keeping me sane and almost sober. Thanks to Tel, Tommy, Wattsie, Bev, Ashbo and Col. Much love to Julie, Danny, Rob, Jenna & Ciara...and the next generation, Harriet, Jesse, Molly & Avery. Stay free kids.

Craig Brackenridge: Thanks to Garry, Paul and Alan for bringing me in from the backstreets. Dedicated to I, P & F along with all the rockers, rogues and Soho sinners out there.

Chapter One: The Lion & The Elephant

It was 1966, a dull and wet Saturday afternoon in Hoxton, the historic core of London's East End. A dark blue Commer van sat stationary in a side street, decrepit and uninviting like an ugly aging toad. You wouldn't ordinarily look twice at such a rusting pile of junk. But, if by chance you did, you would probably assume the men inside were building workers, or maybe road diggers on a tea break. Copies of the *Daily Mirror*, the *Daily Express* and *The Sun* adorned the dashboard, along with a couple of thermos flasks and a large white paper bag full of cheese and pickle rolls.

Look a little harder you might also notice that the newspapers weren't being read, the food was not being eaten, the tea remained un-poured, and some of the crew were far too well-dressed to be digging roads.

Sitting directly behind the passenger seat was Steven Harold Knight, a 22-year-old with a passing resemblance to Steve Marriott from the Small Faces. He had the same haircut, but was six inches taller, broader and looked considerably stronger than the diminutive Cockney rocker. Like a million other men his age, Steve Knight was a mod. But not many of them could afford the Girard-Perregaux Automatic Silver Dial watch he wore so casually on his left wrist or his obsessively polished hand-stitched Chelsea boots.

The transistor radio on the dashboard was playing "With a Girl Like You" by the Troggs but Knight wasn't listening to it. He was lost deep in his own thoughts...

Respect. That was what today was all about. Knowing your place. Knowing who was top dog. Not taking liberties...It was a day to settle scores and not just on a certain hallowed turf thirteen miles away via the North Circular.

Without thinking Steve used his right thumb to tap each of the fingers on his right hand: *1-2-3-4, 1-2-3-4, 1-2-3-4, 1-2-3-4...*

On the radio "Black Is Black" by Los Bravos had taken over from Reg Presley. Steve glanced around the freshly stolen van's dingy interior.

There was a smell of diesel and paint from inside the vehicle and another unmistakeable scent – not of fear as such, more like nervous anticipation. Time to lighten the mood...

'Turn that shit off, Kenny.'

His brother duly obliged.

'Right, so this lion is chasing this rabbit,' Steve said in an accent so Cockney it could have been scraped off the counter of Tubby Isaac's eel stall. 'It goes down an 'ole and as the lion tries to follow it, 'e gets jammed. Now the lion's stuffed. He can't move his 'ead and his jacksie is stuck up in the air wavin' about. An' this elephant wanders past and thinks *why not*?'

Everyone in the van was now smiling. 'So bosh' – *BOSSSH!* – ''e gives the lion a quick one up the khyber. Well the lion don't like it, does 'e, and he starts wriggling and struggling and jerkin' about until finally 'e pulls 'is nut out of the rabbit hole. He's got the right 'ump, this lion, and 'e chases after the elephant. The elephant legs it into an expedition tent, where he sees a pith helmet and a copy of the *Sunday Express*. 'E puts on the 'elmet an' 'olds the paper in front of his boat. This lion charges in and roars "Oi mate, have you seen an elephant in here?" The elephant lowers the newspaper and says "You mean the one that fucked you up the arse?" The lion says "What? it's made the paper already?"...'

The van exploded in laughter.

'Bit later the 'unter, whose tent it was, goes to the doctor complaining of a sore arse. The doc examines 'im and says "My God, how did your arsehole get so stretched?" The hunter says "I got fucked by an elephant." The doctor says "There's a lot of that about. But 'old on, everyone knows elephant dicks are long but they ain't *that* wide." The hunter shrugs and says: "He stuck his finger in first".'

Now the men were in fits. The loudest guffaws came from the Spicer brothers, a pair of keen, thin-faced young middleweight boxers from the manor. They were good lads, Steve thought, and always happy to turn a blind eye to the Marquees of Queensberry's rule book whenever there was a decent drink in it. Like today.

The Spicers were bobbing about impatiently up front with Kenny, who was sitting across from Steve in the driving seat chewing so loudly on a stick of gum that it echoed across the metal roof.

Wrigley's had a slogan: Sealed Tight, Kept Right. That was just how this firm ought to be, Steve thought. It wasn't. Not yet. But it would be.

In the back of the nondescript van were Vic Naboth, Pat McVey, Matty Beeston and Roy Storer – the inner core of the Knight gang – plus Mo, Curly and Larry, three trusted older geezers known collectively as the "Three Stooges", who they had roped in for this afternoon's fun and games.

It was quite a team, but not one that Steve was entirely happy with.

He and Kenny had inherited the firm after their old man copped it. They weren't hand-picked. Apart from his oldest friend Roy, who he'd recruited personally, this lot had been passed down to him like family heirlooms. They'd had value once, but had been knocked about a bit. They were damaged goods.

He'd had this very discussion with Kenny earlier in the week. His brother didn't seem to mind, but Steve had a bolder vision. He wanted fresh blood, a whole firm in their 20s, just like the two of them.

Spank out the old, slam in the new!

Society was changing fast and with a new decade less than four years away he knew the whole crew had to be as dynamic and opportunistic as he was.

Most of the current mob had barely changed their hairstyles since they were demobbed.

With his hair gel, quiff, sideburns and ducktail barnet, Patrick McVey looked every bit the 1950s throwback. The Monday Club was less resistant to change. Pat, also known as "Mad Pat" was useful though. He was a big man with a short fuse and a cleft chin of solid granite; unshaven, with a stare that could strip wallpaper and a face like a clenched fist.

The sort of bloke who would give a bad dream nightmares. "Hulking" was probably the adjective that summed him up best.

Kenny looked at his watch. 'Half-time just ended.'

Steve nodded. 'Give it a few minutes.'

As they sat in silence, McVey reached inside his donkey jacket, pulled out a heavy Colt M1917 revolver and gave it the once-over.

'Do us a favour, Pat,' chortled Roy. 'Where did you get that fuckin' thing? Was "Wild Bill" Hickok having a closing down sale, mate?'

'What else are you packing, Patrick?' asked Matty. 'A blunderbuss? A cutlass stuck down yer almond?'

'Nah, he keeps that in his pantaloons.'

'Cheeky cunts,' snarled Pat. 'It'll do the fucking job, that's what counts, ain't it?'

He flashed two nicotine stained fingers at his detractors. Steve looked over at the three men and raised his eyebrows at Roy. 'I have to say Pat, it ain't gonna do much for our image, mate.'

'Fuck that, by the time they see it they'll be too busy wondering where their kneecaps went to pass comment.'

Pat jammed the gun back into his waistband under his jacket and out of sight.

'I make him right,' said Kenny. 'I don't care what we hit these bastards with as long as they get hit...hard. Our old man put up with these fuckers for too long and now they're taking the piss. If they think they can fuck with us up West then they need a reminder about who is in charge.'

Pat lit a Woodbine. Steve shook his head. Even his fags were out of time. Sighing inwardly he slipped his hand into the right pocket of his black Italian-cut suit. It was a year old but it still looked the business. There was a card in the pocket which he absent-mindedly caressed four times before taking it out. It was a business card bearing the legend Bernard Sternschuss, Diamond Trader, also known as 'Bernie the fence'.

That reminded him, the last time he'd worn this whistle had been at his father's funeral...

'I wonder what the score is?' said Matty, drumming his fingers impatiently. 'Can't we listen to the game on the radio for a bit?'

'Fuck the score,' Kenny snorted. 'Those Jock bastards are probably all in there, waving their little Kraut flags.'

'Yep, that's the point,' said Steve. 'While the Sweaty mugs are all glued to the box getting lathered, watching our boys kick a fucking Slazenger Challenge ball about with the Hun, none of them will be expecting company.'

'It's unpatriotic, that's what it is. Working on a day like this.'

'Shut the fuck up, Matt,' Kenny snapped. 'Just make sure you're ready for this or you'll never see Bobby Moore again. Ever! These bastards won't fuck about.'

Steve nodded. Kenny was right, the McCaffertys were a serious firm. But they had to deliver the message so clearly that a pair of pig-thick Sweaty cow-sons could get it. As of today, they were out of the uppers trade for good.

It was mod that had made the McCaffertys a problem. The gang were a loose collection of exiled Scots who operated out of a spit-and-sawdust boozer on Southgate Road in Hoxton. Barry and Iain "Tug" McCafferty had fled Glasgow in the late 1950s when they fell out of favour with Jock MacDonald, a mobster located in the north of the city. They ended up in the relative safety of the New North Road, a goal kick or two away from Shoreditch Park, and immediately started getting their fingers dirty in whatever murky business they could find.

Arrogant and brutal, the McCaffertys paid scant regard to the firms already operating in the area, and multiple confrontations ensued.

Many ended violently. The Jocks were ruthless bastards with their liberal use of cut-throat razors, the word rapidly got around – avoid this pair like the plague.

A dozen or so victims still walked the streets of London N1 bearing the slash marks of the brothers' "malky" – "Malky Fraser" being Glaswegian slang for "razor". They were a living reminder that messing with the McCaffertys was not good for your skincare regime.

As the new decade dawned the brothers chanced upon the amphetamines market. It had started small-scale but in '62, in Tug's words, it "'took off like Johnnie Johnson' as London's early urban mod elite spawned a mainstream, nationwide cult.

Mod fashion was the new cool and even kids in suburbia were into looking sharp and buzzing about on Vespas and Lambrettas.

"Little pills" officially known as Drinamyl were a vital component of the scene, dished out by quacks to bored housewives, depressive types and greedy bastards who needed to lose weight. These uppers gave users energy and drive.

Amphetamines powered the whole mod underground and were available in different forms. But whether they were French blues, black bombers, black and white minstrels or purple hearts – which were neither purple nor heart-shaped – the kids gobbled them up by the handful to make sure that there was never any chance of letting sleep get in the way of a good time.

The teenage "tickets" had no need of Morpheus, they were already living the dream.

By 1964, business was properly booming and the McCaffertys saw no reason to limit their operation to neighbouring Islington, Highbury and Canonbury. Mickey Knight had warned the brothers not to step on his toes by flogging their whizz on his patch up West but, although they'd agreed to his face, the bastards continued to take liberties and, for some reason, Steven never understood why his father always failed to take action.

That had to stop.

With their old man out of the picture, the Knights knew they had to make a clear statement of intent. The McCaffertys had been a boil on their necks for too long. Putting the Jocks back in their box would show the world that they were in charge and would no longer tolerate dissent from anyone on or around their empire. The "Scottish problem" was about to come MacScreaming *to an abrupt full stop.*

***

The streets outside The Jolly Farmer were remarkably tranquil for a late Saturday afternoon – unsurprising given the importance of the game at Wembley Stadium that was holding England's attention. It was the perfect opportunity to strike the McCaffertys at their most unguarded, the Knights had decided, and nothing short of total victory would do.

It was like 'Flodden or Culloden re-played on home turf,' Steve had said last night.

'What's soddin' "Floddin" when it's at 'ome?' Ken, who read less, had replied.

'It's still quiet out there,' Kenny said softly as he peered through the windscreen and looked up and down the street. 'It's got to be time now, Steven.'

His brother nodded.

'All right lads. Hands off cocks, hands on tools and whatever else you need, this is it.'

The tension inside the van thickened like the London smog as the mob tightened their grips on the array of weapons which they had brought along. It was an eclectic mix of chains, hatchets, clubs and coshes; plus Mad Pat McVey's antique firearm.

'You know the drill,' Steve continued urgently. 'Hit whoever is nearest and if any gutless wonder has it on their toes then let 'em go. Leave the brothers to me and Kenny. Don't hold back though, anyone who stands alongside those Jock cunts deserves what they get.'

'Yes, sir,' muttered McVey in a half-whisper that was meant to be heard.

Steve smiled but his eyes registered minus ten degrees Fahrenheit. Pat's tone, his manner, his irritating fucking presence, made Steve want to beat his fat, Neanderthal face until his knuckles bled. Instead he took a deep breath and tapped the leather cosh in his hand against his leg four times. *1-2-3-4*.

***

The Knight firm burst into the pub like an Atlantic storm. The dozen or so men inside were so entranced watching the football action on the small Perdio Portarama TV set perched up on the bar that it took a few moments for them to register that they were under attack. Barry McCafferty was closest to the door and Kenny took him out of the picture with a single swing of an iron bar. Barry fell badly and landed face down on the floor with his arm hanging loosely over an upturned bar stool. Kenny drove his weapon down heavily on the exposed limb and a sickening crack echoed above the escalating din.

Pat McVey's rusty pistol banged loudly twice and someone dropped to the floor with a flood of claret spreading across his trousers just above the knee. Pat fired again but the gun clicked impotently so he slammed the heavy weapon straight into the face of an oncoming foe, shattering his nose.

Pandemonium broke out as the Knight firm laid into punter after punter with punishing blows. A few "big jessies" legged it, but for the most part the McCaffertys' mob were a game bunch. Most of them chose fight over flight. Knives, clubs and razors were out in an instant and being put to work on the invaders. Preparation, coupled with the element of surprise, worked well in the Knight gang's favour however and the McCafferty cronies were soon leaving crimson patches on the pub's worn wooden floor.

Steve went straight for Tug, the older and most feared of the two brothers. He lashed out with his cosh but the red-faced Scotsman ducked surprisingly sharply and drove a meaty fist deep into Steve's guts.

Every ounce of breath exploded from Steve's lungs and as he bent over gasping for air Tug brought his knee straight up into his jaw. *THWACK!* Then his right arm curled around his neck and tightened into a headlock. Steve struggled, his lungs battled desperately for oxygen, his heart rate rocketed, his eyes stung with sweat. Tug increased the pressure. The room span, and everything drifted out of focus. The void beckoned.

Steve heard his name being shouted and there was a dull thud as Tug McCafferty fell to the ground beside him. The back of his head missed a four-inch shard of broken glass by less than an inch. Roy Storer had crowned "King Jock" with a billy club.

Steve fell too, gasping frantically for air as a sea of boots threatened to engulf them both. The whole room was locked in brutal combat. Steve used the last ounce of his strength to roll on top of Tug and push his fingers around the Jock's throat.

'Yer old man is long deid, Knight, and it's just business as usual for us,' hissed Tug as he struggled to loosen Steve's grip around his windpipe.

'It's not business as usual, you cunt. For you it ain't even business any more,' snarled Steve. 'If you even sell so much as an aspirin between Marylebone and the Embankment you'll be going back to *Glasgae* in a fuckin' wooden box.'

Deep within Tug's eyes Steve saw a flicker of defiance. He needed a final flourish to hammer his message home. The shard of glass was still in reach. Steve grabbed it up and dug it hard into Tug's cheekbone before dragging it down to the edge of his mouth, scarring the Jock the way that he liked to scar his victims.

Tug McCafferty gave a kind of gurgled scream. The glass cut deeply into Steve's fingers too, but he ignored the pain and kept going until the three-inch gash was complete. Tug writhed on the floor, cupping the wound with both hands. His blood was pouring through the gaps in his fingers.

Gulping the air greedily, Steve struggled to his feet. He could feel his own blood dripping from his fingers like warm milk, but the sight of Tug writhing on the ground gave him a rush of adrenalin that washed away the discomfort. He threw back his head and gave a primal roar then slammed the heel of his boot down on the Scotsman's groin.

Still dazed, Steve looked around. The McCaffertys' mob were far from done. They were going toe to toe and tool to tool against his gang. Matty was down but everyone else was still standing, though bald Curly was bleeding heavily from a deep cut above his left ear.

A ginger giant resembling an over-sized, partially shaved Yeti was writhing in agony on the pub floor. His legs were twisted like liquorice but Roy was still smashing away at his knee caps like an angry convict breaking rocks in the hot sun with a sledgehammer.

To his immediate right Steve saw Kenny and Rab Buchan, one of the McCafferty's cousins, rolling apart violently on the floor. The young Jock lashed out at his brother's left leg with a Stanley knife, tearing his Harry Fenton strides but barely cutting his flesh. Kenny clamped down on his wrist with his right hand and slammed Rab's head hard against the floorboard. This stunned him for the moment it took Kenny to roll on top of him and press his own blade against his throat. 'That's you brown bread, son,' he snarled, before knocking him spark out with a clean left.

All three of the McCafferty's top boys were out of the game.

Steve roared and re-joined the fray, smashing into anyone who stood between him and his firm. 'Back! Back!' one of the Jocks hollered as those of them still standing retreated and regrouped in a defensive semi-circle at the other end of the bar.

Steve snarled at them. 'You tell Pinky and Perky 'ere when they come round that if they give us any more shit, the next time we come back none of youse will get out alive.'

He helped Matty up from the deck and supported him as the Knight firm backed out slowly into the street. Inside the pub an eerie quiet descended. Over the groaning of the injured there was only the muffled sound of the TV which had been knocked off the bar in the melee and was now lodged in the sink behind the jump.

'Some people are on the pitch!' it boomed. 'They think it's all over! It is now...!'

***

Kenny and Steve had been up to mischief as long as they could remember. When their mother died giving birth to Steve, their dear old Auntie Eth had tried the best she could to steer them onto the straight and narrow but, with an old man like Mickey Knight, she was pissing in the wind without a brolly. The boys were still in short trousers when they started helping their dad unload hijacked trucks and deliver dodgy packages around the backstreets of Shoreditch.

Steve was a clever kid, much smarter than his father. He could have gone to grammar school, his teachers wanted him to, and so did Auntie Eth. But Steve insisted on going to the local secondary modern like Kenny had. It was where all his mates were going.

By the time he was thirteen, the brothers had graduated to liaising with Fred Prevost, a shop steward in Albert Dock whose network of dockers maintained a constant supply of stolen goods, mostly spirits and clothing. They sold and consumed some of the hooky gear themselves, but were more than happy to flog the bulk of it on via the Knight Organisation distribution network – KO'd *if you crossed them.*

A little later, he and Kenny were collecting the odd chunk of protection money and occasionally delivering bricks through the windows of some of Mickey's debtors. Once he had started shaving, school was elbowed and the boys entered the family business full-time.

They were a handsome pair of lads with a trail of broken hearts to prove it. Granted Kenny had a touch of the Henry Cooper about him, but Steve's matinee idol looks were responsible for more moist gussets than Adam Faith. When Mickey's business expanded into the West End in the early 1960s staying well clear of the Krays operations in Knightsbridge – the lads were in their prime, never less than immaculately dressed and always with that type of ready cash that attracted the crumpet, young and old.

After Mickey's unexpected demise last year, no one expected the boys to step up and continue the family business. That they had done so, with a vicious relish, silenced most of their doubters and detractors. But not all of them.

In the aftermath of the attack on the McCaffertys, Steve and Kenny had laid low for a few days in case of repercussions. None came and within a week they were back in action as a visible presence. The brothers made a priority of visiting all of the establishments which paid for their "services". The message got around quickly. It was business as usual.

Rumour had it that Tug and Barry McCafferty had been patched up and caught the next available bus back to bonny Jockland. The word through the grapevine was that their pub in Hoxton was still in a bad state of repair and was doing very little business. The Knights had achieved the desired effect but it had been a close run thing. Steve knew that if they were to avoid a similar outcome in the future then they needed to stack the odds more heavily in their favour. Vic and Matty were knocking on, and approaching retirement age, and although Mad Pat McVey was up to full match fitness his behaviour was becoming increasingly erratic.

The big man had never really accepted Kenny and Steve as Mickey's successors and was not shy of airing these views in public.

This needed sorting. Fast.

***

Pat McVey sauntered into the Dover Castle just as Chris Farlowe's "Out Of Time" started up on the Rock-Ola jukebox. *You're obsolete my baby...* Apt, thought Steve Knight. Very fucking apt.

'Turn that shite off,' Pat barked at Eric the barman, and then laughed when the little guy meekly ran straight over and unplugged the machine.

It was a Wednesday night but the boozer was deserted, save for Steve, Kenny, Matty, Vic and Roy who were plotting up around a table at the back of the room. Eric nodded respectfully at Pat before bolting the front door and disappearing out the back.

Around twenty bottles of ales – Mann's Brown, Bass Pale and Banks's Mild – sat on the bar next to a bottle of Johnnie Walker Red Label whisky and some glasses.

'Get yourself a sherbert, Patrick, and join us,' said Kenny with a welcoming smile.

'It's a closed shop tonight then, is it?' said Pat as he poured himself a large measure of Scotch and casually glanced back at the door.

'Just a bit of discreet business tonight, mate,' said Steve. 'I'm sure the local pissheads can survive for one evening.'

McVey grunted and glugged down some whisky before he plodded over to join the group. Steve surveyed him like a professional poker player eyeing up his hand. Pat was the hardest of them all, and also the hardest to like. Thickset and unkempt, McVey had an air of repressed violence about him that was never far from the surface.

Even his clothes bore a grudge.

The big man dropped down heavily onto a seat. Up close his face looked like badly laid crazy paving, a mess of scars – some from acne, some from knives and broken bottles.

'Did you hear Pat's got himself a new telly?' Matty said mischievously. 'A big old Pye set...'

'How much did that set you back, Pat?' asked Roy.

'Fuck all!' said Vic, laughing. 'He just walked into the shop, picked it up and walked out again. The geezer said "You can't do that" and what did you tell him, Pat?'

'Who's gonna stop me?' McVey said. Everyone chuckled. Then Pat looked directly at the Knights.

'What's this all about then?' he asked abruptly.

'We'd just like to thank you all for the past couple of days,' said Kenny. 'We know you've been busy out and about letting our "clients" know it is business as usual. It's been a rough week but things are going well, so cheers to you all.'

Kenny raised his glass. 'To us!' he said. The others tipped their own drinks towards him. 'To us!' they echoed, all except McVey who only grunted loudly.

'You all right, Pat?' said Steve as he caught McVey's eye.

'Of course...*guv'nor*,' said Pat. Nobody missed the side order of sarcasm that underpinned his reply.

Kenny spoke quickly in an attempt to steamroller a path through the bad atmosphere. 'Things are going well and we thought it might be time for a little expansion, maybe it's time to bring some new blood on board.'

'More fucking boys,' Pat mumbled under his breath.

'You got something to say, Pat?' said Steve sharply. His patience hadn't quite snapped but, like an unmarried mum with no change for the electric meter, it was half an inch away from breaking point. 'We're all ready for your pearls of homespun wisdom.'

McVey glared defiantly across the table. 'Do you think we need back up do you? What's the matter? Has yer bottle gone?'

Steve's complexion coloured but he remained in his seat, upright and staring McVey in the face. 'There's nothing wrong with my bottle, Pat.'

'Oh yeah?' hissed McVey. 'You weren't very lively the other night. Tug McCafferty had you on the deck right away. If it weren't for Roy here he'd have finished you off. You were fucking lucky to put him down.'

Steve was seething inside but he fought to keep a calm demeanour.

'Now come on, Pat,' yelled Kenny. 'You are fucking out of order.'

'You want to take over London but putting a few Jocks out of the picture nearly done you both in,' spat McVey. 'It's all fucking wrong, if your old fella could see you now he'd be pig-sick.'

'You old cunt,' yelled Roy as he leapt across the table and slammed his fist into the side of McVey's head. It wasn't the first punch McVey had received out of the blue and it wouldn't be the last. Although he staggered as he got up from his chair, he instinctively lashed out and caught his attacker squarely on the chin.

Roy fell back against the wall and onto the ground. McVey slid a flick knife from his pocket and clicked it swiftly into life. Steve and Vic pounced on him immediately and restrained him while Kenny grabbed his wrist and roughly shook the blade from his grip.

'You fucking ingrate,' Steve said furiously as he tightened his arm around McVey's neck. 'You'd pull a blade on your own firm? If my dad was 'ere you'd be heading straight down to Limehouse Basin wrapped in tarpaulin. Get the fuck out of 'ere and don't come back until you've sobered up, you psychotic tosspot.'

Vic released his grip on McVey and Steve shoved him towards the door. The big man staggered forward and regained his balance; then he stood his ground defiantly and glared around the bar.

'I'll go,' he snarled. 'But I'm telling you now I won't be fucking back. This firm is going down the crapper and I'm not going with it. There's plenty opportunity for someone with my reputation in this town.'

'Your reputation died out with the ark,' snorted Roy, still nursing his chin.

Steve had regained his composure and was smoothing out the creases in his Anthony Corbett suit jacket as McVey lingered near the door. He looked at him coolly.

'Just go home, Pat, sleep it off,' he said. 'Come back when you're ready.'

'I'm ready now, you flash cunt,' said McVey defiantly. 'I'll go but I'm telling you now, me and Knights, we're fucking finished.'

'Don't be daft, Pat,' said Kenny with a shrug of his shoulders. 'Where are you gunna go? You're one of us.'

'Not any fucking more. You can stick here with Lulu and the Luvvers, Kenny boy, but I'm done.'

McVey left the pub, slamming the door with a bang that echoed around the bar.

'He's a one-off,' said Vic by way of an excuse.

'Thank fuck for that,' sighed Roy.

'He'll be back,' said Matty.

'I don't think so...'

Steve Knight's words stayed suspended ominously in the air like a freshly hanged corpse at Tyburn gallows. No one answered him; no one met his gaze. Vic and Matty dropped their eyes to the floor. The others exchanged glances that ran from triumph to trepidation. For his part Steve attempted to look impassive. He knew Pat of old. He would hit the Scotch and pick fights with random mugs for a few days as he luxuriated in his own fury. And after that, who knew? Patrick McVey wasn't the type to go gently into that good night.

***

It was Steve who remarked that the evening air was 'as cold as Eskimo Nell's outhouse an' just as fuckin' damp', coaxing a grin out of his companions. He pulled the balaclava snugly over his face, grateful for the warmth that it offered. Kenny and Vic did the same. The three men were standing just inside the long tunnel at the end of Wheeler Street that ran beneath the railway line. Roy Storer was just a dark shape in the distance as he stood watch at the other end.

'Who plotted this delivery route?' said Steve suspiciously. 'Have we got a friend in the dispatch office over at the bond?'

'No,' said Kenny. 'They've been using this way for a while now, and have had no trouble. Like I always say, don't fucking strangle the golden goose. We've left them alone for a while so it has left us some nice easy pickings for tonight.'

'Do you still think this is a good idea?' Steve asked quietly.

'You getting cold feet, bruv?'

'No, but McVey was in on this. We don't want him sticking his fucking snout in or grassing us up.'

'Patrick's no rat,' sighed Kenny. 'That's not his style. I think it's a fucking shame. Having a younger firm is all well and good but Dad's old boys are known and respected. Better than that, they're feared. We could always use a human wrecking ball like Pat McVey. There isn't one of us who could have taken him down one on one.'

'He's a fucking dinosaur.'

'Maybe so, bruv, but dinosaurs ran the world for one fuck of a long time. Pat is fearless, and I'm telling you he ain't no grass.'

Steve snorted through the thick black wool that covered his face. 'I wish I could be sure about that. He's always been a wrong'un. He only married Edith coz he wanted a wife to beat.'

Kenny laughed; Vic didn't.

Steve glanced at Naboth. 'Have you seen him?' he asked. The words had an accusatory subtext, like a teacher waiting for a schoolboy to lie about his missing homework.

'Of course I ain't,' Vic replied angrily. 'I don't know where the fuck he is and I don't care.'

Steve grunted. An air of suspicion lingered in the air like a bad smell. Naboth clenched his fists silently in the gloom.

'Look,' said Kenny, 'He's gone and that's all we need to know. Last I heard he was over Millwall way trying to stir up business with some two-bob firm. Everyone knows he's finished round here, now shut the fuck up, I think I can hear something.'

A truck appeared in the distance and they all watched it approach. When it was just a few yards away, Matty emerged from the shadows and unrolled a rubber sheet across the road with a quick flick of his wrist. The thick black strip was embedded with six-inch nails which glistened for a second in the moonlight before the truck rolled right over them. The two front tyres exploded with a hiss and dragged the spiked track along the road before the whole vehicle ground to a shuddering halt against the wall of the tunnel.

There was a loud roar from the engine for a few moments as the throttle gunned wildly and echoed noisily inside the arches. Then it fell silent. All they could hear now was a hiss and some light clinking in the container.

'For fuck's sake,' Steve shouted. 'Talk about over dramatic. There'll be nothing but broken glass left in the back.'

'It did the job, didn't it?' snapped Matty as he ran towards them. 'You wanted it stopped, didn'tcha? Well its fuckin' stopped now.'

'Less fucking chit-chat,' ordered Kenny. Roy ran back through the tunnel towards them and Kenny barked, 'Get the Spicers to bring the van round. Roy, get up front and check out what state the poor cunt is in.'

The Knight brothers strode over to the back of the truck. The unmistakeable oaky smell of single malt livened up the night air.

'Oh, shit,' murmured Kenny. He lifted his bolt cutters up to the heavy padlock that was securing the door. The metal from the shackle clinked loudly as the cutters bit deep, and then the padlock fell onto the spirit-soaked tarmac. Steve pulled one of the doors open to reveal the booty. Result! At least two hundred cases of whisky were strapped to the sides of the container. Only a few had worked loose in the crash and lay shattered on the metal flooring.

Roy and Matty appeared behind the Knights and simultaneously whistled at the surviving stacks of liquid sunshine.

'See, I told you. No problems. The old ways are still the best,' said Matty smugly.

'Piss off,' laughed Roy.

He jumped into the back of the truck with Steve. Both men whipped out large butcher's knives and started to hack away frantically at the straps which held the cases in place. Tony Spicer backed their stolen van over the grass to the back of the truck then his brother Adrian – "Adey" – jumped out to join the others as they formed a chain to pass the boxes into their vehicle.

Steve kept his eye on the dark, gloomy road behind them as he passed the cases forward. The Old Bill he could handle, but if McVey rolled over the horizon with his new *compadres* then things could get very nasty.

'How's the driver?' said Steve, snapping himself out of his dark thoughts.

'He won't be picking up his pension, let's say that,' said Roy with a streak of gallows humour.

Steve felt a sting of regret. There was no need for that and no need to hurt civilians. He squeezed his left hand with his right four times, taking in a deep breath each time, then continued unloading.

Once they had filled the van, they slammed the back doors closed and ordered the Spicers to drive on to the address they had been given. It was the Knight family slaughterhouse, a small warehouse off Hackney Road which had long been Mickey Knight's safe place to store and divvy up ill-gotten gains.

Before the next day was done the whisky would have been sold on to a network of pubs and clubs...whether they wanted it or not.

Matty and the Spicers clambered into the truck while Kenny, Steve, Vic and Roy followed behind in another car.

The Knights were smart enough never to risk getting stopped by the filth in a truck full of stolen hooch, but the others seemed to neither know, nor care, about the potential consequences.

The road away from the hijack spot was empty, as they had expected it to be at this late hour. Even when they pulled out onto Bethnal Green Road the traffic was light. They stayed a respectable distance away from the truck but only the odd taxi, bin lorry and delivery van were on the road with them.

As they turned off the main drag onto Squirries Street the men noticed the unmistakeable blue light of a police car travelling slowly down the other side of the road towards them.

For a moment time itself seem to slow to a different pace. All of them tensed up but sat stock-still. The cop car decelerated, dropping to the sedate speed of a milk float as it passed the truck. Kenny pushed his head back against the headrest of his seat so that his face was obscured by shadow. Vic, Steve and Roy remained impassive. Heartbeats raced and fingers tightened around tools.

The vehicle slowed down even more as it drew alongside them, they could almost feel the coppers' eyes burning into their faces. *Keep going, keep going, keep going...thank fuck.*

The police car continued on past them, and then suddenly screeched away down the street at speed.

'I think the dozy cunts just heard about the whisky truck,' joked Roy as he expelled a deep breath of relief.

There was a brief giggle from everyone else in the car but Kenny was still watching the cops disappear in the distance. When the car was completely out of sight he whistled loudly and laughed, 'Dozy bastard filth, they couldn't find a cunt in a brothel, fuckin' ars...'

Before he could finish the sentence, a black Zephyr came screaming out of a side street with its headlights on full beam and, shrieking rubber, rammed directly and deliberately straight into them.

The nose of the car hit them right on the driver's side front wheel arch. The Knights' vehicle span with a force that smashed their heads into side windows and left the firm bruised, dazed and disorientated.

In a split second, three young men leapt out of the Zephyr and threw bricks through the car windows which shattered, showering the interior and everyone in it with shards of glass.

Just as quickly, one of the youths threw the entire contents of a tin of matt black paint over the windscreen while the other two slashed wildly at the tyres with bowie knives.

Steve kicked open the car door nearest to him. It clipped the heel of one of the young assailants, but didn't bring him down. The kid staggered for a few steps then sped up into a run. As quickly as they'd appeared, the attack team were gone, leaving their ruined Zephyr standing empty as its engine spluttered to a halt.

In the distance the sound of car doors slamming and a vehicle wheelspinning along the road could be heard.

Steve helped the others from the ruined motor and started to dust himself off. Kenny's car had been reduced to scrap and the Spicers were now out of sight, no doubt oblivious to the fact that they no longer had an escort. Steve spat a mouthful of warm blood onto the pavement and muttered a single word, 'McVey.'

The elephant had just fucked the lion.

***

When the Knights eventually reached the Hackney Road warehouse, it was as lifeless as a rural cemetery at midnight and just as eerie; it felt dark with something more than night, unsettling and foreboding.

From a distance everything seemed tranquil; no movement, no sound. It was only as the firm got closer that they could hear muted groaning from inside the building. Hands on tools, the firm edged slowly towards the entry. There was a small door at the side of the main shutter. Kenny jerked it open and then stood back quickly. The men's eyes strained into the murky interior, its blackness unrelieved by the distant street light; the groaning grew louder.

Steve slipped his hand inside and felt around for the light switch. The strip lights fluttered into life to reveal the only occupants – Matty and the Spicer brothers. The three men were lying flat on the cold, concrete floor, hurt and semiconscious. It looked as if some sadistic bastard had smashed a crate and a half of whisky over them. They were covered in broken glass and soaked in blood and alcohol.

The van was nowhere to be seen.

Kenny closed the warehouse door quickly behind them as the others tried to offer comfort to the victims. They picked the broken glass off their faces and brushed it from their clothes. They were a mess, especially Adey Spicer who looked like he had just undergone some bizarre tribal scarring ceremony. There was barely a square inch of the young boxer's face that hadn't been "decorated" with cuts.

'The dirty bastards,' Kenny growled. He kicked an upturned paint can across the room, strode over to Matty, bent down and gripped him by the collar of his jacket. 'Who was it, Matty, who the fuckin' 'ell was it?'

'Whoa, take it easy, bruv,' said Steve evenly as he tried to loosen his brother's grip and calm him down.

Matty gurgled *'Pagggh...'* and then he lapsed into unconsciousness.

Kenny Knight stood up, teeth gritted. His face was a furious crimson and his lips were so compressed that the flesh around his mouth seemed to balloon out. The sharp, bright light of the warehouse emphasised the veins on the side of his head which visibly bulged and throbbed.

Steve waited for his brother to speak but he didn't. He just stood there, fists clenched, breathing deeply and angrily.

'It was Pat, wasn't it?' said Steve quietly.

Kenny's reply was a long time coming but everyone knew what answer to expect.

'Of course it fucking was.'

Chapter Two: Up West

Kenny Knight sat at the end of the Embassy Club bar with Ted McKeeve, sipping a large Black Bull whisky and taking in the surroundings. A few tired looking showgirls hung around close to the stage puffing at their Player's No. 6. An ageing cleaner with wisps of powder white hair and skin that was creased like vellum swept the dance floor slowly.

'Look at that poor old bugger,' Kenny grinned. 'It looks like the broom is holding him up. What graveyard did you dig him up from, Ted?'

'He came with the club when my father took over after the war,' said McKeeve, a moon-faced northerner. His big bony hands spread over the bar like alien tentacles, which made it impossible not to notice his abnormally large knuckles.

'What? The Boer War or Crimean?' cackled Kenny. 'I've seen more life in a tramp's vest.'

'Old age my friend. It comes to us all.'

'Not me, son. Live fast, die young, that's me. Like The Who said, "I hope I pop me clogs before I get old."'

'Aye, Kenny, and what are the odds Moony, Daltrey and Townshend will still be at it in their 70s?'

Kenny shook his head. 'I just can't see that happening.'

Ted smiled. The older man knew exactly how to play Kenny; Steve less so. The younger brother was much harder to read, but at least they'd never fallen out.

Ted was a genial character with whisky red cheeks and hair the colour of Sloane Steel tweed, but for all his "hail fellow, well met" mannerisms he possessed the brain of a first-class diplomat. The McKeeve family had worked with the Knights for as long as anyone could remember. When supplies were tight during World War II, Mickey Knight made sure that the Soho clubs belonging to the McKeeves had never run out of alcohol. It came at an inflated price, but the McKeeve clan had always coughed up the necessary and consequently they had settled into a long, profitable and occasionally symbiotic relationship.

The Knights still sent through the odd shipment of cut-price, knocked-off booze but their main deliveries to the McKeeve nightclub empire these days were either of the sinewy or the more sensual kind. As well as the occasional loan of a debt collector, Kenny provided a steady stream of high-class call girls to service Ted's three establishments. The women kept the customers happy and, for a not unsubstantial amount of cash, they dished out hand and oral relief to willing participants in the clubs' toilets or in a discreet spot outside.

For anyone looking for a more fulfilling experience, Kenny made sure that the girls had access to a couple of small but plain lodging rooms nearby, neither of them equipped with red lights.

Steve Knight kept away from this side of the business. He found the trade distasteful, although he was quite happy to bank the cash. This arrangement suited Kenny fine; one of his greatest pleasures was "testing" the girls' attributes back at the small flat he had rented for himself in St Martin's Court.

'I understand you are looking for some new recruits?' McKeeve said cautiously.

'Who told you that?' said Kenny; his smile was now fixed but the twinkle had drained from his eyes. How had Ted heard about their McVey related problems? He hated the thought of the Knights' business being gossiped by every Tom, Dick and Harry. Even if he reluctantly accepted that it was par for the course, he was never going to encourage it.

'You know what it's like, Kenny, there's always tongues wagging in this part of town.'

Kenny grunted in disapproval and swigged his drink.

'Anyway,' McKeeve continued, 'I've got a member of the door staff you might like to take a look at.'

'What's that, Ted? A fucking bouncer?'

McKeeve poured out another dram for Kenny and himself then leaned forward conspiratorially.

'This geezer is a bit more than your usual doorman. He's an ex-army type, and not just a square-basher. He did hush-hush stuff in Indonesia and Aden. To be honest, I was thinking of moving him on anyway. I want troublemakers ejected from the club, not fucking handicapped.'

'He's not a nutjob is he? We've got enough problems with senile psychopaths.'

McKeeve looked surprised and not a little peeved.

'He's no lunatic, just ruthless. I'm not trying to foist the guy on you, mate. It's just...well, I think his talents might be put to better use than knocking seven bells out of my gin-soaked regulars.'

'Is he on tonight?'

'Yes, sure. He'll be on from eight. If you want to speak to him then you can use my back room.'

'No, I'll send Steve,' said Kenny with a shake of his head. 'He's more suited to the recruitment caper.'

McKeeve paused and sipped his Scotch. He had something to say but was looking for the right moment. Eventually he decided that the "right moment" might never come along and he broke the uncomfortable silence.

'We had Pat McVey in here the other night.'

'You what? And you never let us know?'

'He was only in for a couple of drinks and then he fucked off. I was glad to see the back of him. He came in with a bunch of geezers from Rotherhithe, or so I was told. A right bunch of scruffy herberts. I didn't say anything because I'm not sure where he stood with you. You hear rumours but...'

'He's fucking out, that's what he is, and if you see him in any of your joints you let us know.' Kenny was growling now.

'I don't want that kind of trouble in here,' McKeeve offered in a respectful tone. 'It's bad for business.'

'We won't fucking touch him in here. I'm not an idiot, Ted. You don't shit on yer own doorstep. But when a place develops a problem with vermin, it makes sense to send in a rat-catcher double lively.'

He stood up and slammed his empty glass on the bar. The sharp sound attracted the attention of the girls at the stage and even the old cleaner snapped out of his coma.

'Rotherhithe you say?' The word pronounced as *Rovverhive.*

Ted nodded.

'Connected to Charlie and Eddie?'

'I think not. No class. Just...'

'...South London wrong'uns! If you see him again you call me, right?'

McKeeve nodded again.

'Thanks for the gold watch.' Stony-faced, Kenny turned and stomped towards the door.

Ted McKeeve watched him go and experienced an unexpected feeling –nerves.

***

Steve Knight had been planning to come into town tonight so he wasn't too put out to take Kenny's call. He liked to let his hair down up West. Steve's teenage memories of Soho had an almost impressionistic quality; he remembered it as a dark, almost unknowable place populated by the scarred and wizened ghosts of the post-war underworld. Although the bright lights twinkled, everywhere you looked had appeared to be bathed in either grey or crimson red. And yet he felt drawn to the place; it excited him. It had an energy about it that he never saw in the kind of CIU and Con clubs his dad dragged him to, where Auntie Eth played bingo on a Friday night and old geezers drank stout.

It wasn't that he didn't like them – they were his people after all – but he had never wanted to end up like that. Steve Knight was destined for more and the West End was where he felt at home.

Soho had changed from his teenage years. These days, it was more like a kaleidoscope. The modern Soho was thriving and alive. The old faces were still there but so were a new breed of bright young things who dressed to impress and had firmly shaken off the cloying shackles of 1950s manners, morality and rationing book austerity.

The whole glorious square mile now pulsed with noise, music and the constant buzz of scooters and sports cars. Fashion was Soho's pulse but pop was its beating heart.

Steve paused just outside the Embassy and lit up a Player's Special Mild, taking in the spectacle that surrounded him.

He had spent many a night up West dancing until the early hours to soul and R&B at clubs like the Scene, which was now sadly missed, the 100 Club, The Flamingo – which called itself the Allnighter – and La Discotheque. He'd seen the Yardbirds at the Crawdaddy club in '63 and enjoyed them but he much preferred imported sounds from the likes of Sam Cooke, Clyde McPhatter, The Shirelles, Martha Reeves and the Vandellas, Booker T. & The M.G.'s... Sheer class.

For reasons Steve couldn't quite fathom, the music of Black America touched something deep inside of him.

A lot of other young working-class Londoners shared his passion. These were the mods, a tribe apart. Originally known as modernists, the mods were as hated by the courts and the media as villains were. Steve liked the scene and loved the sounds, but found the elite mods' intense attention to detail and ever-evolving fashions too much of an effort to keep up with.

He preferred a classic, smart look with a modern twist. A two-tone mohair whistle suited him down to the ground, the more fanciful colours and flares, that he noticed as the young pace-setters sought to distance themselves from the herd, weren't for him.

The in-crowd called themselves "stylists" rather than mods these days. They could call themselves the ponces for all he cared. As long as they bought his pills, Steve could not give a monkey's toss. But he knew his love of soul, of dressing well, and the mod's can-do attitude would stay with him until the grave.

***

It had been no big deal to detour to McKeeve's club. He wasn't convinced that Ted's "intel" would bear much fruit but there were worse places to start a Friday night.

He took one more lungful of his cigarette, flicked the butt into the gutter and went inside.

Ted McKeeve welcomed Steve with a broad smile and led him through a large pair of mirrored doors at the end of a corridor. The Starlight Suite was a seldom used function room at the back of the club and it had not seen the business end of a paraffin heater for some time. There were families of fur-clad Eskimos who would find it a bit on the chilly side. The bar shutters were down and only a few strip lights struggled to illuminate the cavernous space.

'Classy atmosphere you've got here, Teddy boy. Reminds me of a clap clinic.'

'Well I dare-say you'd have more experience of those places than I have, Steven.' Both men grinned. Ted paused and added, 'Kenny seemed a bit on edge earlier...

'Everything's fine, top of the world. You know Kenneth, he always gets a bit cranky when it's his time of the month.'

Ted laughed and gestured towards a small table that had already been set with a bottle of single malt whisky and two gleaming tumblers. Steve sat down and McKeeve walked back out. Less than a minute later, Arthur Bennett walked in and Steve rose from the table and welcomed him with a handshake. The doorman was tall and barrel-chested with a strong grip and a military bearing.

'Arthur? Pleased to meet you. I'm Steve Knight.'

'I know who you are.' Arthur Bennett was a big man in a bad suit that looked as if it had been bought off the peg in a drunken haze. He seemed uneasy in the clobber and that discomfort only added to his air of constant irritation. His natural blonde hair was cut short but was still thick and wavy and he had a bushy pair of sideburns which ended just below his ears. With a large chin, he resembled a pissed-off three-dimensional incarnation of Desperate Dan. Even when he was standing quietly there was an aura about him that suggested that this was a man who could blow his top at any minute.

Steve motioned to Arthur to take a seat and poured two thick measures of Ballantine's out into the glasses.

'Well this is nice, eh?' said Steve with an ironic smile. He raised his glass towards the large silent figure across the table.

'With the greatest respect, do you mind letting me know what the fuck this is about, Mr Knight?' The words came with an unspoken subtext of 'why are you wasting my time?'.

He was a good few years older than Steve and the words 'Mr Knight' spat from his mouth as if he was ejecting a gob full of mucus.

'Please Arthur, call me Steve.'

'Ok then, what the fuck is this about, *Steve*?'

'I'll keep it brief then...'

'That would be nice.'

Steve's hackles rose slightly. Awkward he could take, bad-tempered was cool too. But gobby would be a problem. For now he'd let it ride.

'What it is, Arthur, is strictly business. Our family is moving forward since the tragic loss of our father, may he rest in peace, and we are looking to expand our personnel a little. Some of our firm are getting a little close to retirement age and we need an injection of new blood.'

'Doing what exactly?'

'Doing what is required to keep our affairs in order...for which you'll make a fucking lot more than the peanuts you get doing monkey work on the door at this joint.'

Arthur's attitude was getting on his tits. Was he wasting his time here? He started to touch the fingers of his left hand with his thumb. *1-2-3-4, 1-2-3-4, 1-2-3-4, 1-2-3-4...*

Arthur noticed but didn't comment. 'You mean you want to pay me more than I'm getting at the moment just to hurt people on your behalf?'

'That's about the size of it, yeah,' said Steve with a shrug. This was going nowhere. 'There are a few other aspects obviously.'

'I'm listening,' said Arthur with a smile.

***

Arthur Bennett's reputation had gone before him. Word was the big man was a loose cannon, a tough nut, and generally hard to control. But as the whisky flowed and the barricades came down, Steve saw another side to him. The real Arthur was complicated. He was a good man with a dry wit, frustrated by where his life was going. He craved direction as much as he did stability. The army had given him both but hadn't satisfied his hunger any more than working the doors in central London ever could. His army training had also provided Arthur with a set of skills that were woefully underused. This was a man Steve could work with. He had to hand it to Ted McKeeve, he'd delivered a prime candidate for an apprenticeship.

Steve trusted his instincts and they had seldom failed him. In the same way that he had a feeling, even as a nipper, that there was something not right about Pat McVey, he now felt sure that Arthur was worth a punt.

'I think you'd be a good fit for us,' Steve said finally. 'I'd like to introduce you to the rest of the firm. Together we can go far.'

'It's a high-stakes business, then?'

'That it is.'

'And where are you heading? What do you actually want?'

'Want, Arthur? What do *I* want? I want it all, my friend. All or nothing at all.'

Arthur nodded, a faint smile playing around his thin lips, and raised his glass.

'All or nothing sums me up, Mr Kni...Steve.'

He held out his hand and they shook firmly. Steve picked up his cigarettes and lighter and packed them into his jacket pocket. Arthur cleared his throat.

'I don't suppose this recruitment drive of yours might extend beyond me, would it?'

Steve smiled. 'We might be in the market for more talent. Have you got someone in mind?'

'My mate Butch...Del Kelly...is looking for a career change and he might be worth considering. Things ain't been too good for him either since he left the forces. He's got a job up the Tottenham Court Road but he hasn't settled.'

'Where is he working? In a nightclub?'

'No,' said Arthur who turned his head and stared at the floor. 'In a butcher's.'

Steve laughed, he couldn't help himself. But he stopped when he noticed Arthur's face redden.

'With all respect, Arthur, I don't know if we really need anyone on the firm in a white apron unless 'e's on the square or capable of performing surgery, though I might be in the market for some of his tools.'

'He's a very handy man with a blade,' Arthur said persuasively. 'Very comfortable around bloodshed. He can make short work of any carcass if required.'

Steve's interest was piqued. 'Why did he leave the kate then?'

'It wasn't really his choice. He had a, eh...disagreement with a young Hooray Henry type officer, you know the type, followed by a visit to the glasshouse then a one-way trip back to Civvy Street.'

Steve nodded. If his instinct told him Bennett would be a good fit, why not trust the man's judgement and bring his mate onboard as well? The firm needed new blood to flourish and expand, and if his old man's old cronies couldn't see that then they would just have to move aside.

'All right,' said Steve, breaking the silence. 'You bring your mate along to the Dover Castle on Sunday. It's a pub just down from Bethnal Green station. Do you know it?'

'I know of it.'

Steve smiled and stood up from the table, smoothing his jacket down as he did.

'You bring Del the butcher along then. Just after seven. Tell him to leave his pinny at home though. I'll see you soon, Arthur. I think this could be the start of something special and don't worry about Mr McKeeve, I'll make sure you get a decent severance package.'

Arthur smiled and muttered a quick goodbye. The way Steve had said 'severance' had given him an unusual feeling. Part elation, part trepidation. For some reason an old Chinese curse sprang to mind – "May you live in interesting times".

***

Steve stepped into the Soho night air and paused beside his Vauxhall Victor to have a quick lung-full of nicotine and soak up the atmosphere again. It was the usual parade of sharp young types going somewhere and sleazy old cunts going nowhere. On a whim he left the car and walked down Old Burlington Street, turning left into Burlington Gardens, passing Savile Row and on to Regent Street when he stood stock-still and let the crowd wash around him like water around a rock.

Mostly the passers-by were tourists and out-of-towners, easily distinguishable from Soho's permanent population – the pimps, pickpockets, prossies, poets, pissheads, shifty porn merchants, small shopkeepers and pansies. You didn't need to hear the funny accents to tell them apart. The bad clothes, gaping jaws and gawping looks gave them away. "Grockles" his mates on the south coast called them; Joe Soaps from all over the country, down to see the capital's nightlife and lose their wages in the process.

In Soho there was any number of ways to part a billy – *a Billy Bunter, punter* – from their hard-earned. That's why Steve loved it. No matter if they were after a handful of pills or a blow job from a backstreet brass, it was odds on that some of that lovely dough would eventually roll back into the Knights' pockets.

Class mattered less and less these days. Most people could be divided into two distinct groups – the mugs and the non-mugs. Steve knew which one he was, but mentally thanked God for the fact that the former proliferated everywhere. One day in the not too far distant, the mugs were going to make him seriously rich.

Steve felt a warm glow in his stomach as he flicked his fag end into the gutter and started back towards his motor. The old jam-jar had been through more than a few of his adventures but he knew it was no longer the type of vehicle he should be seen in. He'd trade it in for an S-type Jag. If the Knights were to be seen as kings of the West End then they had better start fucking look the part.

Something caught Steve's eye. Or rather someone. A mod girl strolling along in a black and white polka dot mini-dress, with white boots that came up to just below the knees. She wore her blonde hair in a bob and she looked like class personified. She also looked vaguely familiar.

'Hey!' Steve shouted across the traffic.

The girl looked over and flashed him a smile that could have melted a cheese sandwich at thirty paces. Yeah, he knew that face, but from where?

'Steve! Oi! Oi!'

Steve had started to cross the road to catch up with her when a familiar Cockney voice shouted his name. He looked around and saw Roy Storer waving from the corner of Savile Row. When he looked back the girl had gone.

Steve waited, watching his friend saunter through the pedestrians. He wasn't alone. Roy was with a fresh-faced youth wearing a red James Dean, Jim Stark Cordura jacket and drip-dry denim jeans. The kid had thick, slicked back black hair and the arrogance that comes with looking great and knowing it.

'What you doing here?' smiled Roy. 'You ain't meeting big-arsed Beryl from Berwick Street again are you?'

'No, Mr Storer,' laughed Steve. 'Strictly business tonight. I've no time for pleasures of the flesh; I'm too busy getting some new blood on board to make your job easier.'

'Thank fuck for that,' said Roy, winking at his young companion. 'If I have to spend another night with that rotten bunch of old *see you next Tuesdays* we have now I'll go barmy.' The youth laughed and Roy took the opportunity to introduce him.

'Steve, I'd like to introduce you to Billy here. He's my Auntie Carol's eldest from up the Colville Estate.'

'Nice to meet you, son,' said Steve warmly. He shook the kid's hand and then thrust a thumb towards Roy. 'Are you sure you are related to him? You don't seem ugly enough.'

'Piss off,' said Roy as Billy chuckled quietly. 'How did you get on anyway? Kenny said you were up here looking for talent.'

'It wasn't a wasted journey, Roy, I'll say that; but we can talk about it down at the Dover.'

Roy's cousin nudged him. 'I was wondering...while we are at it, what would you think of Billy here joining us? He's a good lad. Dependable.'

Steve looked a little taken aback. Billy picked up on his expression right away.

'No, it's alright, Mr Knight, I understand,' said Billy quietly.

'It's Steve, please. How old are you, son?'

'I'm seventeen, Steve.'

'Christ, my Kenny's got string vests older than that.'

'I'm a good grafter, Mr...Steve. Roy's told me what to expect and I reckon I can handle it.'

'He's a decent boxer, Stevie. Junior champion a few years back,' said Roy. 'Don't be put off by his good looks, they just prove the little bastard's too fast to hit.'

Steve smiled but paused for thought. If things went to plan then they would have a lively new firm but things were going to get messy first, especially now that McVey had thrown his lot in with another mob. He wondered whether it was right to drag this young kid into all that. He looked fit enough but he also looked like he should be at school waiting for detention to end. He had a Marvel comic – the Avengers for Christ's sake! – poking out of his jacket.

He remembered though that he and Kenny had seen, and done, a lot of villainy even before Billy's age so who was he to starve the boy of opportunity?

'What do you want from life, son?'

Billy smiled. 'What do you want if you don't want money, Mr Knight?'

'Good answer. If you've got the dough-ray-me everything else follows, am I right? Okay fair enough, Billy. You come along with Roy on Sunday night and we'll see what's what then.'

They said their goodbyes but Steve had only got two yards away when Roy was back in his ear.

'Cheers for this, Steve,' he said quietly. 'You've made his day. The boy won't let you down.'

'I hope not, Royston, because it'll be your bollocks on the block if he does.'

***

You could have cut the atmosphere with a chiv. Vic and Matty sat nursing their pints in a corner of the Dover Castle while the three new boys sat opposite looking either slightly embarrassed – Billy and Butch – or, in Arthur's case, pissed off. Steve was at the bar with Roy and Kenny. 'What the fuck is wrong with Vic and Matty?' he said. 'They look like the East London branch of the Lingering Resentment Society.'

'For fuck's sake,' he shouted over to them. 'You lot need to join hands and contact the living.'

Steve turned his back to hide his smile. His heckling seemed to break the ice nearly as efficiently as the light ales did. As the pints and shorts flowed, the conversation from the corner became louder. Eventually laughs followed.

Steve had taken an instant liking to Butch. His face lean and weathered but his eyes were alert and his war stories were worth hearing. He and Arthur took about twenty minutes to win over the doubting duo with tales from their time in Aden, just as Steve knew they would because he'd heard their stories the day before and they were both truly sick and very funny.

'Squaddie humour takes some beating,' smiled Arthur. 'A lot like the fucking terrorists we snatched...'

When the evening was over and they all drifted off into the night, Steve and Kenny stayed behind for a lock-in.

'Well that went well,' said Kenny.

'It was touch and go for a while but I knew it was gonna work as soon as Arthur got them laughing.'

'Matty gave Billy no end of stick, asking if he'd be able to get up in time for his paper round. What a classic.'

'That was the funniest moment, that and when he bought him a glass of milk when he got a round in.'

'So, success?'

'That's the first hurdle cleared. They get on and they've clearly got potential. The next stage is to put those skills to the test.'

Chapter Three: Bricking It

The old Volkswagen campervan pulled up close to the pavement and came to a grinding stop. Arthur, Butch and Billy – nicknamed "the Baby Firm" by Kenny Knight, even though two of them were older than he was – spilled out right into the bustling heart of Aldgate's Brick Lane market. The vibrant melting pot of stalls, smells and sounds felt exotic. Even though the sun was starting to set, the activity on the streets showed no sign of abating. Some traders had their wares laid out on the pavement, shoes, handbags, women's clothes and the like. Billy watched an old Jewish stall-holder drawing a crowd to his crumpled mess of suit jackets spread out on a simple wooden barrow with his patter.

Billy smiled, but Arthur was clearly less impressed. Casting a distasteful eye over their surroundings, the big man wrinkled his nose as if he had just stepped in a freshly deposited cowpat at a cattle market.

'I hate this fucking part of town,' he said vehemently, and spat on the pavement to prove his point. 'Hardly no proper English left...'

'Well let's just do what we came for and get going then, shall we?' said Billy diplomatically. He looked down at a small slip of paper which had an address scrawled on it. 'I think it's just down here,' he said as he pointed to an old printer's shop a few doors down.

'You know what this is, don't you?' said Butch, readjusting his long coat slightly so that the machete he had slipped into his waistband was less noticeable. 'It's a fucking test isn't it? The brothers want to see if we're any good before we join the firm.'

'They never said that,' Billy pointed out.

'Yeah, but that's what they fucking meant, ain't it, Arthur?' Butch persisted.

'I don't care what it is,' snapped Arthur. 'It's got to be better than kicking posh pissheads with more money than sense out into the street for a living. As long as we get paid then I don't give a flying fuck, so let's get it done and get the fuck away from this khazi.'

They walked towards the shop front. Its large floor to ceiling picture window was covered in yellowing posters, peeling at the edges but completely obscuring their view of inside. The name emblazoned across the door said "Paterson's Printing" but the shop was a front for Mirko Falzon, a Maltese low life who traded in "white cargo", bringing young European girls into the country to work as tarts for his small network of pimps and madams.

The odd batch of printing creaked from the ancient presses in the back shop now and again but that was only to keep up appearances. All the locals knew that you were more likely to get a blow job inside than a freshly produced letterhead.

Falzon had paid Mickey Knight for the right to work his stable in certain spots around Shadwell, Bethnal Green and Knight territory up West. Since Mickey's demise, payments from the Malt had become increasingly erratic and in the last two months they had dried up altogether. The new recruits had been given strict instructions – persuade Falzon to agree to a new payment plan and bring back a healthy chunk of cash to cover his arrears.

Arthur opened the shop door and its old bell broke the silence. The three men entered and surveyed the shop. You will have seen tidier rubbish tips. It was rank. The serving counter was covered with unopened letters, strewn papers, coffee cups and unwashed plates with remnants of festering food. Filthy. From the rear came strange smells, smoke and gusts of raucous laughter. Billy shut the door behind them and turned the little sign on the window so that the word "Closed" faced out onto the street.

A stocky, middle-aged man with slicked-back silver hair emerged from the back shop and welcomed them surprisingly warmly. His sharp double-breasted suit bore no traces of printer's ink.

'Gentlemen, welcome! Mirko Falzon, what can I do for you?' he said with his palms outstretched as if he was welcoming them into a restaurant.

The trio stood apart menacingly in a wide arc.

'We are associates of Kenny and Steve Knight,' said Billy in a businesslike manner that belied his youth. 'We understand that you have some accounts outstanding. The brothers would like to give you the opportunity to correct this oversight. We are instructed to tell you that they are keen to re-establish the payments.'

Falzon smiled broadly but the bonhomie did not reach his eyes.

'Gentlemen, gentlemen. I'm sure there has been some mistake. If you could return to the brothers and inform them that I am no longer in need of their services then I am sure they will understand. The past is the past. I'm just a humble printer my friends, and the only business I am engaged in is legitimate. So I have no need for their type of service, grateful though I am for their continued friendship.'

Arthur pulled a large claw hammer from inside his jacket. 'Listen, you fucking Malt ponce,' he roared. 'You owe the Knights big time and you know it. Now get your fingers in that fucking Jack and Jill and hand over a down payment on what you owe or I swear I will nail your hands to that fucking counter.'

Falzon let his mask of respectability slip off his face. 'I pay Mickey Knight, not his fucking boys.'

'You'll pay us, you greasy wop cunt,' growled Arthur. 'New management. What was Mickey's now belongs to Kenny and Steve and that includes your monthly insurance contribution.'

'You'll get no cash from me, you bastards. Tell the boys that, *ux*? Now get the fuck out of my shop.'

'We've asked nicely,' hissed Butch as he slid the machete out dramatically from beneath his Crombie overcoat. 'Now we'll just take it.'

Unfazed, Falzon pulled an ancient shotgun out from under the counter and levelled it at Butch's chest. They all froze. Falzon laughed.

'You fucking amateurs. It's not going to be so easy with me, boys. You should have done your homework. And you really shouldn't have come down here on poker night.'

He turned his head slightly while still keeping his eyes on Butch and shouted into the back shop, *'Attakka! Ejja!'*

Six heavy-set dark-haired geezers burst through the door behind the counter. The three debt-collectors took a step back and braced themselves. Then the door behind them opened and another three sturdy Maltese men came in through the front entrance, cutting off their retreat.

They were unarmed, not that it made much difference.

Butch's machete made a few contacts, ripping flesh wounds into arms and bellies, but it was soon knocked from his hands. Billy was beaten to the ground before he could even reach for his weapon, while Arthur managed to hold onto his hammer long enough to knock one of the enemy spark out, but there were just too many of them in the small space and a fierce uppercut followed by a winkle-picker to the bollocks cut him down. He fell onto the filthy, stained lino where he remained curled into a defensive ball.

Angry men began to pound into all three of them with fists and boots, until Falzon started to shout above the racket. *'Dan huwa bizzejjed!* ***Biżżejjed!*** Enough! We want them taught, not killed.'

His mob dragged the blooded Baby Firm into the street and rolled them deliberately into the filthy gutter. Then, laughing loudly, the Malts uttered a few hearty insults in their own language, before filing back into the print shop and slamming the door shut, leaving the three outsiders face down in a steady trickle of rain water, dog piss and God knows what else, which at least washed away some of the blood dripping from their faces and staining their clothes.

The Knights' apprentices lay groaning while pedestrians hurried by them without stopping, pretending not to see or hear the blooded wretches. There were no Good Samaritans in this godforsaken part of town.

Eventually Arthur started to pull himself up from the ground. 'Well that went down like the *Lusitania*,' he said with a half-smile.

Butch gave a dull moan. Arthur got to his feet. 'I'm creaking a bit,' he said, as he helped Butch up. 'We could have done with our old SLRs in there, mate.'

'I'd have settled for a Mills bomb.'

Billy was still semiconscious. They dragged the younger man to his feet and began to stagger slowly together towards a parked van for a moment, almost holding each other up, and then their heads started to clear.

'Where the fuck is Malta anyway?' Billy groaned.

'South of Sicily,' grunted Butch.

'This ain't going to look too good,' said Billy. 'Going back to the brothers all fucked up and empty-handed.'

'Who's going back empty-handed?' demanded Arthur.

'Yeah,' agreed Butch as he turned to Billy. 'What fucking school did you go to? Ain't you never heard "if at first you don't succeed".'

'We can't go back in there,' protested Billy. 'There's hundreds of the fucking Malt bastards.'

Arthur touched a gash on his forehead gingerly as he looked at something across the street and smiled. 'Wrong answer. It's try, try again, Billy boy. Try, try again.'

***

Falzon and his mob sat around the broad kitchen table at the heart of the back of the shop. The air was thick with laughter and cigarette smoke. The playing cards had been cleared away and in their place were bottles of good Maltese hooch – Anisette and Bajtra shots, to be washed down with cold bottles of Cisk beer.

'Did you see their fuckin' faces?' Falzon laughed. *'Liema mazz ta 'telliefa!'*

'Losers!'

'Gidra!!'

'We've asked nicely,' Falzon's cousin Eugenio said with a grin, mimicking Butch in a high-pitched accent. 'They won't be back.'

'Maybe we should expand a little ourselves,' said Falzon. 'Take a look at some of these places the Knights are into up town...'

He raised his glass. *'Għall-kaptani l-ġodda!'* he said. 'The new masters!'

'The new masters,' the assembled voices echoed loudly. So loudly that they failed to hear the gunning of a diesel engine outside the shop.

What happened next was harder to miss. A hot-wired Post Office van suddenly crashed through Falzon's shop window showering the entire front shop with shards of glass and splinters of wood.

The impact sounded like a bomb going off. A cloud of dust swept through the door into the back shop, sending the men around the table into a panic. The Maltese mob were busy coughing and waving away the dust when Arthur's voice rang out.

'Delivery for Falzon...you spic cunt!'

A hastily constructed petrol bomb in a milk bottle sailed through the door and shattered on the floor next to the table, its freshly siphoned contents igniting into a ball of fire. The flaming liquid spread across the room and burned the feet and legs of the Malts who screamed and panicked, adding to the confusion. Spilt liquor on the table was set alight too.

Some men made for the back door while the others ran from the makeshift furnace to the safety of the front shop...where Butch, Arthur and Billy were waiting with pickaxe handles and clubs – their faces obscured by damp handkerchiefs covering their mouth and nose. They looked like old-time bandits from Hollywood's version of the American Wild West, with their very own Billy the Kid at the forefront.

The trio rained their weapons down hard on their fleeing Maltese opponents. Falzon, desperate to escape the heat and fill his straining lungs with fresh air, knocked over his own cousin to get out faster, only for Arthur to grab him by the scruff of the neck and throw him roughly onto the floor behind the shop counter.

The back shop was now almost totally ablaze. The flames were licking through the door and setting light to some of the posters on the wall.

'Arthur! Time to go,' shouted Butch.

'Not till we get what we came for!'

Arthur stuck the toe of his boot deep into Falzon's stomach. 'Where is that fucking cash?'

'There's no money,' groaned Falzon, almost delirious with pain. 'It's been a bad week.'

Arthur spat on the ground as the smoke was starting to curtail his breathing. 'Well it's going to get a lot worse.' He looked around for some inspiration then he tugged at the heavy cash register on the counter until it crashed down across Falzon's shoulders. The Maltese villain hissed like a burst tyre as every breath in his lungs was expelled. The drawer of the till sprung open and a handful of coins tinkled across the floorboards. Arthur bent down and scooped up every bank note that he could, including the ones that were stashed beneath the coin sorters.

'This is just a down payment,' he said.

Falzon did not reply. Only his groans could be heard above the crackle of burning timber.

'For fuck's sake, let's go,' yelled Billy.

Arthur jumped over the now smouldering counter and waved towards a gap in the window at the side of the van. 'Come on. We've got what we came for.'

Throwing their masks into the gutter, the men slipped through the crowd of onlookers who were gawping at the blaze, dusting themselves off as casually as they could to try and look like innocent passers-by. As they turned into the side street where they'd parked up their car, they heard the dull explosion of the Post Office van's petrol tank catching ablaze. The watching throng gasped loudly as if they were watching a high-wire act at the circus that had gone horribly wrong.

Arthur and Butch exchanged grins. 'Who needs Guy Fawkes?' smiled Arthur.

'You geezers are headcases,' said Billy.

'And the old Maltesers are stretcher-cases,' Arthur replied.

***

The trio laid low in a caravan park at Reculver, in Kent, where the Knights owned adjoining caravans for use as a bolthole. But there were no repercussions either from Falzon or the police.

On the fourth day they got the phone message via the guv'nor of the adjacent King Ethelred pub to head back to the Dover Castle.

Ninety minutes later.

'Here they are,' shouted Kenny as the three of them hobbled into the bar, still bearing visible marks from their debt collecting mission. 'The fucking bomb squad are back in town!'

'The wanderers return,' said Steve as he waved his arm towards a table that was already set up with drinks.

Vic Naboth and Matty Beeston were already sitting around it but they did no more than nod towards the three new arrivals. With everyone settled down, Kenny probed for more information on the attack of Falzon and his mob. He had never liked the flash Maltese bastard and he smiled broadly when Arthur relayed the full details of the violence that had been visited upon him.

'You did a good job,' said Steve.

'Even though you didn't leave much to protect,' laughed Kenny. 'I've heard Falzon has fucked off back to Malta and the whole fucking gaff is only fit for demolition now.' He paused for breath. 'Tell me, what was Falzon's poker face like?'

Billy mimed an expression of anguish and pain. Kenny laughed like a drain.

Steve looked a bit more serious. 'As entertaining as my brother finds all this, it is worth thinking about how we go about things. In this instance the "bull in a china shop" approach probably did the job and sent out the right message. But it has also cut off a nice regular earner so I don't think this should become a standard occurrence. It's always better to get a bit of dough before we spill some claret. I'd rather they were scared shitless and coughing up rather than on their Bromleys, or in a coma with their wallets shut.'

Arthur, Butch and Billy looked as deflated as a burst tyre.

'This can't happen again,' he continued solemnly. 'Arson, explosion, multiple casualties...that's going to get noticed. That's gonna start mouths flapping. That'll get the filth sniffing around. We need reliable people, sensible people on this firm; people who know how far to go and not a step further. And you, Billy, I don't want you getting into the 'eavy stuff too quick. I want you to liaise with our friends in the docks, Roy will make the intros. I'd rather you were handling knocked-off continental quilts than noxious continental cunts like Falzon...'

'Yeah, yeah, yeah,' Kenny chimed in. 'Now stop pissing about and put them out of their misery you big fairy.'

Steve smiled and offered his open hand across the table. 'But apart from that small oversight...welcome to the firm, boys.'

Backs were slapped, hands were shaken and glasses were raised and clinked. The mood became friendlier. Even Vic and Matty managed to crack a couple of grins as Billy retold selected highlights from the battle of Brick Lane.

Then Steve pricked the party atmosphere.

'You understand that was just for starters, don't you?' he said solemnly. 'Now it's time for the main course.'

Everyone looked suitably glum. Then Steve laughed.

'C'mon,' he said. 'Let's go up West and celebrate properly.'

***

They ended up in Walker's Court, an alley off the tail end of Berwick Street market. Steve knocked three times on a door which was opened slowly by a large black man, not much shorter than a lamp post, with a scowl that could turn milk sour. He took one look at the brothers and smiled broadly, displaying a mouth half-full of solid gold teeth.

'Well, well, the Knights,' he chortled in broad Cockney. 'And some friends! Come in girls.'

'Cheers, Tiny,' said Steve. 'I think Nellie is expecting us.'

'She better be. I've been turning billies away all night on account of a certain "private party".'

'That would be us,' smiled Kenny, slapping the big man on the back.

'Likkle more, walk good!' shouted Tiny in cod-Jamaican as he watched the firm follow Steve up the stairs to the first floor. The extraordinary Nellie greeted him immediately with a bear hug. She was a large, short woman of 55, nearly as round as she was tall, but her smile took years off her. Not that many men noticed it too swiftly as she also possessed breasts like Barnes Wallis's bouncing bombs.

'Steve,' she said. 'It's been too long. I suppose you'll be wanting upstairs...'

'Yes, Nell, can you sort out the boys?'

'Silly question!'

Nellie clapped her hands and six very naked girls came out of the adjourning room. This alone made Billy gasp. He'd never even seen one of them before. Two of the women were holding trays of bottled beer and Scotch which they placed on a small table.

'Sit down boys!' said Nellie.

The firm did as they were told and the naked women began to drape themselves around them. Nellie singled out one, a pretty brunette called Raquel, who was young and curvy with coffee-coloured skin and full lips, and pointed a long red finger nail towards the stairs.

Steve watched the woman climbing them slowly, admiring her perfectly arched back and her fine arse which was gyrating slowly to the sound of the Beach Boys' "God Only Knows".

'God almighty,' whispered Billy, half at the view, half at the fact that his cock had just been grabbed by Monique, an Afro-French stripper who was moonlighting from a strip club in Old Compton Street.

Steve half-ran up the stairs behind Raquel and came for the first of five times within moments of reaching the master bedroom. Three hours later and three orgasms in, he lay back and let his mind wander as she dozed off beside him. The smell of the women's reefers drifted up from below. The Beatles' "Rain" was playing downstairs on *Radio Caroline*; he could just hear it above the laughter of the firm as they partook enthusiastically of the many pleasures that Nellie's menagerie had to offer. The boys were happy. He was happy. Wasn't he? He had money. He had status. He could have whatever woman he desired... What more could he want?

A whole fuckin' lot. Steve Knight had ambition by the bucket. But for starters he wanted the hot blonde mod stranger whose face he visualised every time he reached his vinegar, and who, for the moment, seemed as out of reach as his big crazy dreams.

Chapter Four: South of the Border

The Rotherhithe mob were a loose collection of thugs, mugs and herberts who had tended to restrict their nefarious activities to their home turf – some light house-breaking, low-level protection rackets, dipping, working the doors and so on; a couple of their mums were on the game. That all changed the day Charlie Richardson had his collar felt on the day of the 1966 World Cup final.

The fall of the Richardson gang had switched on a metaphorical light bulb in the mind of Stuart "Stu" Blackmore. While the big cats were away, giving Her Majesty pleasure, the mice – better make that rats – would play.

Blackmore and fellow gang leader Reggie Glover, both ex-boxers, had targeted Eddie Richardson's fruit machine game to begin with. Racketeering and the scrap metal business would surely follow. They were hard bastards, who had cut their teeth minding Sir Oswald Mosley in the Kensington North by-election of 1959. They weren't afraid of any opponent, in or out of the ring.

Word of their expansion and ambition spread quickly around the London underworld and didn't take long to reach the ears of Mad Pat McVey. Blackmore and Glover aside, the Rotherhithe mob weren't particularly tough but there were a lot of them. They were effectively a small army, and one that someone like Pat, whose reputation was like a welcome mat in underworld circles, could first infiltrate and then command...

The Empress Of India sat right in the heart of the mob's manor in Rotherhithe New Road. The place had seen much better days, but its large bars had potential. When the landlord, Big Billy Truckle, had cut his losses and sold the place in March, Stuart Blackmore had snapped it up with the intention of turning it into a dancehall.

This wasn't set to be anything to rival Hammersmith Palais however, just a functional spit-and-sawdust joint where the local mod and teens could gather each weekend, dance to the well-known Stax, Motown and Blue Beat hits the DJ played, and fuck or fight depending on their luck.

***

Two vans pulled into the stretch of the road at the side of the Empress Of India, a back alley unblemished by pedestrians or street lights. The old guard of the Knight firm occupied the lead vehicle, a Bedford CA. Arthur, Butch and Billy shared the second, a Commer Walk-Thru, with a few chaps from the manor, a handy mob who loved a rumble and were happy to steam into anyone in return for a night on the pop in the Dover courtesy of the Knights. The Spicer brothers were usually top of this list but the lads had barely been seen since they left hospital following injuries sustained during Mad Pat McVey's attack on the Knights' slaughterhouse. The loss of the heisted whisky hurt a lot more.

This lot were younger than usual for a reason – none of them had any connection to McVey. All together, they were a dozen strong.

Kenny corralled everyone together behind the vans, out of sight of the venue, gesturing to them to keep quiet. Roy Storer unlocked the back of the Bedford and opened the lids of two large wooden cases packed with hammers, coshs, shivs, tyre irons, lengths of piping and other useful tools.

'Are you sure there's going to be anyone in there to do over,' Roy asked Kenny quietly as he took a pickaxe handle for himself.

'Do I look like a fuckin' amateur, Roy? Of course there's someone there. The tip-off I got was solid. Every Monday night they all meet up in here, regular as clockwork to divvy up the weekend's business.'

Roy felt the satisfying weight of his weapon in his black-gloved hands.

'Good. But it don't look too lively, Ken.'

'That's because they're doing the place up,' Kenny sighed. He pointed at a very small lit window high up on the building. 'See? Somebody's in, who do you think it is? The fucking holy ghost?'

Roy screwed his eyes up and thought for a second that he could see some movement inside the illuminated room. 'I think your snout was right, Kenny. There's definitely somebody there.'

'There had fucking better be, or somebody else will be getting a visit tonight.'

The fifteen men strode purposefully through the gloom towards the darkened building. Kenny's brief was simple – 'hit anyone in the joint and hit them fucking hard'.

The gang lined up against the side wall adjoining the back of the building. Kenny glanced round the corner into the alley that ran across the back of the Empress. There was one man watching the back door, a bald geezer in his thirties, built like a docker with arms like legs of mutton. He didn't hear Arthur coming. He didn't see the glint from his knuckledusters. He didn't feel anything until Arthur's fist rammed hard into the side of his fat head...although, had he still been awake he would have definitely heard the blood-curdling crack of the impact.

The watch-out fell and hit the ground like a sack of spuds.

The next sound was the creaking of the back door's hinges as Kenny opened it cautiously with his boot, just in case any more Rotherhithe goons were behind it. There was no one. So much for security.

They walked quickly but quietly through the back of the pub. The building seemed so still, so ghostly silent that even Steve started to wonder if their intel had been kosher.

As they passed through the deserted door and into the main hall, the extent of the refurbishment became clear. The place was a dusty mess, with piles of rubbish littered around, chairs stacked haphazardly at the back and sides, and workmen's tools scattered here, there and everywhere. Arthur helped himself to a hammer.

'We burn this down and we'll cause a hundred quid's worth of improvements,' whispered Roy.

Steve silenced him with a glance. The derelict room seemed to shudder around them. The stage was just as filthy, with the tatty remains of the dark, red velvet curtains that once hung grandly in front of appreciative audiences. The only living inhabitants appeared to be spiders. There were great net curtains of cobwebs everywhere.

The men exchanged glances. Steve gestured to them all to keep quiet and pointed towards a door at the side of the stage. A flicker of light emanated from it and faint mumbling could be heard.

As they moved towards it, Kenny produced a lemonade bottle from his jacket pocket and unscrewed the lid. The whiff of petrol was unmistakeable. He jammed an old rag into the neck of the container, and gave the gang a signal to stay put.

They tensed and gripped their weapons as he crept cautiously through the doorway into the near darkness. What came next was as exciting as it was inevitable. It began with the crack of broken glass, the quiet boom of fuel meeting flame and Kenny's thundering footsteps as he burst back into the hall with the Rotherhithe mob in close pursuit.

'Oi, Kenny,' Steve shouted. 'So much for reining it in!'

Loud, agitated figures came pounding down the smoke-filled corridor, coughing and spluttering and spilling onto the stage. They knew they were under attack and had improvised weapons in their hands, but their eyes were almost squeezed shut with pain from the flames and fumes. Half a dozen of the Knight mob set upon them furiously.

Through the melee Steve noticed Butch at the heart of the action, both Ghurkha Kukri blades whirling furiously and hitting their targets while his face remained as impassive as a cigar store Indian's.

Fury and fear of the inferno drove more of the Rotherhithe boys onto the stage. Butch was knocked off his feet by the sheer weight of numbers, joining the others falling or leaping onto the dance floor. They must have been fifteen, maybe sixteen strong.

The second wave of the Knight firm rushed forward and a full-scale ruckus erupted across the large empty space. Pat McVey was suddenly visible in the crowd, his face hard, scarred and ugly, like a bag of mistreated spanners. He scanned the crowd for Steve Knight, found him and headed straight towards him with a crowbar gripped tightly in his hand.

Before McVey could reach his target, Arthur brought him down with a heavy swipe of his hammer. The metal head whacked against McVey's shoulders and he fell to his knees with a cry of pain.

The Rotherhithe mob's two top boys did not seem to have any specific target in mind. Reggie had a leather-covered cosh with a short handle which was covered in East London blood before he even reached the middle of the room. Blackmore seemed to think he was Errol Flynn. He had an old sword in his hand but he was swinging it so clumsily that he drew claret from his own gang.

Billy caught him with a powerful punch to the temple that belied his size. Blackmore stumbled forward, his weapon falling to the floor with a clang. Reggie turned back quickly to protect his mate. His cosh hit Billy's face so hard that a three-inch wound split open like a ripe tomato.

Kenny dived in before Reggie's cosh hit its target again, driving the toe of his steel-capped boot hard into his enemy's groin.

Steve gestured towards Butch and they joined Kenny in pounding the Rotherhithe's top boys into unconsciousness.

Despite the hammering, McVey had managed to regain his footing on the increasingly blood-stained dance floor. He grabbed an old Dulux paint can and launched it at Arthur Bennet's head. Arthur instinctively ducked but the heavy tin clattered against his shoulder and the impact made him drop his hammer. Before Pat McVey could reach it, Matty rugby tackled him to the floor. The two old friends grappled together in the dust.

McVey's yellow teeth dug deep into the skin at the top of his ear. Matty screamed in agony, writhing where he lay. McVey leapt up again and kicked Arthur solidly in the jaw as he reached across the floor for his weapon. Before Arthur hit the deck, McVey was on Matty again punching him in the face. He then dragged him to his feet and launched him into a pile of chairs before viciously kicking his old pal in the back of his head.

Matty was out for the count from the first blow but Pat McVey continued to put the boot in savagely and mercilessly. From across the melee, Steve watched the attack in horror and mounting anger. Matty would be lucky to get out of this with a fractured skull.

The same thought seemed to occur simultaneously to McVey who stopped kicking and pulled a large steak knife from his jacket pocket. Without hesitation, he plunged the blade hard and deep into Matty's chest.

For Steve Knight, time seemed to go into slow motion. His mouth opened to shout but no words came out. Instead he watched a crimson arc shoot from Matty's body as McVey pulled out his weapon. He knew right then that it was too late to save his friend's life.

The concept of berserker rage originated with the Vikings and refers to certain warriors who were able to fight in an uncontrollable trance-like fury. When the rage kicked in, these berserkers were driven entirely by blood-lust. They could fight longer and harder than other soldiers. According to Old Norse literature, they were Odin's special warriors. To the enemy they seemed invincible.

Berserkers were said to go into battle wearing the pelt of a wolf. Steve Knight wasn't. He was wearing a suit. But in every other aspect, his wrath right now made him just as dangerous as any marauding Norseman.

Powered by anger and disgust, Steve dispatched the Rotherhithe thug he had been tussling with a single headbutt and, his adrenalin accelerating into top gear, he propelled himself through the mass of tussling bodies towards Pat McVey.

Nothing and no-one else mattered.

Steve swung his cosh at McVey's head with every ounce of his strength...just as another member of the Rotherhithe squad stuck his boot out and tripped him up. His blow glanced McVey's temple and Steve crashed onto the hall's dusty wooden floor. His attacker, a young kid called Ron Rouman, jumped on top of him and took a swing at his jaw. Steve blocked it and fought back in a frenzy; unleashing a barrage of hard, sharp blows that knocked his young opponent spark out.

His sole focus was to break free and take out McVey. The object of his hatred had started to limp off clutching the back of his head. He was making for the adjoining bar. The good news was he seemed to be losing a fair bit of claret.

'McVey, you old cunt,' screamed Steve. 'Get back here!'

All around him the tide of battle had turned against the Rotherhithe. Steve heard Kenny's voice ordering his troops to withdraw from the advancing cluster bombs of smoke, but all he could think of was Pat McVey's retreating form.

He followed him back through the bar. A few yards in front of him he saw the back door rocking on its hinges, and increased his pace. He could hear voices behind him as the rest of his firm started to follow him out.

Caution thrown to the wind, Steve hurtled out of the back door into the cold, wet night determined to make McVey pay. But Pat was nowhere. The backstreet was empty. The only sound was the rain that pelted down hard and relentlessly, like Noah's worst nightmare.

Bollocks. Right? Left? Which way to turn? There were no clues. The downpour had washed away any trace of spilt blood.

Kenny and Butch rocketed out of the building, followed by the rest of the firm. Bruised, battered but still standing. Sirens sounded in the distance but were getting closer. They would not be alone for long.

'Steve, let's go,' yelled Kenny.

Steve stood his ground. 'Without Matty?' he said, quietly.

'It's too late for him, bruv. We've lost him. Now come on.'

'McVey's out here somewhere. *I CAN FUCKIN' SMELL HIM.*'

'Not now, Steve, come on for fuck's sake. We'll get him later.'

Kenny tugged at Steve's arm but could not shift him. He leaned into his brother. 'Now is not the time,' he said in a tone so quiet and controlled it was almost otherworldly.

Steve let out a single agonised scream and then booted the back door so hard that spikes of pain shot up from his ankle to the top of his thigh.

'I'm coming for you, McVey,' he screamed.

Ken draped an arm around his brother and steered him back towards the vans as one. By the time the police arrived they found nothing but chaos and casualties.

And a single, tragic corpse.

Chapter Five: Diversions

Steve found sleep hard. After a few restless hours he drove into town and parked up on the Embankment. His rage had subsided but the grief had yet to kick in. He just felt...empty.

He took a slow walk up into the centre of Soho and ordered breakfast in an Italian cafe in Frith Street. Eggs, bacon, fried mushrooms and black coffee revived his spirits. Full of pent-up energy Steve walked briskly back towards Chinatown. As he passed the corner of Greek Street and Romilly Street he noticed the doors to a few walk-ups were open. The first had signs saying "French lessons given" and "Beautiful butterfly needs mounting". But the next one "Large chest for sale" caught his eye. This advertised the services of a brass he knew who called herself Sabrina in honour of the famous fifties actress with 42 and a half-inch breasts. She'd do.

Sabrina, real name Kathy, recognised her latest punter immediately.

'Mr Knight,' she said with a purr worthy of Eartha Kitt.

'Sssh please, Kath. Don't talk. I'm not feeling too sociable. I just need...'

She put a finger to his lips. She knew exactly what he needed. Skilled fingers undid Steve's shirt buttons and slipped inside. Her lips followed, working their way down. When she reached his navel she stopped, stood back up and felt his excitement.

Sabrina removed her blouse and black Berlei bra, and let his eyes soak up the full glory of her breasts. Her fingers returned. A smile played around her soft rosebud lips.

Moving quickly she unbuttoned his flies and flipped him out. He was rock hard and her mouth engulfed him hungrily.

God she was good.

But as ever, when Steve reached his climax another woman's face flashed before his eyes. His mystery mod.

***

In the weeks following Matthew Beeston's funeral the word was out that McVey was a wanted man – wanted by both the Metropolitan Police and more avidly the Knights. Steve and Kenny were determined to get to him before the filth and had a more medieval form of punishment in mind for him. The plan was inspired by a conversation in the Cheshire Cheese near Fenchurch Street station and involved four powerful motorbikes and four strong chains. It was no coincidence that the Knights had been discussing the cruel and very public practice of being hung, drawn and quartered at the time.

The brothers had let it be known that a "nice drink" would be forthcoming for anyone whose information led to Pat's capture, but so far nothing. All they could gather was that he was still breathing and still somewhere in or around London – Canning Town way, according to some sources; Petts Wood "with the pikies" according to others.

Steve knew that patience was the only course of action. If they waited long enough McVey would surface. As his late father used to say, 'when water stops moving the scum always rises'.

Steve sat at a pavement table at an Italian cafe in Berwick Street, waiting for his brother. He smoked two Gauloise cigarettes with his first cappuccino. In the background Vic Damone was crooning "On The Street Where You Live" on a jukebox or wireless. Very fifties but pure class. It occurred to Steve that he could live quite happily in a street like this. He sat back contentedly and watched Soho flow past him. Two dolly girls walked by; their miniskirts combined would probably make a good tea towel. Steve grinned and ordered another fancy coffee. Damone had moved on to "Begin The Beguine", suggesting it was an LP playing. Take your time, bruv, he thought. If I sit here long enough that little blonde mod sort might even put in another appearance.

***

By coincidence, less than a mile away another hard man was waiting less patiently over a pint of bitter. The TPA Club in Denmark Street was an afterhours drinking establishment frequented largely by musicians, villains, duckers and divers.

Rodney Huggins had the look and build of an armed robber but his warrant card told a different story. Huggins was 42, just like his waistline. The detective was based in Islington and wasn't too happy this far off his manor but his snout had insisted on it.

He and his fellow cops called Eddie Morgan "Little Pig" because he had big ears – both literally and metaphorically. But based on his looks alone, Morgan was generally and more accurately described as "rat-like", an epithet Huggins thought thoroughly unfair on rodents. Skinny with a pinched faced, he had a slight chin, a prominent nose and an unwashed smell heavy with last week's sweat. As well as the big flappy ears.

Morgan's red hair was generally cropped as short as his stubble. He had hardly any eyebrows. He was a small-time thief who liked to hang out in circles where they played by big boys rules. He was a regular in villain-friendly pubs including the Dover Castle where recent events had, he calculated, made his gossip about the Knights and their associates worth a bob or two to the filth.

Rodney Huggins's pint had been refreshed twice by the time Morgan scampered up to him. There was nothing likeable about the man. Even his grip was clammy.

After they shook hands, Huggins felt the need to subtly wipe his on a beer towel; and then again on the back of his trousers.

The detective bought Morgan a rum and black and walked him to a quiet table. The pubs were open now so the TPA was fairly deserted. Even so, Little Pig's eyes were everywhere, looking for potential trouble.

'So what's the word, Eddie?'

'A lot happening, Mr 'Uggins,' he replied, sounding for all the world like Uriah Heep's most degenerate descendent.

'With the Knights?'

'You've heard?'

'We'd be a bit fuckin' useless if we hadn't heard about exploding print shops, wouldn't we, son? So what do you know?'

'That little blaze down Rotherhithe way was down to them too.'

Roy nodded, impassively. *That* he didn't know.

'I'm not sure if they knew those brothers had been doing a little bit of work for Demirci.'

Another nod. The Turk!

'Pat has fucked off and he's fucked them off.'

'McVey?'

'Yeah. Mad Pat.'

'But he's their enforcer.'

'Was their enforcer, Mr 'Uggins. They've got new boys in now, a couple of ex-army geezers. Very 'andy around a can of petrol, know what I mean?'

'Names?'

'Butch and Arthur.'

'Surnames?'

'I'll get onto it.'

'Is the McVey business clouding Steve's judgement?'

'Not so you'd know it. Takings seem to be up. No one's knocking 'em for their bills no more. A lot of people thought they'd go tits up after Mickey popped 'is clogs, but Steve is one smart fucker. 'E's expanding. What with the twins away and the Richardson's banged up, word is the pair of 'em will be running the town soon.'

Rod Huggins thought about that for a moment. It had the ring of truth. The *Twins* aside, who else was there? The Nash brothers, the Dixons, the little mob around East Lane, Harry May in Bermondsey, the Turk of course, that bunch of tearaways down the Old Kent Road...all tasty, but not empire builders. Steve Knight had the ambition and the brains to make it a reality. He'd already expanded the enterprise far beyond anything Mickey Knight had accomplished. Give him a year, eighteen months and he would have left any dirty business well behind. It wasn't such a big leap from tailored suits and wads of readies to legit businessman.

'Is Kenny happy with the way things are going?'

'The brothers are close, Mr H. Different but rock solid. Kenny as you know would be 'appy enough with things staying as they were as long as he gets his leg over and gets to see West 'Am. But 'e's going along with this expansion. Steve 'as sold 'im on it.'

'The others?'

'Vic ain't 'appy. He's lost two of his closest mates, Matty and the big fella. Word is McVey was the one who plunged 'im. They won't forget Matty, Mr 'Uggins, they won't. That score will be settled.'

That's their weakness then, thought Huggins. That could be all the opportunity he needed to get them bang to rights and put 'em away.

'I heard Matty's funeral was something else,' he said casually.

''Undreds there, Mr H. Proper solid. The 'ole manor turned out. Beautiful 'orses.'

***

Kenny had turned up eventually. He and Steve moved on to the Embassy and chose a discrete booth at the back. A busty waitress brought them over a fresh bottle, courtesy of Ted McKeeve. They raised their flutes to the club owner and then clicked them together.

'To Matty,' said Steve.

'Matty,' Kenny echoed.

Over on the small stage on the other side of the bar, a 20-stone cabaret singer the wrong side of 40 had started to warble her way through Shirley Bassey's version of "You'll Never Know".

'And she never will,' laughed Kenny.

Steve cast an eye over the woman. She was a big'un. She had hair like Brynhildr, a dress that was tighter than Scrooge and her make-up looked like it'd been slapped on by Liberace in the dark with a trowel. Right now she was showering a silver-haired punter with maximum-force come-hither looks that could easily be mistaken for gurning or the onset of a stroke.

'Christ,' he said. 'Does she want to fuck that old cunt or eat him?'

Kenny laughed.

'This is it, bruv,' said Steve as he clinked his glass against Kenny's again. 'The fruits of our labour.'

'Yeah,' said Kenny wistfully. 'The old fella set us up nicely, God rest his soul.'

'He set us up, Kenny, but we've put the graft in. This is our thing now, we fucking worked for it.'

Kenny grunted his approval.

'We can do anything we want now, Kenny boy, whatever we decide. Dad left us with a solid foundation for the business but now it's up to us where it goes.'

Kenny said nothing.

'Cheer up for fuck's sake, what's wrong with you? Ain't you been getting enough or something?'

'Enough? 'Ow about any? There are priests getting more leg-overs than I am.'

'Since when?'

'The summer, bruv. July. I've not had the fucking chance, what with all the changes in the firm. I ain't had a chance to think let alone get me wick dipped.'

Right on cue, Brynhildr burst into *'I, I who have nothing. I, I who have no-one...'*

'Fuck me,' said Steve. 'She heard ya!'

'I'm just a no-one, with nothing to give you...'

'Ain't that the truth!' grinned Kenny. 'Steve, bruv, if I ever get so pissed I make a move on that, knock me sparko and send me home in a sherbet.'

Steve laughed loudly and he slapped his brother playfully on the back.

'So when was the last time you 'ad a bird…who wasn't a brass?'

'That night we went to Nellies.'

'Christ.'

'The only *Richard* I've 'ad up the flat is Carla the cleaner.'

'The 'eavy-'anded one who's always breakin' things?'

'Yeah.'

'And you ain't banging that?'

'Leave it out, Steve, she's Roy Shaw's bit on the side.'

'But he's away.'

'Even so...'

'So why keep her on?'

'Because she cleans my gaff in the tightest leather miniskirt you've ever seen an' is very thorough, especially when it comes to stretching up to do the cobwebs or bending over the back of the settee to get at the winders...arse like a peach.'

'You plum!' Steve laughed and stood up. 'Right, I'm going for a gypsy's, you keep your minces open for some nice bits of stray.'

***

Brynhildr was mangling "The Impossible Dream" when Steve finally got back.

'Where the fuck did you get to?' asked Kenny. 'I was ready to send out a search party.'

'Me guts were playing up something rotten and there was a queue for the khazis, but never mind that, have some of this.'

Steve plonked a fresh bottle of Moet in their ice bucket.

'Nice.'

'So, any sorts?'

'A few birds tried it on with me, as they would, but I told them I was waiting for me boyfriend.'

Steve laughed loudly.

'To dream the impossible dream...' chirped Brynhildr.

Both brothers were now in hysterics.

'Well something has tickled your fancy,' said a big brassy woman who draped herself around Kenny and kissed his head. 'And I wouldn't complain if you tickled mine...'

'Hello, Lil,' Steve chuckled.

"Diamond" Lil Barrymore had been a big noise in the clubs of Soho in the fifties and even though a steady diet of gin and Gitanes over the years had taken their toll, she was still a full-bodied and glamorous woman. In a favourable half-light...

'Hello, boys!'

Lil squeezed past Kenny and plonked herself between the two of them.

'Why don't you have a seat, Lil,' said Kenny sarcastically. He smiled and let one eye ogle her heaving bosom which was busting out of her skintight velvet dress.

'Don't mind if I do,' she said as she nodded towards the champagne. 'Any of that coming my way?'

'Sure,' said Kenny. 'Be my guest.' The smell of her perfume was as overpowering as the swell of her breasts. He felt her thigh push against his, causing a sudden involuntary tightening in his Y-fronts. 'Wait and I'll get you a glass.'

'No need,' said Lil as she fingered the stem of his glass as if she was gripping a thin cock. 'I'll get my lips around yours if that's alright.'

She drained Kenny's drink, leaving a garish red lipstick mark on its rim.

'You are a very naughty woman, Lillian,' laughed Steve.

'Do you want to see how naughty?' she asked coquettishly. Her hands slid across and up both of their thighs, coming to a rest on each of the brothers' crotches.

'What now my love?' Brynhildr sang plaintively.

Kenny shook his head but made no effort to move a muscle. 'Listen, Lil, it's been a busy week and I'm in no mood for a prick tease.'

'Who mentioned teasing?' she purred in a comical but sultry Mae West drawl. The fingers on both hands settled into a slow, kneading movement just to prove she was not joking. The results were instantaneous.

'I do love a *hardened* criminal... Maybe we should move this party into the VIP lounge, I'm sure Mr McKeeve wouldn't mind.'

Steve shrugged. 'Why not?' said Kenny. They got up from the table and with two bottles of champagne in hand they followed Lil across the room towards a door that was covered in upholstered leather. It was set apart from the rest of the venue by a small, crimson rope.

***

Kenny and Steve emerged from the Embassy club blinking as the first rays of sunlight illuminated the silent streets of Soho. Kenny coughed and then spat a mouthful of dry phlegm into the gutter as he did up his cashmere overcoat. He belched loudly.

'Strewth, have you been eating fish?' said Steve who laughed and added: 'Silly question... I saw you go down on her at least three times. 'Ere, 'ave a gum, bruv, your breath smells like a dying seal.'

'Was she a brass?' Kenny croaked as he watched Steve button and unbutton his suit jacket three more times.

'Of course not. Lil just helps them out when they get busy. She's another one of our admirers. A devotee of our modern style of business.'

'Bollocks. I bet you slipped her a drink on your way back from the shitter.'

'What if I did? You got your money's worth, didn't you?'

Lil had been more than accommodating, keeping the brothers entertained in a number of unusual and occasionally eye-watering ways.

'I've never had a fuck like it. Where did she learn to do all that...?'

'All I know is she spent a lot of time in an upmarket Shanghai brothel catering for very rich clients with unusual tastes.'

'Did she work there, or teach there? Talk about any hole's a goal. There was stuff going on there that definitely weren't in the Kama Sutra.'

'I wasn't keen on the pissing, but the riding crop...that was a bit of me.'

'A bit of you? She had a *bite* of me!'

'Never thought I'd be in to that, but...'

'Worked for me, bruv.'

'The body was pretty firm for an older bird. Her Jack and Danny had a mind of its own.'

'Strewth. It gripped like Shirley Crabtree. I reckon she could have gone all morning too.'

'And 'alf the afternoon. Like Eskimo fucking Nell.'

Kenny laughed and lit up a cigarette and proffered the open pack of Player's Navy Cut to Steve.

Steve declined and stepped out into the street. 'If you are feeling good, Kenny boy, then that was a worthwhile investment. Now I'm off to make another one.'

'Do you want me to come with you?'

'Nah. You get 'ome and get cleaned up, you sweaty bastard.'

Kenny shook his head and laughed quietly as he flicked his fag end into the path of an old street cleaner. 'Cheeky cunt.'

***

Billy was sitting in the Dover flicking through a copy of the East Ham Express when the Knights arrived in high spirits.

'See this?' said Billy. 'This jewellers in the 'igh street celebrating 100 years in the business?'

Kenny glanced over. 'Yeah, so?' he shrugged.

'I know the son, Albert. Look, this puppy-faced prat' – Billy pointed at the floppy-haired teenager posing with his family. 'He buys 'is bit of Bob 'Ope off us.'

Kenny grunted.

'It says 'ere 'e's running the show while the rest of these Addams family lookalikes enjoy a "well-earned three week break" over in Majorca.'

'Again, so?'

'So Albie Phillips couldn't run a fuckin' bath.'

Steve walked over from the bar with three pints on a tray. 'And joining the dots, you're saying it'd be a piss of piece to have the gaff over,' he said.

'Spot on. Saturday morning. Sweet as...'

'A smash and grab in broad daylight? That ain't our game,' grunted Kenny.

'No but listen. Albie's a proper Billy No-Mates, see. 'E's never 'ad a Richard let alone a Donald as far as I'm aware. He drinks in the Black Lion. I'll send a little sort in, get 'is attention...'

'What are you thinkin'?'

'Get 'im in that shop flying high on acid. I'll be nip down there on a scooter with a jack 'ammer. Bish, bosh. We've got the lot.'

Steve nodded. 'More Tom than Jerry could handle...'

'No risk. No danger. An' Plod ain't gonna keep up with a Lambretta on a Saturday afternoon.'

'I don't like it,' said Kenny.

'Why bruv? What's not to like?'

'His old man ain't back for a week,' added Billy.

'Plenty of time, let's get cracking.'

Kenny shook his head. 'I'll come with you, just in case.'

'What could possibly go wrong?'

***

Albert Phillips had been flattered by the attention of Sandie Ivens when she had accidentally bumped into him in the Black Lion, spilling his drink and then dabbing at the stain on his trousers more thoroughly than it justified. Of course he wouldn't dream of her replacing it. He'd bought her a fresh one instead. Later that night they'd shared a joint and she'd kissed him on the cheek before she left.

Albert was even more delighted when Sandie had turned up at the shop the next morning unannounced. He gave her a guided tour and in the stockroom, she'd encouraged him to try LSD for the first time – 'a titchy bit, just to take the edge of, gets yer through a borin' day'.

Billy and Kenny were parked up in Shelley Avenue, just 100 yards from W. Phillips & Co in High Street North. Butch was window shopping casually outside. As soon as Sandie left, Butch went in and found Albert behind rolling around behind the counter experiencing the full, heart-pumping terror of a bad trip that was getting rapidly worse. Butch grinned broadly. He turned the sign in the jewellers shop window to Closed and strolled casually to the top of Shelley Avenue where he gave the waiting men a discreet thumbs-up.

Kenny sitting on a stolen Vespa nodded imperceptibly and pulled a balaclava on followed by a borrowed helmet, making sure the fabric fitted snugly around his face. Billy on a borrowed Lambretta opted for a red bandana.

The plan was simple: go in, grab all the Tom, and fly off down Wordsworth Avenue like hot shit off a shovel. Perfect.

'Ready?'

'I'm ready.'

In and out. This had to be fast. Two minutes top whack. Then back into the high street, onto the scooters and straight down Wordsworth Avenue towards Plashet Park and the B165 to Upton Park. Any passing cop car would be caught up in the inevitable jam of Saturday afternoon shoppers. What could possibly go wrong?

When Billy burst through the door he was startled to find the jewellery shop wasn't empty. Albert Phillips's maternal uncle Roger "Slugger" Hobbs had arrived seconds before to check how his soppy nephew was coping and had found him writhing about to the left of the shop door with specks of foam bubbling around his mouth.

Hobbs, an ex-pro middleweight, reacted immediately to the intruders by giving Billy a solid kidney punch. Kenny pushed past the younger man and waved his hammer at the unexpected inhabitant only to be rewarded with a face full of fire extinguisher. As the Knight team turned tail and ran, Hobbs went behind the counter and dialled 999.

Billy guided Kenny onto the back of his Lambretta, leaving the stolen one behind, and followed the escape plan, driving left from the shop and turning right into Wordsworth Avenue...only the road ahead was not clear. Billy braked so sharply, Kenny fell off the back of the scooter. All he could see through his stinging eyes was an impressionistic mess of colours, vivid reds and dark blues swirling around like a bad Monet. The reds were the banners of the marchers leaving the park, the blues were uniforms. It was a political demo with a large police escort.

'Oi!' shouted the nearest cop.

Kenny scrabbled back to his feet and climbed back onto the scooter as Billy span it round. They drove back towards the High Street with uniformed officers in pursuit.

Butch, who had watched the chaos from a distance, had toyed with idea of scooping the other scooter up off the pavement until Roger Hobbs came out of the shop glaring. Butch turned sharply and walked away at a pace that was steady but unhurried. He reached Plashet Cemetery as the first police sirens rang out in the distance.

Later that evening back in the Dover, Kenny sat with a face like a boiled lobster nursing a large Scotch.

Steve shook his head. 'I dunno Ken, that plan was perfect on paper...it was just a shame it played out on concrete.'

No response.

'Strewth. "Slugger" Hobbs. What were the odds of that? Any other bugger would've run a mile...'

Nothing.

'It coulda been worse. It could 'ave been Old Bill in the gaff.'

Nada.

'No harm done though, eh? A nice day out, some fresh air and a story that'll get funnier every time you tell it.'

Kenny looked up and narrowed his eyes like arrow slits. 'Never a-fuckin'-gain,' he snarled. 'That's the last time we do things your way.'

Steve nodded as if in agreement and patted his brother's back. No point rowing about it now. Kenny would come round when he needed him to. Right now he had something else on his mind.

***

Roy Storer was struggling with a particularly well-worn wheel nut on his car when he noticed a gleaming silver Jaguar 420 pull up behind him. It was magnificent; the ultimate compact

Jag. The engine seemed to purr with pleasure at its own beauty.

Roy assumed the flash, brand new jam-jar belonged to some old toff who had strayed off the beaten track into his manor; a banker perhaps, or maybe a stock broker who'd got lost on his way to the golf course. Then the thought struck him that it could be Pat McVey paying him a visit. He reached for the tyre iron beside him and tensed. The car's engine was still running and no one got out.

The driver sounded his horn impatiently. *BEEEP!*

Roy ignored it and continued wrestling with the wheel nut. He could easily afford a mechanic but he liked to keep his hand in. *BEEEEPPP! BEEEEEEPPPPP!* Two more horn blasts, longer and harder than the first. Roy threw the tyre iron down in frustration and got to his feet.

'Fuck off, you noisy cunt, I'm busy,' he yelled.

The window of the Jag rolled down smoothly. 'I say, you Hoxton oiks are terribly rude, what?' said the driver snootily.

It was Steve. Roy smiled widely and walked towards the Jag.

'Very nice, Steven, very nice indeed,' cooed Roy as he ran his hand lightly along the bonnet.

'Keep those filthy paws off, Storer,' laughed Steve. 'This is a precision piece of British engineering, this.'

Roy's expression clouded.

'What's the matter, mate? You worried it's going to overshadow that old clunker of yourn?'

Steve turned off the engine and stepped out of the Jag. Roy still hadn't replied.

'You don't think it is too soon after Matty, do you?' Roy said eventually. Steve looked a little shocked at the suggestion.

'Things move on, mate,' he said quietly. 'Especially these days. I haven't forgotten about Matty. None of us have. That account will be paid in full with a bucket-load of interest as soon as we track McVey down. But the geezer is like a rat. A fat, fucking rodent feeding off everyone's misery and plotted up in some godforsaken shithole somewhere. But we have to be seen to be moving on, Roy, so that people round here get it into their thick fucking heads that there's a new way of doing things...our way.'

Roy nodded. 'I suppose you're right.' He didn't sound convinced.

Steve laid a reassuring hand on his mate's shoulder. 'I'm not going out of my way to look flash, Roy, but if we keep growing maybe we can make sure nothing else happens to any of us. We need to lay down the law; we need to show the world that the Knight firm are still in business but under new management. Aggressive new management. In fact I've just signed the lease on our next venture...'

'Lease?' said Roy. 'Are you getting us another warehouse?'

'No, mate, we have just taken over the Cat's Cradle.'

Roy was incredulous. 'That old fleapit? You've got to be fucking joking? That's not a dance hall; it's a fucking bear pit.'

'Not for long, mate. We are going to strip it back to the brickwork and create a new joint. No expense spared, a little bit of West End glamour right on our doorstep. I've already picked the name...Aphrodite's Palace.'

'Aphrodite's nightie,' Roy scoffed. 'Fuck off, Steve. That sounds like a Turkish brothel.'

'It will be a house of pleasure all right,' smiled Steve, 'But not for scrubbers. No expense spared. Modern designed interiors, good quality booze, no herberts – a real chance for the hoi polloi to get a taste of the East End in surroundings they are used too.'

Roy knelt back down and started to work on his car's wheel again. 'Well, if you're sure, Steve,' he sighed.

Steve knelt down beside him and passed him the tyre iron. 'This is for all of us, Roy. It's not just my flight of fancy. My old man had plenty of big plans but he never acted on them. Right at the back of 'is mind he thought that ambitious ideas were "not for the likes of him" but I don't feel like that, mate. I don't think any of us should. We can do exactly what we fucking want and no one can tell us any different. We've just got to have the bollocks to do it. Do you know what I mean?'

Roy nodded. 'Of course, Steve, it's just all happening a bit fast but I'm with you mate...all the way. I just wish that cunt McVey was out of the picture.'

'He will be soon.'

Steve stood up and dusted down his slacks. He looked slowly around the street as if he was going to find McVey peering from behind some door or window.

'He'll stick his snout out sometime, Roy, and when he does we'll make sure he's fucking brown bread before he can scuttle off into hiding again. Now what about this 420?'

'It's class, Steve. Though personally, I'd have gone for a Porsche 906.'

'Of course you fucking would. A cunt like you would look shit in a T-series Bentley.'

Chapter Six: Cradle To Grave

The Cat's Cradle was an imposing building situated on the Bethnal Green Road. It had been a booming cinema in its pre-war heyday but the glamour seemed to drain away from it as each new television set arrived in house after house around the area. By the mid 60s young couples were more likely to be peering at Bruce Forsyth through a 14" Rediffusion TV screen than taking in a dinner dance or cabaret.

The local Roxy had reeled off its final celluloid performance in 1964. The doors reopened after a hasty renovation job and The Silver Garter nightclub was born. Despite booking big turns, including such world famous American showbusiness icons as Sammy Davis Jr and Neil Sedaka, the club remained woefully out of step with the rapidly changing decade and failed to encourage regular crowds.

In a bid to keep afloat, bar prices dropped...and so did their standards. The club became a regular haunt for every hothead, violent drunk and punch-drunk thug for miles around. A little gang off the nearby Cranbrook estate made sure that every outsider ran a gauntlet of pain. Even a change of name to The Cat's Cradle could not save it.

This is where the Knights came in. Steve had always been able to sniff out an opportunity, especially if it doubled as a front to launder illicit cash. Buying the club seemed like a foolproof investment.

The small fact that the cravat-wearing owner, former Major Lee Wilson, was both a serious alcoholic and a hopeless gambler deeply in debt to the brothers helped as well.

As soon as Steve and Kenny Knight took over, the Cat's Cradle sign was ripped down and the word went out around the neighbourhood that this was to become a more elite venue where violence was verboten – unless it was being dished out by the doormen.

The days of a pie, a pint and a punch-up in the company of a pair of plain Jane strippers were well and truly over.

Steve took the lead in the club's makeover, taking his inspiration from upmarket joints up West like The Bag Of Nails and La Discotheque with their bold design and modern outlook. He didn't want to settle for the old conservative ways of black suits, dicky bow ties and birds done up like cut-price Audrey Hepburns. That was yesterday. The new crowd were to be his generation and younger – fashionable, forward-thinking, buzzing with inspiration and aspiration...writers, models, actors, musicians. Not the old working class who wanted no more than a crate of brown ale at the weekend and a week every summer in Southend On sodding Sea with a bowl of winkles, but the new working class who did not accept any of the ancient boundaries and no longer recognised England's antique class system and the archaic barriers it had in place to stop you from being whatever and whoever the fuck you wanted to be.

Today's young London proles had no interest in living their life as factory fodder or road sweepers. They weren't going to be some poor desk drone in an office saying 'yes sir, no sir, three bags bloody full sir' to a fat, arrogant middle class boss until they fucked them off with a gold watch either.

They wanted the world!

The Life! All or Nothing!

They wanted what their so-called "betters" had – because this was their time. And they wanted places to party where they could look flash and hot; hip places with colour, bright lights, loud music – the latest Black American sounds – and a big fuck-off dance-floor with lots of nooks and crannies around the edges to sit in and conspire, romance and reach whatever narcotic nirvana they chose to enjoy.

Steve would serve it up to them in spades with modernist decor, free-flowing space, streamlined bars and subtle psychedelic flourishes – at least that's what Mixi, the interior designer he had paid nearly five grand, told him. If truth be told he did lose her when she started banging on about the 'tectonic qualities of textiles', but he knew she dug what he wanted – and what he would not stand for.

It was no middle earth but Steve definitely didn't want a load of smelly beatniks and birds with CND bloomers dossing about. It was designed to be for a crowd that were going places and Steve felt more than a small sense of achievement when it was ready to be unveiled to the world.

***

Fifteen minutes before the grand opening of Aphrodite's Palace, Steve Knight called the club's staff and security, along with most of the firm, to the Swan Ballroom. Once they'd all been given a glass of champagne, Steve climbed on a chair and called for quiet.

'Aphrodite was the Ancient Greek goddess of love, beauty, pleasure and procreation,' he boomed. 'In other words, she was a bit of a goer.'

A ripple of polite laughter ran around the room.

'She was identified with swans, doves, roses and myrtles, which explains our tasteful decor. But she was a warrior goddess too. Like a proper East Ender, she weren't afraid to 'and out a few clumps when necessary. But there won't be any of that tonight. Because tonight is about the future, about West End style done the East End way; and it's also about love. Yes, love. Aphrodite's Palace is built on it, my friends, and with your help, it's going to be the in-place for a generation of faces...'

He raised his glass and went on. 'Ladies and gentlemen, I give you the future.'

'The future!'

Backs were patted, hands were shaken, and then Steve led Kenny, Roy and Butch up to his office on the second floor.

'Nice speech, bruv,' said Kenny. 'All for love, eh?'

'In my case the love of all the mountains of pretty green this gaff is going to generate,' Steve smiled.

'Did you know Aphrodite was the patron saint of drippers?' asked Butch.

'Thank you, professor, I did not.'

Kenny laughed. 'Well the only things getting screwed tonight are the billies,' he said.

'Oh really? That's a shame,' said Roy. 'I had me heart set on that little blonde barmaid with the pixie cut...'

Steve grinned. 'Yeah. Lovely sort. But Kenny's right, it's the Billy Bunters we've got to worry about tonight. Here, Butch, turn the light out a minute will you, mate? Let's watch 'em pulling up.'

The office windows looked down onto the street. Before long, an Austin Princess limo turned up containing the first VIP guests – the Stepney born composer Lionel Bart with Cockney pop star Helen Shapiro. Like the actors, actresses, cabaret singers, boxers, footballers, comedians and models – some genuine, others tarts – who followed them, the stars stepped onto a strip of red carpet that led from the pavement into the club's cavernous entrance where they were greeted warmly by comedy legend, South London born Max Wall playing the part of Professor Wallofski for a hefty fee.

A good turn-out of locals clapping and cheering helped give the evening the feel of a West End film premiere. Some had gone to the trouble of wearing dress suits and gowns in the hope that there might be space for them inside at this star-studded event on their own patch.

Steve smiled to himself. He had a good feeling about this place. There was more to it than even the gang knew. He'd had a hidden door installed disguised in the bookshelves behind his desk, and one side of the room had been redesigned to accommodate a kind of priest's hole – a safe area between the original brickwork and a solid plasterboard wall, with basic creature comforts stored inside.

If he ever needed to lay low no one would ever find him there because no one else knew that it even existed.

A second limo pulled up down below as Arthur burst into the room.

'What's this, a blackout?' he chortled. 'Are we expecting the fuckin' Luftwaffe back?'

'We're just admiring the spectacle, Arthur,' said Steve with a smile. 'Taking a little time to savour the occasion before we head down to the melee.'

'Fuck that,' said Arthur. He fumbled for the light switch and the office flooded with light. The other four sighed almost collectively and turned away from the window.

'You're like a bunch of peeping Toms,' Arthur snorted.

'What? Like that sneaky bastard who's been creeping around your mum's gaff trying to get a butcher's at her in her Littlewoods catalogue girdle?' laughed Roy.

Arthur grimaced. 'If I ever find that pervert he'll be fuckin' sorry. He'll have a job peeping with no fucking eyeballs.'

'It's being so 'appy that keeps you going,' said Kenny with a smile.

Steve strolled over to the desk and sat down on a large leather chair. His chair. He picked up a silver lighter from the top of the desk and clicked it into action four times, *1-2-3-4*.

'Anyway, Art, nice to see you have come suitably attired for tonight's affair,' said Kenny, with a glimmer of a grin playing on his lips.

'Yes, Arthur,' smiled Steve. 'Very smart. Undertaker's chic I believe they call it down the King's Road.'

'What do you mean? You said dress smart, this is smart, ain't it?' He gestured down at his worn black suit, white shirt and scuffed black boots. Only his thin tie looked like it came from this side of demob day.

'It's the same fucking gear you wear all the time,' said Roy as he gestured around the room at the others. 'At least we've made a bit of an effort.'

Butch ran his hands gently over the side vents of his three-button tonic suit then tightened the knot slightly on his silk tie.

'This whistle is straight out of Lord John mate. Roy's too. Top class clobber and no mistake.'

Arthur scanned round the room but seemed unimpressed by their sartorial splendour.

'Fuck off,' he rasped. 'You look like a bunch of playboy poofters.'

They all laughed and even Arthur allowed himself a broad grin. Steve nodded to Butch who walked over to a small fridge at the back of the office and pulled out a chilled bottle of champagne.

'Anyway, gentlemen, fashion tips aside, I think we should celebrate this new milestone in our organisation,' said Steve as he lifted the bottle carefully from Butch's grip.

He casually twisted the bottle round in his hands four times. The rest of the firm sighed inwardly but knew not to pass comment...apart from Kenny.

'Never mind fingering the fucking thing,' he boomed. 'Get it fucking open, my mouth is as dry as an Arab's jockstrap.'

Steve glared at his brother for a moment then his face broke into a smile worthy of Sid James in a room full of randy nurses.

'A glass for my big brother first please, Butch,' he said. 'Never let it be said that I've ever stood in the way of Kenny and a light ale. We have to keep him pissed in case he sobers up and discovers how fucking ugly he is.'

Everyone started laughing, including Kenny, although he still made a throat slitting gesture towards Steve.

'I don't have any problems in that area, pretty boy,' he laughed as he looked over at Steve. 'The ladies round here like a man that looks like a man. Not some puffed-up ponce wearing a girlie blouse.'

'This is from Irvine Sellars you fucking philistine,' laughed Steve as he touched the collar of his bold paisley patterned shirt. He gestured towards the glasses that Butch had just filled. 'Gentlemen please, raise a glass to us. The Knights, the kings of E2 and all we survey.'

'The Knights!' they echoed back.

'Kings of the fuckin' world,' added Roy, with a smile.

***

"B-A-B-Y" by Carla Thomas was oozing out of the speakers as the Knight firm arrived in the club's busy main room. Thomas's seductive Memphis vocals complimented the party atmosphere perfectly. Most of the gang were glowing with the vintage champagne that was settling inside them. Only Arthur had refused the "fizzy shit" and made his way straight to the bar for a pint of mild.

Butch and Roy drifted off to work the room, greeting their family and friends who had all been invited to the opening night celebrations. The DJ, spotting the firm, slipped Otis Redding's "Respect" on to the turntable. Dicky Harris, a pirate radio star, was only too glad to spend a night on dry land for the money the brothers were paying him.

Kenny and Steve scanned the room in silence and breathed in the rarefied atmosphere.

'I've got to say, bruv,' said Kenny, breaking the silence, 'I think this could work.'

'Oh ye of little faith,' smirked Steve.

'I wasn't sure that creating a meeting place for arty-farty trendies and soppy toff layabouts was a good idea. But I think you could be on to something here, Steven.'

Steve placed a hand on his brother's shoulder. 'Things are changing, Kenny boy. Money don't look like it used to. Everything is up for grabs now. The working class are dressing up, the upper class are dressing down and getting with it. Believe you me, another few years and you'll be growing your hair and wearing bell-bottoms.'

'Fuck off! There's no fucking chance of that, son. This is all just a flash in the pan. Models with no tits? Pot-puffing layabouts? Bank managers on LSD? It'll all be over by Christmas, Steve, you mark my words. But if you can make us a few bob from it now then fair play to your elbow.'

'Only time will tell, Kenny, but I think this is a sea change, mate; it's the start of something big. Not necessarily good, but lucrative.'

Kenny slapped Steve on the back and winked at him before he moved into the heart of the club to greet some old friends. Steve stepped back against a wall to soak up the atmosphere.

This was it! Wasn't it? His warm glow of satisfaction began to be eaten away by a hollow, grinding feeling in his stomach. He pulled his solid gold Buccellati lighter gently from his pocket and sparked it into life four times until the panic subsided. As he slid the lighter back into his pocket he noticed a girl close to the bar watching his every move.

Not just any girl. *The girl.*

It was the leggy mod girl he'd spotted off Regent Street a few months ago. He'd recognise that profile anywhere.

As soon as he made eye contact with her she began to make her boldly way towards him. "Sashaying" was the word. She looked even more stunning in this setting, he thought; especially in that classy orange and white Mary Quant miniskirt.

When she smiled at him Steve felt like his heart was melting.

He had never been one for overly romantic thoughts or soppy gestures but for a moment the rest of the room seemed to blur out of focus. All he could see was *the girl.*

As she moved, her mini dress gripped different parts of her shapely form and seemed understandably reluctant to let go.

Steve snapped back to attention just before the vision of perfection reached him.

Bollocks. It wasn't her. She still looked stunning but her hair which had been cut razor-sharp, Cleopatra style, was too long. She was just as pretty. Facially they could have been twins. Maybe a little taller? Close but no cigar...

'Were you sending out a beacon there?' she asked playfully. The voice was cut-glass, public school, almost certainly Roedean; Home Counties, head-girl posh with a side order of jolly hockey sticks. The smile that played around her lips was loaded with an attitude he couldn't quite relate to. Steve understood immediately that she was referring to the business with his lighter but he kept his cool.

'Yes, love,' he said with a faint grin. 'It's a throwback from my days in the merchant navy. We were always signalling some bugger or another.'

'All hands on deck, was it?' she purred.

'You definitely said deck then, didn't you?' replied Steve with a beam that skirted around a leer. She smiled back but her smile was far more seductive. Her eyes, he noted, were as dark and smoky as a prison chimney.

'You know, I don't think you ever were in the navy, Mr...Knight.'

'Well I've certainly done a bit of business down at the docks, darling, but nothing more. How do you know my name anyway?'

The girl stood back slightly and slid her arms behind her in a move that accentuated the firm curves of her ample bosom. 'I like to know who is inviting me out on a Friday night.'

Steve looked a little puzzled so she continued.

'I'm from the Parker Davidson Model Agency; we received an open invitation to this soiree.'

Steve had never been used to girls being so upfront with him, unless they were on the game, but this girl wasn't a tom. She had real form, knockout looks and the confidence that had clearly come from generations of feather-bedded bourgeois respectability.

He nodded coolly. Give nothing away, he thought. Play it aloof. There were plenty of beauties around tonight. As his old man used to say; never settle for the first thing that's on offer, no matter how tempting it might be.

'My name is Anthea Sellers,' she went on. 'I must say this place looks beautiful, Mr Knight. Not what I was expecting at all.'

Steve let the thinly-veiled insult drift by. She won't sound so fucking snobby when I'm stuck up her other "Quant", he thought; when she's yelling my name, clawing my back, biting my neck and begging for more.

He fixed his gaze on her gorgeous boat.

'My interior was styled by Mixi Sakamoto,' he said evenly, very matter-of-fact. Anthea's eyes opened slightly wider.

Steve smiled. She was obviously thinking how did this brute even know what design was, let alone be in a position to hire one of the most chic interior creators in London... He loved to play with people's expectations of him, and wrong-side their prejudices. It was almost as satisfying as chinning a copper.

'Well she has certainly worked her magic here, Steve,' she purred. 'You don't mind if I call you Steve, do you?'

'By all means. We're all friends here.'

'Yes, we are,' she replied, her tone skirting around coquettish. They stood in silence for a moment, eyeing each other up like a pair of panthers until she broke the silence. 'Ah, well. One must mingle, Steve.'

'One must,' he replied with the merest hint of sarcasm.

She leaned forward just enough to brush those firm breasts against his chest and kissed him on each cheek.

'Very continental,' he said coolly. Anthea laughed and began to slink away through the crowd. Steve watched her go. Later, he thought. She wasn't the one, but tonight she would do. He looked around, the place was heaving, the atmosphere convivial. Everything was tickety-boo.

***

The Aphrodite's Palace launch night was an incredible success. Knockout! The club was still humming three hours later. It was already looking as if it could be the new place to be seen; the coolest draw in the capital's clubland. Dicky Harris was playing Mable John's "Your Good Thing (Is About To End)" but Steve knew it wasn't. How could it? This was it! The gateway to the new life! The future!

He spotted a local Labour councillor, a smart fella in his early thirties very much on the way up. The word was he was seen as a future player, possibly even prime minister material...

'Councillor Watts,' he said, extending a hand.

'Call me Seamus,' the man replied, applying what Steve recognised as a Masonic handshake, not that he was on the square himself.

'And this is?' He nodded at the blonde by his side who looked about half his age.

'My fiancée, Anita.' Steve leaned over and kissed her left cheek. Definitely still a teenager, he thought.

The music changed gear. *'Oh she may be weary,'* sang Otis Redding sweetly as "Try A Little Tenderness" kicked in.

'I would love to talk to you about a new building project,' Steve said. 'I've got this idea and it's a proper corker. It's going to be...'

There was a sudden crash from the club entrance followed by a growing commotion, a mess of shouts and screams.

'Excuse me, Councillor,' Steve said politely. 'I'll be right back...' He caught Kenny's eye from across the room and nodded towards the foyer. 'I just have to check something.'

The brothers moved towards the source of the racket but did not even reach the main doors before Pat McVey and the remains of the Rotherhithe mob piled into the club like a poisonous tidal wave. Through the swinging entrance doors, Steve got a quick view of his doormen beaten and Through the swinging entrance doors, Steve got a quick view of his doormen beaten and battered on the bright new carpet, their crisp white shirts decorated with splatters of claret. They looked as broken as the noses at a boxing club reunion.

McVey's gang clearly had carnage on their mind. Blades flashed and clubs swiped at anyone they could reach, regardless of age, colour or creed.

Panic set in immediately. The venue emptied at a frightening rate as the toffs, socialites and self-regarding "artistes" who had turned out for the vicarious thrill of the association of violence baulked at the horrifying reality of the real thing.

McVey's aim was simple – to smother the reputation of Aphrodite's Palace before it even had a chance to breathe.

For a few seconds Steve froze, torn between his new image as a genial host and the reality of what he did for a living. But as he saw his beautiful club reduced to swirling chaos his dark side took over.

'Everyone! Behind the bar,' he roared. 'Now!'

The Knight gang moved almost as one, following Steve behind the jump. He reached down to a wide cupboard under the bar and fumbled with the small lock that was securing it. He was shaking with so much fury his fingers could not even grip the key he needed to open it.

'Stand back,' roared Arthur who launched a powerful boot at the door and shattered the wood into splinters. Steve smiled to himself momentarily. Who the fuck wears steel toe-capped boots with a whistle? Good old Arthur. They all grabbed one of the wide range of available weapons that tumbled out of storage and dived into action.

'Wipe these fuckers out,' screamed Kenny.

A vicious toe to toe battle ensued. Any innocent parties capable of movement had long since left the room and all that remained to be seen was a head on tear-up between the two firms.

Where once they had fought on the cobbles or terraces, now they fought in the arena of the upmarket club but little else had changed.

The Knight firm were fresh to the battle and they struck hard and fast. Steve in particular was almost delirious with anger as he battered and swiped his way through the intruders, determined to get to McVey.

The bastard was trying to destroy his business. It would take the best part of a year to persuade any of the classy clientele to venture back east again after tonight. Maybe years...if fucking ever.

One of Pat's firm had taken a tumble in front of him. As he staggered to his feet Steve booted the bloke's arse so hard that his vertebrae seemed to ripple. He went crashing down chin first, and he stayed down after Arthur took the precaution of jumping directly onto his head.

Steve smiled savagely, bearing his teeth like a hungry tiger as he lashed out at every rotten McVey nobody he came across. He was in the zone. A machine. Invincible. But it was Pat's septic mug that he was after, not these scumbags.

Where was the no-good, two-bob pig-ugly cunt? He could do with a few more tramlines.

To his right, Steve saw Reggie Glover overpowering young Billy in the corner of the room. He'd do for now. With a single swipe of his crowbar, Steve opened up a wide gash in the back of the Rotherhithe mob leader's head. Before Glover could drop to the floor Steve shoulder barged him against a fire exit door, sending him tumbling out into the night air. He landed heavily at the bottom of a metal staircase. Steve pounded the iron bar down a few more times on his back and shoulders then delivered a solid kick to the ribs that propelled Glover head first into a metal step. He was unconscious but he hit him again and again. Steve felt no shame, and definitely no mercy. Pat McVey would be next.

'You come into my club with McVey and your shower of cunts! You ruin my big night? You fucking no-mark bastards are finished!' he ranted, accentuating every second word with a solid kick into the stricken figure on the ground.

A voice cut through the darkness but it took a second or two to penetrate through Steve's red mist. It was Kenny behind him. 'Steve! Get in here, the Old Bill are almost at the front door.'

'You think you can finish us off, do you?' Steve hissed at the unconscious Glover. 'It will take more than your firm of syphilitic nobodies to take us out of the picture.' His tone rose to a near scream. 'You're nothing. *NOTHING! The shit on my shoes!'*

'Steve, for fuck's sake, get in here.' Roy had joined Kenny in the doorway.

Steve's mind emerged from his hate-filled haze. He looked over at the pair of them and nodded. But before he moved he took one last look down at Reggie Glover. His body was lying in a puddle of piss, blood and dirty water but his left arm was raised off the ground slightly as it rested on the first step of the metal staircase. Even though he knew that Glover was out for the count, Steve growled 'You tell McVey I'm coming for him.'

Then he lifted his foot high into the air and brought it down on his opponent's exposed arm.

The crack of bone echoed around the empty alley as the shrill ring of police cars grew in the background.

***

The opening night of Aphrodite's Palace made the papers for all the wrong reasons. Twenty-seven people had been hospitalised, three including Glover were still in a coma and the CID were sniffing about all over the gaff. It took days after the attack for Steve's volcanic rage to subside. In the end it only stopped because he made himself compartmentalise it, chalk it up to experience and lock it away in the box room of his mind.

He had to do that, he reasoned, because he had to get on with the more important business of saving face and keeping things going. *Keep calm and carry on*, as they used to say in the War.

The hate had to be kept on a back burner until it was needed because if you let it take you over it will blind you to everything else.

The Knight gang and many of their associates had spent the first forty-eight hours after McVey's raid turning up unannounced around the clock at every pub, club, dive bar, brothel and strip joint that Pat McVey was known to frequent; pretty much every rock he might have crawled under was lifted and examined. But it was fruitless, and on the fifth day, Steve and Kenny called time on the manhunt and ordered everyone back to work. Business as usual was the best way to repair the damage.

Revenge could wait. The retribution would be no less fierce if it took a few weeks to track down the treacherous quisling; or months.

***

Steve Knight had another reason for moving on, a strange compulsion that had been gnawing away at his heart and mind for days – he just could not get Anthea out of either his head or his dreams. He felt bewitched by the woman, almost obsessed.

Steve had many a good-looking "sort" on tap but Anthea was different. The way he saw it, this smart, sussed but slightly stand-offish chick was a cut above the rest. Out of his league perhaps, but then Steven Harold Knight loved a challenge. He resolved to find her and test her mettle, if only to satisfy his curiosity. And if he satisfied his lust at the same time, it would be the cherry on top of the pie.

Inside he knew a woman like her was trouble, but that was part of the attraction. She could even be *the one.*

***

The model agency wouldn't play ball but Steve eventually tracked Anthea down to a flat in Holland Park Mews with the help of Jack Houghton, an old school pal and a fairly recent member of the constabulary. It was always handy to have plod on the firm, especially when they were from the manor and shared a mindset.

He took a trip over to West London on a bright Sunday afternoon, parking his Jag on the cobbled street in the nearest available space closest to her place.

Holland Park was posh by East London standards; just the other side of Kensington and the right side of the festering shithole that was Shepherds Bush. Steve walked down the wide cobbled path and peered at the house numbers. His heart had already started to beat a little faster. This surprised him. Getting good-looking women to drop their drawers had never been a problem for him, but this one would be more of a challenge.

He had not felt this kind of impulsive attraction for some time. Okay, granted there was a young brunette round his way that he had cast an admiring glance at on more than a few occasions but she was such a sweet, unspoiled little thing that he could not bring himself to let her get involved in his lifestyle.

Anthea looked capable of handling it. In fact she looked capable of handling a lot of things. Just the thought of it gave him half a stalk.

Steve looked at the scrap of paper in his hand and then the number of the door he had stopped at. This was it.

From inside he could hear some seriously weird music; quite haunting but strange...a bit similar to the kind of thing the Beatles had done with "Love You To" on *Revolver* but less structured. Asian was it? He banged the heavy brass knocker on the door three times, waited for what seemed like an age and then banged again.

'All right! All right!' A woman's voice came from inside the house. 'It's open, come in for goodness sake.'

Steve let himself in and allowed himself a slight whistle. Almost all of the flat's internal walls had been removed, revealing a single large open space decorated almost entirely in shades of white, orange and yellow. The walls were covered with framed posters of French films. *Alphaville* caught his eye, then *Viva Maria!* and then *Three Rooms in Manhattan*.

He recognised the smell immediately as hashish; the minimal furniture was straight out of Habitat. There were no chairs, no settee. Instead there was a large sunken area in the middle of the room decked out in thick white carpet and a selection of huge cushions.

Anthea was sprawled across them puffing on a Jamaican Woodbine. She was dressed only in a black silk dressing gown that looked a few sizes too small for her. The model's long, sun-tanned legs were bared to about an inch below her panty line and one of her bristols peeped out seductively from beneath the sheer fabric.

Even without make-up the woman looked stunning.

'Why, Mr Knight, what a surprise,' she purred. 'How on earth did you track me down? Was it Morag at the office? She is such a slut! That girl will do anything for a handsome stranger...especially if he's handing out fivers.'

'Well thank you for the "handsome", you ain't too bad looking yourself for a plain girl.' He kept his face straight but the twinkle in his eyes gave him away. 'But no. It was another source.'

Steve glanced back at the movie posters on the wall, partly because they were fascinating but mostly to stop himself leering at her amazing figure. The Italian comedy flick *Casanova 70* looked quite alluring.

'How mysterious... Tell me, do you know any of these films, Mr Knight?'

'I saw *Yo Yo* last year.'

'Really? What did you make of it?'

'Okay. Sad millionaire's son runs away and joins the circus, falls in love with Claudine Auger, as you would. French film, obviously, directed and co-written by Pierre Étaix, funny in parts, never really gels...not as good as *Le Soupirant...*'

'Well I never. And there was me thinking your favourite film would be *Carry On Screaming!*.'

'And there was me thinking you'd be a patronising, stuck-up cow...'

Anthea smiled and scrunched the remains of the joint into an oversized earthenware pot.

'Touché,' she giggled. 'Well said that pleb.'

Her hair was different from the opening night, Steve thought. Shorter, almost boyish. An array of polystyrene head dummies on the other side of the room solved that mystery. Each one had a different wig, including the short blonde one she had been wearing the first time he saw her.

She was the mystery mod after all!

His perfect girl.

'Nice syrups,' he said, nodding towards the mannequins. 'And a nice drum.'

She looked blank, but only for a moment.

'Syrup of figs – wigs? Is that right? Yes?' she asked, with a giggle. 'One day you will have to teach me your quaint Cockney slang, but for now won't you come in and sit down instead of standing there dithering like an anxious rent collector?'

She patted a cushion next to her and beckoned him over. Steve closed the front door behind him and walked slowly across the room, soaking up its exotic splendour.

'I don't suppose you see too many rent collectors around this part of town, do you?' he said, stepping into the seating area and plonking himself down just inches from Anthea.

'Father takes care of those things. I find it all so frightfully dull.' She sounded bored. 'Who wants to talk about money anyway? It's very vulgar.'

Steve raised his eyebrows slightly. But the sweet smell of her hair and the close-up view he had of her silken curves stopped him from getting too het up about her spoilt child drawling.

'What about all these modelling jobs? They pay don't they? Pretty handsomely from what I've heard. You don't just do them for a laugh and a bowl of lentils do you?'

Anthea laughed and let her hand drop onto Steve's shoulder. 'No, I suppose you are right, Mr Knight, how very astute.'

She pointed over at a small coffee table near the huge picture window that illuminated the room with natural light. It was entirely covered with cheques, coins and bank notes with French francs and Italian lira mingling with sterling denominations, mostly cockles – tenners – with a few Jacks – fivers.

'I have to live, Steve. It's all over there if I need it but I don't think you came here to offer me financial advice did you?'

She sat up and looked at him full in the face. He felt himself getting lost in those big brown eyes. Anthea smiled and ran her free hand over his thigh until she was cradling his crotch. In a moment she let her right thumb and forefinger toy with the top button of his flies while the other three fingers of that hand descended gently on to his manhood.

Steve sat impassively, trying to conceal his surprise. He had not expected things to move so quickly and was trying to take stock of the situation.

Good East End girls didn't act like this. Just the bad ones.

'You're not big on the art of conversation, are you?' he said with a sly grin.

'Talk comes later,' Anthea whispered. 'I'm a scholar in the art of lovemaking.'

She pressed her fingers more firmly over his groin, feeling his cock strain heavily against the fabric of his strides. Their lips locked together and Steve helped the front of her dressing gown slip open with only the gentlest tug on the loose silk strip that was holding it together. He ran his hand firmly but gently over her pert nipples which pulsed warmly. Anthea gasped loudly as he let his fingers slide down her body and sink smoothly into her welcoming moistness. He started to move them steadily inside her pushing slowly deeper, as her hands undid his belt and fly buttons.

Steve stopped abruptly and stood up, getting shot of his clothes as quickly as he could without ripping anything, while Anthea lay back and used her own finger to massage her clitoris. She closed her eyes and smiled dreamily. Steve was already aroused, almost to bursting point. His cock stood out so hard and firm that she could have used it to play quoits.

He had to slow things down, take his time. Make it special.

He sunk to his knees and began to massage the top of her chest, then the tops of her arms and those inviting breasts, finding a gentle rhythm as he tuned into the seemingly endless sitar track. Her skin was as smooth as buttermilk. Perfect.

Anthea squirmed on the thick carpet and more than once tried to pull Steve's hips onto hers; but he continued to stroke, lick and kiss her while keeping his manhood at arm's-length. He let his finger-tips splay out moving softly over her stomach, then on and down teasingly slow to where she most wanted them.

She groaned. Then she groaned again. When her groaning grew loud enough to rouse the neighbours he moved into position and placed only the tip of his cock between her warm pussy lips. She shook in anticipation but he pulled back and then repeated the process three more times.

A long, slow, primitive growl built up from the back of her throat until it exploded.

'Fuck me, you bastard,' she screamed. 'Do what you came to do and fuck me, you big brute.'

Steve did as he was told, plunging hard into her tenderness, then finding a constant pounding rhythm until they both collapsed in an exhausted state onto the sweat-drenched cushions just as the setting sun bathed the room in a soft, orange glow.

Later as they talked into the early hours, he discovered why Anthea had looked so familiar the first time he'd seen her. It turned out that before her modelling career took off she had been a dancer on ITV's *Ready Steady Go!* He started singing '5-4-3-2-1' and she took it as an invitation to start fucking again.

***

It had been a heady six weeks, Steve Knight reflected as he settled onto a bar stall in the Dover Castle soaking up the boozer's quiet normality. He was knackered and in need of a fix of reality. With Anthea as his guide and by his side he'd plunged head first down a series of rabbit holes into worlds as mind-blowing as any imagined by Lewis Carroll. Sometimes she'd drag him to high society dos, stuffed with retired majors and baronets; other times he'd end up talking to bohemian poets and artists, out and out ponces whose every whim was subsidised by mater and pater, or weird kids – earnest and loaded – who banged on about the peace movement and the iniquities of the Vietnam War.

His preferred music, Stax and Tamla, was out the window. These odd-balls listened to Californian bands like the Grateful Dead and Jefferson Airplane. Not the majors obviously, it was either big band jazz or classical composers for the proper nobs. Horrible old pony. Give him the Four Tops any day. "Reach out, I'll be there"...

A grin began to play around Steve's mouth as he thought about Anthea. He'd be there all right. He had never had sex like it, real marathon sessions that left his legs wobblier than a *Crossroads* Motel TV film set. She was a connoisseur of carnality. She even kept a copy of the *Buddhist Love Book* in her khazi.

The girl was changing though. Now she only seemed to want sex when she was out of her nut on Lebanese hash or when her back teeth were floating in gin and it. He wouldn't be surprised if she were on something stronger, like opium, when he wasn't around.

She denied it, but there were times when she seemed so doolally Steve wondered if she even remembered getting shafted. Yet the bird had a funny kind of hold on him, one that he had never experienced before...

'Hello, stranger!'

Kenny bowled into the pub, disturbing his thoughts.

'How is life on Planet Posh, son? We thought you'd forgotten us, the poor hardworking hoi polloi.'

'Leave off, I'm in touch every week and you know it.'

Kenny laughed. 'Only fucking briefly,' he said, giving his brother a playful punch. 'And the last time you gave me a bell was nearly three weeks ago.'

'Anything I should know?'

Kenny pursed his lips. 'Well, the income is good...'

'But?'

'Those new boys, Steve, fuck me, they have given this business a proper punch up the trousers. Arthur and Butch went in hard and heavy from the off, and that set the tone pretty quick. People are more inclined to pay up on time than they ever were. No arguments. No excuses.'

'And Billy?'

'The kid is bloody useful, bruv. He's the bright one. Brains out here!' – he gestured with his hands about a foot away from his forehead. 'He's like you, Steve. He knows that jaw-jaw can sometimes bring in better than war-war...especially if you're jawing from a position of strength, like we are. He has solved a few disputes with the old grey matter that would probably have cost us money if we'd gone in fists first. Though he can have a row when he needs to. He may not hit as hard as the other two but when he has to it is no holds barred.'

'Yeah?'

'Yeah. In a little dispute we had with the manager of a shoe shop over near Haggerston Park he beat the little fucker so severely with the wooden contraption they use to measure kiddie's feet that Butch said he thought he was going to smash his brains out onto the carpet.'

'Ha. That's what I would call "fitting",' Steve grinned. He was about to add that Billy would be ripe for promotion over the next couple of years but he decided against it. He knew Kenny did not share his enthusiasm for moving the firm away from street thuggery and into legitimate businesses. He loved his brother but his head was stuck in a time capsule. Kenny was all about the old rules. Yet the old rules no longer applied, and the new rules were still to be written – and by the Knights.

The firm's future was definitely going to be more Richardsons than Krays. A well-oiled, money-making machine.

'Here, try this, Steve, – sling us that bottle over, El, and a couple of glasses.'

Eric produced a bottle of Scotch from under the bar. It had the look of a Johnnie Walker, but Steve noticed it had "Jackie Walker" written on the label. Kenny poured them both a glass. It looked darker than real whisky.

Steve took a sip and spat it straight back out.

'What the fuck...'

'Butch has got his cousin knocking them out.'

'It tastes like paraffin.'

'Well, I wouldn't go near it with a fag on, but it does the job and every working man's club from here to Dagenham is stocking it for a nice mark up.'

'Very enterprising. Eric, another light ale please, son.'

'The network is up and running too, Stevie,' Kenny went on. 'We are getting a steady stream of good tips for truck hijackings and warehouse break-ins. The word is out there that the Knights are back, stronger than ever.'

'So all is good?'

Kenny hesitated. 'All except for the drug side. Sales of pills and weed have started drying up, especially up West. I can't figure it out. That's where the demand was always at its highest and now it's falling through the floor.'

'McVey?'

'Nah. Pat's too fucking dim to do anything discreetly. We did think it might be the McCaffertys up to their old tricks.'

'I thought they'd been quiet since the World Cup?'

'Yeah they have. They've sneaked back down but they're minding their own. The only time they crossed our paths it was by accident one night in a pub up on Cremer Street. It got a bit naughty so Butch removed three of the older brother's fingers with a hatchet. After that the word was they had fucked off back to Glasgow for good.'

'So Tug's not tugging so well these days.'

'He ain't. Ha.'

'No. Ha-ha. So, not the Jocks and not McVey...'

'I've been doing a bit of digging while you've been off dicking toff totty but all I've found out is that someone new is dealing to the *smart set'* – he said the two words with a hefty side order of sarcasm – 'but even greasing palms, I could not get a name...'

Steve gripped his brother's shoulder. 'We'll find it. And I do mean *we!*

Give me a few days to cool things down with Anth and I'll be back full-time. Deal?'

'Deal.' They shook hands. 'Just make sure you do her up the 'arris once for me. It's what Dad would've wanted.'

Steve laughed. He missed his brother's dirty mind and vulgar badinage. He might appear to be a lone wolf a lot of the time but Steve knew a wolf's real strength wasn't its jaws or its claws, but its pack.

***

Steve was sitting up in the bed taking in the eclectic array of pop art and movie posters that adorned the walls of Anthea's bedroom. She lay beside him, puffing on a slim brown cigarette. He studied one about an all night rave that had been put on to launch "new underground newspaper *International Times*" that promised "Strip, Trips and Happening Movie...pop art masked ball" with a couple of bands he'd never heard of.

'Soft Machine?' he said to himself.

'Oh I don't want a soft one,' she giggled.

He felt Anthea's hand slip under the blanket and rest playfully just above his pubes. He glanced at her. Those firm breasts of hers glistened under a thin layer of perspiration and he couldn't help but notice that her nipples were pointing impertinently in his direction like a pair of chapel hat pegs. He gently ran his finger around each areola four times in a clockwise direction, then repeated the ritual anti-clockwise. Anthea assumed this was a prelude to another coupling and began to rub her thighs together lightly under the bedclothes. Steve felt a tingle in his groin and kissed her gently. John Thomas was standing to attention for the third time that day when a loud bang from the front door suddenly cooled his ardour.

Steve's first thought was to reach for the razor that he carried in his jacket pocket. He had no intention of getting caught literally with his pants down.

Anthea sensed his alarm and rested a calming hand on his chest.

'Who is it?' she shouted.

'It's just me, darling,' came the reply. An older man strode into the room, caught a glimpse of Steve and walked straight out again.

'Oh my,' he gasped from the living room. 'I can see you are busy, precious. I'll come back later.'

'Don't be silly,' shouted Anthea, 'Come in and talk to us.'

'Oh no, love, it's not the Turkish baths. I imagine you've got your hands full. I'll see you later, sweetheart.'

The front door slammed and the flat was silent once again.

'Who the fuck was that?' exclaimed Steve. 'Shirley Temple?'

'Just my friend Christian,' laughed Anthea. 'He's always popping round.'

'So the Kensington smart set don't bother to knock before they barge in?'

'How dreadfully plebeian you sound, Steven.'

Anthea sighed. Her tone set his teeth slightly on edge.

'My house has an open door to any of my friends and any of their friends. I love to share.'

Steve snorted in derision but he could not stay mad at her. She had already moved a smooth leg over his as her nimble fingers once again drifted softly over his hips. Within seconds he was making a tent under the thin silk sheet and Anthea giggled as she kissed his chest gently then slid her head down under the covers to investigate. That was the kind of sharing he could live with.

***

Twenty minutes later he declared himself 'cream-crackered' and slumped back into the luxury duck feather and down pillows. She wrapped a leg around him.

'You will come this evening, won't you?'

'What? Again?'

'No silly, to the soiree.'

'I can't.'

'You can.'

'I've got something on.'

She lifted up the sheet and looked down and sang 'The King is in the all together...'

He laughed.

'You can,' she said with head girl firmness.
'Not this time.'
'Uh-huh.'
Anthea whipped off the sheet and straddled him, then bent down to kiss his neck sensually pushing her breasts into his chest.
Steve groaned but made no attempt to stop her.

***

Rodney Huggins had called on the meet with Little Pig just for a catch-up. But as he watched Morgan slurp his Guinness, dribbling much of it down a foolishly chosen white shirt, he began to regret it. The Ship Tavern in Holborn was one of his favourite boozers. It served a good pint and had an incredible history. It had been built in 1549 to refresh field labourers, and during Henry VIII's reign, Catholics would sneak into the pub to hear Mass delivered from behind the bar by outlawed priests. Hard-working men and God-fearing rebels...all a damn site more deserving of a pint than the snivelling snout who sat before him now nibbling a cheese and pickle roll.

'Thanks for coming, Eddie,' he said in a tone as natural as he could make it.

'My pleasure, Mr 'Uggins. Always lovely to do business with your good self.'

'Right, let's skip to business then. Where's McVey?'

'The brothers don't know. Word is they've given up looking. Mate of mine swears blind Pat's got his head down with some gypos down in Kent. St Mary's Cray, he says, but I don't know that for sure.'

'He hasn't gone over to the Krays?'

'Not a chance Mr H. Ronnie can't stick 'im.'

'Gypos then? So the Knights are letting him get away with it?'

'No, no, no. They just ain't bothering to look for him. I heard Roy tell Eric in the Dover that they were just sitting back waiting for Mad Pat to resurface. Besides, Kenny's keeping busier than a dog with two dicks running the business...'

'And Steve?'

'He's away with the fairies, guv. The way I hear it, he's too busy shafting some marble-mouthed deb over Notting Hill way to give two stuffs at the moment. Loved up, 'e is.'

The detective laughed. 'Steve Knight in love with something other than money? That's a first.'

He slipped the informant a brown envelope.

'Thank you, Mr H.'

'It's only a pony, Eddie, but I appreciate you taking time out of your busy day.' The sarcasm was lost on the grass.

'My pleasure.'

'Okay. I've gotta dash but I'll put another pint in the pipe for you.'

'Thank you. You're most gracious. I'll give you a bell if I 'ear any more.'

'Please do. Oh and Eddie, you might want to brush yourself down a bit. You've got half a roll down yer dicky and the butter clashes with the Guinness stains...'

***

It was typical of Anthea. Arrogant, presumptive, unreasonable...because she knew he had other business to take care of. So why did he suffer it? Surely not because when she wasn't monged out she banged like a shithouse down in a dysentery ward?

He grinned. You shallow bastard, Knight.

Steve resigned himself to sampling her erotic delights once or twice more. Maybe three times. Who's counting?

There was something to be said for a posh boarding school upbringing. And they hadn't called her head girl for nothing. Anthea was nothing like the girls he'd grown up with, girls who begrudgingly dished out their favours before becoming consumed with guilt.

***

Ten minutes later, Anthea screeched the car to a halt outside a three-storey townhouse in West Kensington. The Tiger was a wonderful piece of engineering but Anthea ground the gears and pushed it through the streets of W11 with scant regard to pedestrians or other road users. It was a wild ride, but Steve had sat in the passenger seat impassively and let the wind blow through his hair.

There were a few scruffy types lounging around on the steps outside but the real action was obviously happening inside. Every light in the house was on and moving silhouettes could be seen behind each window.

They cruised in through the open door and Steve was dismayed to find yet another mammoth gathering of chinless wonders and weirdos quaffing free drinks and getting high on whatever they could get their manicured hands on.

The gaff looked like a stately home with expensive bronzes and vulgar mock-Greek statues scattered about. Someone had thrown a few silk scarves over the antique lamps to give the place a more "groovy" ambience and loud trippy music filled every room. Psychedelic, they called it.

He noticed a short, large breasted brunette was looking at him with barely disguised interest. He winked as Anthea near enough dragged Steve away and on through the hall and across the main room on the ground floor towards a flamboyant middle-aged man in an open-necked paisley shirt that was at least two decades too young for him. His thickly coiffured hair looked as if it had been moulded onto his head.

'You simply must meet Christian properly, he's my muse,' Anthea simpered as she steered Steve towards her friend.

Steve wasn't exactly sure what a muse was, but suspected it was upper class speak for "a right horrible ponce".

'Oh, *bona*,' squealed the man in a voice that was a bizarrely reminiscent of Julian and Sandy from *Round The Horne*, confirming Steve's suspicions. 'You must be Anthea's latest beau. How lovely to see you when you've got your clothes on, darling.'

Steve recognised his voice immediately. It was the same old iron who had interrupted their bliss back at her flat.

Steve had met many homosexuals – "brown-'atters" – in his line of work, especially in the clubs of Soho, and found them okay and often very funny, but few were as hoity-toity and over the top as Christian Somerville.

'Oh there's Binky,' yelled Anthea as she looked across the room then turned back to Christian, 'Take care of him for me darling, will you?' Steve gave her a look that said 'Don't you dare', but Anthea just planted a warm kiss on his cheek and ran off.

'So you are Anthea's latest are you, handsome?' cooed Christian. 'You must be fucking exhausted, love, she's a real live wire.'

His voice was posh, but camp posh. Like a bent bishop.

Steve smiled but said nothing. He was in no mood to discuss his relationship with strangers. He had barely mentioned anything in detail to Kenny or Roy so he wasn't about to open up to some passing ginger.

'Strong and silent, are you? Very butch, dear.'

Christian thrust a lit joint towards Steve. 'Get your lips round that, Steve dearest, it makes all this palaver more bearable.'

'Not for me thanks.'

Steve looked around the room suspiciously.

'No shortage of gear in here tonight though is there? Have you got someone that keeps you all supplied?'

'Oh yes, darling, we've got our "little man" who sees us right. You'll meet him soon. Victor. "Victor Victoria" I call him. Such a toughie, a rough diamond like you, Stevie.'

Christian squeezed his bicep suggestively and Steve did him the small favour of not chinning him.

'He's at all the soirees and he's very discreet if you know what I mean. Once he brought his friend Kemal along, from

Cyprus I believe, face like a leather jockstrap. He's in the same game.'

Steve nodded. Whoever was supplying this snobby mob must be doing good business while taking some coin out of the Knight firm's pockets at the same time. He looked directly into Christian's eyes.

'Do you think he could get me something tonight?'

'He can get anything you want, darling,' said Christian as his face flushed slightly. 'Uppers, downers, inners, outers, blues, black bombers, nigger minstrels...whatever your bag is, baby.' Christian fluttered his eyelashes at Steve who stood impassively in front of him.

'Cocaine, Mr Somerville. I'd like some of the old Salvador Dalí.'

Christian took the knock-back on the chin.

'Christian, please. Actually he's here tonight honey if you fancy a little...something special. I think he's in the games room.'

He pointed over to a heavy panelled door at the far end of the room that was very slightly ajar.

'I might well do that,' smiled Steve politely. 'Nice to meet you...*Christian,* but do excuse me.'

'My pleasure.' Beat. Leer. 'And it would be...'

Steve's pleasure at that moment would have been to serve the great fop up a solid right-hander. But instead he smiled wanly and strolled across the room, distracted only by the unmistakable sight of Kit Lambert chatting to a man who looked remarkably like the Earl of Snowdon in a dark corner.

Once he was at the doorway, one nonchalant look was enough to establish that the pusher was indeed present. He was perched on the side of the snooker table with some bags of pills, powders and dark green marijuana in front of him on the baize as if he was running some kind of narcotic jumble sale. Business seemed to be going well as a gaggle of punters were waiting to pass over their readies and a small pile of notes had already built up on the polished wood over the top cushion.

The pusher, Victor, had his back to him but when he turned sideways Steve gasped silently and moved away from the door as quickly as he could. His face had already started to redden with fury.

The dealer was Vic Naboth.

Steve had to get away. Moving quickly, he headed back towards the main door. Neither Anthea nor Christian saw him, but the busty brunette was blocking his way.

'Going so soon?'

'Yeah, something has come up.'

Her eyes twinkled suggestively. 'That's a shame. Here...' she grabbed a scrap of paper from her bag, wrote something on it, and stuffed it into his hand.

'Thanks...' he looked at it. '...Charlotte. Be seeing you.'

'I do hope so.'

***

Pat McVey woke up with a grunt and took stock of his whereabouts warily. He was in a single bed with a sleeping woman's right arm draped over him. He had woken up in the same place every day for the last few months but it usually took him a few moments to remind himself where he was and why through his throbbing dark rum hangovers. Two empty bottles on the bedside table told the story.

The tart was snoring. He shook her roughly and she rolled onto her back. About 40, he guessed. Blonde with dark roots. Quite pretty except for the black eye. Wonder where she got that. Oh yeah.

He reached for his fags and lit up. He was grateful to Kemal for setting him up in this poky council flat just off the Old Kent Road, a minute's stroll from the Dun Cow. And he was grateful for his promise of protection – 'You are my guest, and as my guest your safety is guaranteed indefinitely,' the Turk had said. But fuck was he getting bored. At least Vic was coming over later. They'd have a pint or ten in the

Green Man, see a stag comic and fuck a couple of strippers. Happy days.

***

Vic Naboth sat on a hard wooden chair in the office above Aphrodite's Palace. His body language was relaxed. Almost cocky. Across the desk from him Steve sat in his much grander leather chair. Kenny stood at the window with his back to both of them. Butch and Arthur were waiting outside, primed and ready.

Downstairs the DJ was spinning the Beach Boys hit "Good Vibrations" unaware of the irony.

Vic glanced from one brother to the other. Steve was stone-faced but still a prick. Kenny looked uncomfortable, and so he fucking should be with them dragging him in like a naughty schoolboy. Kenny was his mate, his ally; he knew what was what. Steve was out of his depth and always had been.

Vic took a swig of his brown and mild and decided to break the silence.

'So what's this all about, son?' he barked, knowing full well that would wind up the younger Knight brother good and proper. Steve didn't react.

'It's about business, Vic,' he said calmly. 'And the way we do things now. There are too many loose ends on the firm and we need to consolidate.'

'What the fuck are you talking about? We're villains, boy, not fucking Barclays Bank. We do what we need to do to make money and if anyone gets in the way they get battered.'

'Who do you think makes the most dough, Vic? The man who robs the bank or the man who owns it?'

'Kenny! Are you listening to this shit?'

'He's right, Vic,' said Kenny with a sigh. 'If we want to move onwards, and upwards, it's the only way.'

'You see, you are a blunt instrument, Vic, but we need a surgical scalpel,' said Steve quietly. 'We need to cut out the cancer that is eating away at our profits not batter it until it gets critical.'

The veins in Vic's forehead were glistening under a thin layer of sweat.

'I can't listen to this bollocks...'

Vic stood up.

'Sit down,' Steve barked.

Vic continued to stand defiantly. Arthur opened the door and popped his head around the door.

'It's okay, Arthur. All cool.'

'Come on, Vic, sit down for fuck's sake,' said Kenny. 'We just want to talk.'

'I was your father's partner, just you remember that,' said Vic as he sat down reluctantly.

'We all know that that ain't true, Vic,' said Steve with a patient sigh. 'But we have no intention of trying to play down how much you meant to our old man. Not just as an associate but as a friend.'

Vic seemed to relax a bit. He reached inside his jacket, causing Kenny to tense up and Steve's right hand to slip below the desk.

Vic pulled out a packet of Player's No.10 and lit one up. Kenny relaxed.

'Losing Mr McVey to our, eh...competitors shall we say, has lost us a lot of money, Vic, as you well know,' Steve said calmly. 'He was a good friend of yours, wasn't he?'

'Pat is okay,' growled Vic. 'He's all right.'

'All fucking right?' snapped Kenny. 'He killed Matty. He raided our opening night and fucked this place up. If I see the cow-son ever again he will be six foot under, on my life.'

'He always was loyal to your father,' Vic answered defiantly. 'He just doesn't believe in all...all this.'

Vic waved his hand vaguely between Steve and Kenny.

'This little foetus firm you've got running here.'

'And that is exactly our problem, Vic,' Steve said evenly. 'All this, as you put it, is our way of doing things. As much as I wish my old man was still about, the reality of the situation is that he has gone and we are in charge now, and as much as we have no desire to break up the old firm we need everyone to pull in the same direction.'

'Things were fine the way they were!'

'The way they were, Vic, was everyone doing their own thing under the Knight firm name. There were lots of loose ends and twisted alliances. You even did business with that cunt Wilson for fuck's sake!'

Steve paused for a moment to regain his composure then he continued in a measured tone. 'Anyway, whatever went before is a foreign country to us now. Pat McVey can never be forgiven but we want everyone else to stay with us, to grow with us, but on our terms. We are going to all make more money than ever before but we need to stand together and have a clear way forward that we are all working towards.'

'Piss off,' Vic hissed.

Steve looked a little surprised and sucked his teeth slightly. 'Piss off? Is that it, Vic? Is that your sole contribution to the discussion? I don't think there is any more to say then.'

'For fuck's sake, Vic,' yelled Kenny with just a hint of desperation. 'Listen to what Steve has to say. Things are changing; the whole fucking world is changing. The Ruskies have just landed on the moon…hippies are rioting, there are dope smokers and angry fucking students banging on about Ho Chi Minh. It's not all brown ale and demob suits any more, mate. It's a new world with new markets and new opportunities...for all of us. We don't want to break things up in this firm, we just want a bigger slice of the pie. No more pissing about for a few tanners here and there. This city is the centre of the world right now and we deserve a part of it.'

'And how are you going to get that, eh?' Vic roared. 'Poncing about like a couple of Carnaby Street tarts and forgetting about the way we used to do things. Things that made us money. Things that got us respected in this fucking town.'

'I've had enough of this,' said Steve, almost to himself. 'This conversation is going nowhere.'

He pulled his hand up from the side of the desk and slammed a fairly worn Beretta 950 on the desk. He flicked the button on the side of the gun to release the magazine. It was fully loaded and after a brief glance at it he slid it straight back into the weapon with a loud click.

'So this is where I get threatened is it, son?' leered Vic. His voice was hard but a tell-tale bead of sweat trickled down his left temple.

Steve slipped the magazine out of the gun once more then drove it straight back in again. And again. His face was expressionless. Vic noticed Kenny turn away to look out the window and began to shake.

'Four times, eh? Are you still at that, you fucking mental case?' spat Vic. 'Your dad said you weren't right, even when you was a nipper.'

Steve released and reloaded the Beretta for a fourth time then, without a word, he pointed the barrel of the gun at Vic Naboth's chest and fired four times. *Blam! Blam! Blam! Blam!*

The older villain dropped to the floor immediately with a look of bewilderment frozen on his face.

Kenny looked across the room at his brother, his ears still ringing. Steve was running a silk handkerchief over the gun before placing it back in the drawer.

'I've got to get meself a silencer,' he said. He looked as bothered as if he had just swatted a fly.

'Butch! Arthur! Get in here – now,' Kenny shouted, 'And bring a fucking mop.'

***

Downstairs the bars of Aphrodite's Palace looked busy but even a casual observer would notice how dramatically the club's clientele had changed since the opening night fiasco. There were no Chelsea girls here, no skinny models or politicians; and certainly no slumming posh boys hanging around for the visceral thrill of associating with the underworld – they loved the image but the reality of Mad Pat McVey's violent gang raid had terrified and traumatised the poor souls.

The new clientele were a different league of flash. They were second-hand car dealers, house breakers, confidence tricksters, ticket touts, scrap metal merchants, counterfeiters, pickpockets and market men. And the women who weren't wives and girlfriends were all on the game. Not streetwalkers – they were classier than that. These were what passed for high-end whores in this part of town and they were the only reason the club also attracted clerks, bankers and the occasional clergyman.

The toms paid a portion of their hard-earned cash to the Knights and received pleasant surroundings to work in, as well as protection from the vicious Maltese pimps who preyed on street girls. Those who did not have flats in walking distance were able to rent one of the spare rooms upstairs by the hour.

Kenny and Steve pulled up seats at the bar and drank whisky, with Kenny soon finding his lap occupied by Rita Shaw, a jobbing actress with peroxide tints and magnificent knockers.

She put her Martini down and giggled.

'I need a slash,' she said and tottered off in her four-inch heels.

'So ladylike,' laughed Kenny.

'You won't mind when those long legs are wrapped around your boat later.'

Kenny turned in to him.

'So briefly, Pat?' he said quietly.

'After we find him?'

'Yeah. You still thinking death by Norton ES2s?'

'Nah. Too showy. Either we hunt him down, shoot him like the rabid dog he is and he ends up like Vic will be tomorrow, sunk deep in a fly-over or...we could be a bit smarter.'

'How do you mean?'

'We make him a deal, bruv. We give him something to play with. A club off the manor say. We give him licence to run somewhere we're not interested in, like Lewisham or Catford. That'll end the feud, keep him busy, keep him out of our way... '

'But he killed Matty...'

'The more I think about life, bruv, the more I think it's more like a game of chess than draughts. You can steam in jumping everything in your way or you can play a long game.'

'He'll build up a firm and come back after us again.'

'Listen. We set Pat up, maybe we even help him dispose of any small-time rivals. We know where he is and what he's up to. We trade with him. And when he's convinced bygones are bygones, when his guard is down and he suspects nothing...'

'Show time!'

'Exactly. Queen takes castle. Check-fucking-mate.'

'You're either the smartest man alive or completely round the twist.'

'Or both, bruv. Or both.'

Rita staggered back, her bosom overflowing.

'Oi, are you going to rabbit all night?'

Kenny kissed her full on the lips.

'No. We're gonna be at it like rabbits all night.'

She giggled and they left.

***

Five Days Later

Pat McVey was strolling down Hackney Road in the dimming early evening light without a care in the world. This was his third public outing in as many days. He had been holed up in a safe flat down the Old Kent Road courtesy of Kemal Demirci, AKA the Turk, ever since the attack on Aphrodite's Palace but he had started to fret when Vic

Naboth had failed to show up for their regular meet. It was time to put his face about on his old manor again. If the Knights wanted to know, they could come and find him. Fucking wankers. They'd probably lost their bottle, assuming they had ever had one to begin with.

He'd track Vic down and get the SP. For the moment he chose to brazen it out and show the world that Pat McVey would never tremble at the feet of a pair of flash cunts who were living off their old man's reputation.

Pat, on the other hand, genuinely loved violence. McVey had killed his first victim when he was thirteen, pulled a bloke off his bike in Cherry Tree Wood and snapped his neck. *KWAK!* It wasn't premeditated and he'd had no real motive other than that he was bored and in a rotten mood. He didn't even rob him.

Just remembering that moment excited him, just as it had at the time; killing that scrawny man – so weak, so worthless – had given him the first erection he could remember. It had happened when he'd plunged Matty too. Bang on! Hard as a fucking nail. He hadn't lost a minute of sleep over it.

McVey visited a few pubs along the way, knowing the right people would clock him. People with small brains and big gobs. He made his way quietly to the snug bar of each boozer, ordered a single Scotch, downed it and moved on, fully aware that every barman who served him would probably be straight on the blower to the brothers.

It was not long before McVey spotted Billy Storer laughing and joking with some young friends in the saloon bar of the Crown & Anchor in Temple Street. Pat walked straight out of the boozer and into a cafe across the road where he soon sat nursing a steaming mug of tea and a growing ball of anger festering deep in the pit of his stomach.

***

Rodney Huggins did not take kindly to meeting in a Coventry Street Wimpy Bar, but Eddie Morgan had insisted. 'For convenience,' he had said, adding equally unconvincingly that he was 'working nearby'. In truth Little Pig had only recently discovered the joys of the Wimpy Bar and would happily pull any stroke for the chance of a free one.

'You should have a Brown Derby after this, Mr H,' Eddie said as the waitress brought over their Wimpy Grills and Morgan's coffee. The sight of the tall hexagonal mug alone seemed to delight him.

'I have eaten in a Wimpy before, Eddie,' Huggins replied with an air of disdain. 'No bar, most uncivilised.'

He leaned forward. 'Now,' he said. 'What have you got for me?'

'McVey,' said Eddie solemnly. 'He's back.'

***

The streets outside the cafe on Temple Street were dark and quiet. Gloomy even. McVey gazed out of the window across at the pub. Three empty mugs sat in front of him, and Joe, the joint's owner, was making an exaggerated show of tidying up for the night. As an attempt to dislodge his last customer it was pretty fruitless but he knew of Pat McVey's reputation and didn't dare ask him outright to sling his unwelcome hook.

Finally he said: 'One more tea before we close, sir?'

McVey stood up suddenly. The scraping sound that his old wooden chair made as it was thrust across the tiled floor made Joe flinch.

He hawked and spat onto the table. 'Your tea tastes like cat piss,' he growled. The owner recoiled in fright.

McVey took a few coins from his pocket and tossed them into the spittle with a grin before he stormed out.

***

Billy Storer and his two young friends strolled down the street laughing and joking with each other. Bert Turner and Ricky Davis had been Billy's pals since school, but since Billy got involved with the Knights they had seen much less of each other. It had been a rare treat to spend an afternoon together and mull over old times.

They were a smart bunch, clad in the best clobber 1967 had to offer – most colourfully the bold green plaid trousers the pair opted for, topped with casual roll-neck pullovers. Unlike their younger brothers, who went for French crops, they'd let their hair grow, Kinks style.

A close observer would have noticed the redness around their eyes. None of them had spent much time in the last 72 hours anywhere near a bed.

'You've changed, Billy,' said Bert with a grin. 'You've stopped moaning.'

'Prick.'

'You do seem a lot happier now you're holding folding,' said Ricky.

'You should try grafting a bit harder,' Billy laughed. 'Since I've been with the brothers, I've never been short of a few bob.'

'How's your mum about it?' asked Bert.

'You know. Worried at first but she perked up when she saw the money I was making. When I told her I was taking driving lessons and was thinking of buying a jam-jar she convinced herself that I was in a nice steady job with prospects...'

'As opposed to being an apprentice hoodlum...'

'Fuck off! Listen, when you're at Upton Park putting the boot into some Millwall scumbag you're doing it for the thrill. When I get stuck in I get all the enjoyment and a pay packet...'

'Money to boot... to boot!' laughed Ricky.

The three lads stopped in front of a small alleyway where a couple of Lambrettas were parked.

'Are you still driving those things?' Billy said, in a lightly mocking tone. 'You'd have trouble getting a bunk-up on the back of one of these.'

'We get around, mate,' said Ricky with a wink.

'Yeah,' piped up Bert, 'At least we ain't fucking walking like you.'

Billy smiled as he touched the polished glass of the speedo on Ricky's Li150.

'They still look great, mate, but I'm going to get meself a...'

Smash! A house brick struck Billy's jaw sending his body crashing onto the grimy paving slabs along with two of his teeth.

Pat McVey continued his vicious attack swiftly, pounding Billy's face with heavy kicks from his hob-nailed boots, smashing his nose out of shape.

He was focused so sharply on reducing Billy's features to a bloody pulp that he paid no attention whatsoever to his friends.

Ricky immediately leapt on to McVey's back, trying to topple him. But the bigger man shrugged him off like a sleepy gorilla dislodging an unwelcome infant, sending him flying into a pair of overflowing dustbins, spilling their contents over the pavement.

Bert was more prepared. He went straight to the leg-shield of his scooter, and reached for the length of lead piping he kept tucked away up there.

'Get off him, you old cunt,' he shouted swinging the piping hard and precisely, catching McVey just behind the left ear.

A spurt of blood splashed onto Bert's moccasins and McVey dropped onto his knees, dazed by the force of the blow. Bert gulped. That should have knocked the bastard clean out. He lashed out again, striking his prey smack bang between the middle of his shoulder blades. McVey groaned in pain but still refused to collapse. Bert raised his bar to deliver him again, harder, and heavier...

'Leave him, Bert! He's mine.' Billy was slowly rising to his feet; his handsome youthful features were almost invisible under a thick veil of blood. He somehow managed to get upright again and bounced lightly from foot to foot as he adopted a weary boxing stance. Bert and Ricky stood at either side of him, aching to grind their attacker into the cobbles.

'Come on, McVey, toe to toe,' Billy continued. 'Let's have it. Face me, you sneaky cunt, let's see how you do it when you ain't got a fucking brick in your hand.'

McVey was still on his knees. But his back was straight and his head bowed, as if he were praying. He emitted a low growling noise. Billy stood directly in front of the crouching figure, prodding him with the toe of his shoe as if he were baiting a bear.

'Come on, you ugly fucker. Come and try again. Steve always said you were a no-good piece of shit.'

Pat McVey leaned forward onto one arm, then swiftly straightened his knees and leapt to his feet. A dull street light briefly illuminated the long blade in his other hand before it sank deep into the soft skin under Billy's chin. The kid's eyes opened wide with shock and stayed open in a cold lifeless stare.

McVey withdrew the blade and laughed. 'Ugly beats dead, cunt.'

Bert and Ricky leapt backwards, crashing into their scooters and knocking them onto the hard pavement. Billy's body fell to the ground with a dull thud.

Glowering, McVey pointed the blood-stained dagger at Ricky then Bert but said nothing. Both tensed for the battle to come, but McVey just grinned and growled 'When you see Steven and Kenny Knight tell them I'll be waiting for them. Tell them I'm in with a new firm, and we'll slice them open like a kebab. *Anlama*?'

McVey turned and walked away. His grizzled unshaven face had rarely looked so happy.

His hard-on took an hour to subside.

Chapter Seven: The Judas Pig

Two days later.

Lizzie Davies was lost in a daydream as she removed the wooden pegs that were securing her underwear and a few blouses on the washing line in the small square of grass that passed for a garden at her mum's house. It had been a warm day and she was just starting to think about how "Swinging London" was passing her by when a booming voice behind her snapped her back to reality.

''Allo, darling.'

She spun round a little too quickly and noticed it was Kenny Knight, resplendent in a razor-sharp dark blue suit which jarred with the backdrop of her parents' modest two up, two down. He placed a hand gently on her shoulder to steady her.

'Easy, love, I'm not here for the rent,' he said with a broad smile that made her blush.

Kenny was a good-looking man in a brutish sort of way, despite his hair being prematurely thin and a face that looked as if it had survived eight rounds with Henry Cooper.

It was his brother she was really interested in. They had both been to the same school as Lizzie, even though they were years above her and seldom there. From an early age she had admired Steve's boyish good looks and that feeling had grown into a full-blown crush as she matured; a crush she dismissed as ridiculous as she had never even spoken to him and he had certainly never seemed to have noticed her.

Kenny had always given her the time of day though and never failed to stop for a chat whenever their paths crossed. Admiration is too strong a word, but Lizzie had always had a soft spot for the Knight brothers. She knew they were hard, she knew they were dangerous, but round her way people had a grudging respect for them. They opened doors for ladies, gave generously to local charities, bought raffle tickets, threw spare change at the local tearaways and, more than that, they seemed to keep the real undesirables off the street – as the elderly child molester who was working as a lollipop man outside Shoreditch Park discovered to his painful cost only last month.

She had heard tales of them dispensing a little homegrown justice to any burglars or car thieves that operated in the area too, thieving off their own.

But she had also heard far more blood-curdling stories as well. Maybe it was all just a mix of truth, half-truth and myth.

'Kenny! You made me jump,' she said with a giggle. 'You like sneaking up on women bringing in their smalls, do you?'

Kenny glanced at Lizzie's underwear on the line with a greedy eye as if he were picturing her wearing them. She noticed her mother at the kitchen window, looking like a startled cat.

'Go away, mum,' Lizzie shouted.

'The curtains are always twitching around here,' Kenny laughed. 'How you doing anyway, Lizzie?'

'Fine, Kenny, thank you for asking. Plodding on as usual.'

Kenny sucked in a disapproving breath through his teeth and sighed.

'A good-looking girl like you shouldn't be plodding, Elizabeth. You should be treated like a queen. It's all happening out there, Liz, and you need to get a slice of it.'

'I do all right; I get up to the clubs most weekends.'

'Weekends?' he gasped in mock shock. 'That's old hat, darling, they're at it seven nights a week up West. It's a twenty-four-hour party town.'

Lizzie looked down at her feet. 'Well I ain't seen much of it.'

Kenny paused to fish some snouts out of his pocket. He offered her one, which she declined, and then took another sly glance at her underwear on the line before he lit up – red lace lingerie set; who'd have thought it?

'What about your club? How is it going?' she asked even though she knew the answer.

Kenny's face immediately darkened. 'That poxy place. That's Steve's baby and he's fucking welcome to it. If it wasn't for me putting a bit of business in there it would have been boarded up months ago.'

'How is Steve?' Lizzie asked tentatively.

'You know Steve, he's doing fine although I don't see as much of him these days. He's got some posh new bird up in Kensington.'

Lizzie's shoulders drooped slightly. Kenny carried on regardless.

'Nice looking girl but a fucking wrong'un. The crowd she hangs about with are a right shower...hippies, queers, Commies, you name it. Proper druggies too.'

He noticed that the sun had set on Lizzie's previously cheery mood and smiled.

'Anyway, I'll tell you what I came for, darling. We're having a little party on Friday and I wondered if you could meet a friend of ours and bring him along. It's a surprise type of thing and there will be a few bob in it for you.'

'I'm not a flaming scrubber,' Lizzie said angrily.

'No, no, it's nothing like that!'

Kenny raised both hands in an exaggerated sign of surrender. She had a bit of fire in her then. A good East End girl – and you knew where you were with them.

'All we want you to do is bring him along to the old hale and hearty on the night without him realising what you're up to. Once we know where he is going to be, we'll give you a bell and you can roll up, give him a bit of bunny and then suggest you both move on to your mate's do. He's an ugly old bastard, if he thinks a tasty looking bird like you has taken a shine to him he'll go goggle-eyed.'

'And that's it? Just bring him along to the party?'

'That's it, just that. And if I know Patrick he'll follow along behind you like a dozy old mongrel.'

Lizzie's frown evaporated. God, Kenny thought, she was a pretty little thing when she smiled.

'Here...' he fished inside his pocket and pulled out a slip of paper with some bank notes folded neatly inside. 'That's the address where it's gunna be. I've got your number, just sit tight on Friday and stay by the dog and bone.'

Kenny thrust the bundle into her hand, leant over, kissed her cheek roughly and started to leave. Then he paused and said, 'You're a good girl, Lizzie, I won't forget this.'

She smiled. Maybe Steve would be there. And maybe his posh bitch of a girlfriend wouldn't be. Maybe he'd notice her.

Suddenly Kenny was back. His mood was darker.

'Once this is done, Lizzie, you need to forget about this whole conversation though. It never happened.'

'Of course, Kenny, whatever you say.'

She was puzzled but his broad roguish grin reappeared. He took the opportunity to peck her cheek again, waved goodbye and disappeared through the back gate. Lizzie studied the handwritten note for a full five minutes after he'd gone trying to figure out exactly what she had gotten herself into. She felt nervous but also strangely invigorated. Her, little Lizzie, helping out the Knights? Blimey. Somehow just the thought of it suddenly made her feel more alive.

***

Steve Knight stood in the lift of the Granville Court flats trying not to breathe too heavily as the acrid stench of stale urine drifted into his nostrils. This was no way to live, he thought; stuck in a concrete box up in the sky with God knows what kind of deadbeats and low life scumbags as your neighbours. No wonder people here were alienated and dehumanised. What kind of dirty degenerate would empty his bladder inside his own building? They'll be shitting on their own doorstep next, literally.

The number *15* illuminated on the panel at his side and after a loud ding the metal door slid slowly open with a pained creaking sound.

He stepped out onto a bijou landing. It was filled with old folk who were milling around one of the four doors on that floor, dressed in black.

Steve made his way through the crowd of mourners as respectfully as possible, ignored the hateful glares he was attracting from a number of them – if looks could kill, he thought, I'd be brown bread.

When he reached the open door he stepped through it. In the living room he saw a middle-aged woman sitting in a chair sobbing uncontrollably while another woman who looked like a relative prodded her with a cup of tea, that familiar East End cure for all bad things. She was probably in her early forties but in this light, and with her face blotchy and damp with tears, she could have passed for someone just a kick in the arse away from a state pension.

The crying woman raised her head up slightly and as she noticed Steve her wailing increased in volume. He was about to speak, but Roy Storer suddenly appeared at his side and steered him through the room and out onto the small concrete balcony with its neat selection of potted plants.

Roy closed the door behind them, shutting out the tears.

Now all they could hear was the relentless hum of the city – engines, car horns, people shouting, kids laughing and the cry of a rag and bone man... '*Raaaaggg n boonnneeeesss! Raaaaggg n boonnneeeesss!*'

The sounds of life; of normality. Despite the daylight and their high vantage point, their view of the manor was obscured by the heavy morning fog. Beyond the next block, the city was just a grey blur.

'What the hell are you doing here, Steve?' said Roy as he looked through the window of the flat at the tableaux of grief. 'Fucking Hitler would be made more welcome in here than you are.'

'I wanted to pay my respects.'

'You can pay your respects by telling me where that cunt McVey is. I'm going to finish him today.'

His hand drifted instinctively onto the Luger pistol that was nestled in the inside pocket of his jacket.

'That's all in hand, Roy,' said Steve in a calming tone.

'In hand? You should have done the cunt before you done Naboth. Vic was selling a few pills outside the firm. So fucking what? McVey is a rabid fucking animal, and he should have been put down long ago. Billy should still be here now. For fuck's sake, he was only eighteen...'

Roy tried to push his way past towards the door but Steve grabbed hold of him by the shoulders.

'I know you're angry, Roy, but we'll sort McVey out for good, I promise you.'

Roy broke free of Steve's grip. 'It's too fucking late now. I'll do it myself. That wrong cunt will be dead by dinner time.'

Steve grabbed Roy by the arm again and Roy instinctively lashed out with his fist. His knuckles hit Steve firmly on the jaw and he staggered back with a look of surprise and indignation in his eyes. Roy instantly knew he had made a mistake but he would not back down. He stood there defiantly, shaking with righteous anger.

Steve did not move; he did not make a sound. He too stood stock-still, like a statue, his face hard and immobile. Only his eyes told a different story as the battle raged in his head. To retaliate, to meet fire with fire, and rain a furious vengeance down on his friend or...to understand what he was going through, and forgive and forget like a bigger man...

Roy steeled himself for an onslaught that didn't come. Instead, Steve shook his head and spoke softly.

'Now, I'm going to put that down to a breakdown in communication, Royston, but you had better listen... I can see that fucking Luger under your jacket and if you think you are going to go after McVey all guns blazing in broad daylight then you can fucking think again. You might get him but you're going to get yourself banged up or killed at the same time. We will sort McVey out – together. But we'll do it right so you need to calm the fuck down. Now!'

Roy teetered on the edge of anger and deflation for a moment before his shoulders dropped. Steve had a point, no matter how painful it was to take.

'Eighteen years old, Steve. Eighteen. My fucking Aunt Carol is in pieces. It ain't right...'

Steve placed a comforting arm around his old friend's shoulders and wiped a splodge of blood from his nose with his free hand.

'I promised her he'd be okay. I promised I'd look after him, I promised...'

Roy's sobs drowned out the rest of the sentence.

'We'll sort it, mate, all of us. That piece of shit is a dead man walking, I promise you.'

***

Mad Pat McVey sat with his back to the wall in the far corner of the Dover Castle. He had a clear view of the door and a newly purchased fully loaded 9mm Luger was tucked satisfyingly close in the right-hand pocket of his trousers, covered by his black bomber jacket.

Pat stubbed out a Player's Navy Cut directly onto the table top even though a large glass ashtray was inches away. He had other plans for that if push came to shove. He took a deep gulp from his pint of bitter and scanned the room.

It was after nine o'clock on a Friday night, but the bar was sparsely populated and not a single punter was willing to meet his gaze. McVey rested back onto the worn fabric of his chair and smiled to himself. Here he was bang in the middle of Knight territory and there was not even a ripple of protest to be heard. No aggression, no condemnation, nothing.

The killing of Billy Storer would be almost old news on this manor. No arrests had been made, no suspect announced, but the locals all knew that McVey was the killer. And yet here he was, bold as brass, out drinking in the Knights' heartland without a care in the world.

McVey was taking liberties and he loved it. He wanted to be on these streets. He wanted to show the Knight brothers up and let them be seen as the pair of feeble half-men they were. And more than anything he wanted to front them up if they came a-calling and take them down.

He, Pat McVey, would put them in the ground but first he would have them squealing for mercy right here in front of everyone who knew them.

His only regret was that he had not done them both in that night at Aphrodite's Palace.

The Dover was different though. He could blow their fucking heads off right in the middle of the boozer and not one punter would see a thing when the law came a-calling. Witness myopia, it was an East End thing. This might be Knight territory now but when he takes it over the locals would just shrug their shoulders and carry on with their lives.

People can be very accepting if there is a real and present danger that they can get hurt...badly.

After a few more pints, McVey shifted grumpily in his seat. Where were the two shitty-arsed poofs? He was getting bored waiting around being ignored. With every minute that passed he became more convinced that the Knights had been warned that he was here and had gone to ground. The gutless wonders were running scared! And that realisation filled him with a feeling of anger rather than pride.

The pub door opened and Pat stiffened in anticipation, but it was just some young bit of skirt. He watched her make her way to the bar and order some shit in a glass with a bit of lemon in it. Gin? Vodka? He couldn't tell. She was a tidy little thing, though, the only bright spark in this dreary shithouse. Her light blue mini-dress clung to where it touched, but not in a tarty way, and her shapely bare legs slid into a pair of black patent shoes with a tiny heel on them.

The bird was naturally pretty; what little make-up she had on had been subtly applied. Her cherubic face was framed by long brown hair, but the thing he noticed most about her was her eyes, which were as dark and brown as a cup of hot chocolate.

McVey eyed her up and down greedily. It had been years since he'd had a tart this tasty. When she threw her hair back and giggled at some lame joke that Eric's son, John, behind the bar had cracked, Pat growled inwardly with a primitive desire.

After a few minutes she glanced around the bar and met his stare. She gave a small, coy smile. That was all he needed. The Knights could go and fuck themselves tonight, he had a warm itch in his Y-fronts and this cute little bint would certainly scratch it.

As McVey approached the bar with his empty glass in his hand he heard the barman mention the girl's name as he handed her some change for the jukebox.

'So you are Liz are you?' he leered as he plonked himself on a bar stool next to her.

'Earwigging were you, you cheeky sod,' she replied playfully. 'My dad warned me about blokes like you.'

'Well you're dad was right,' Pat held out his hand. 'I'm Patrick.'

Lizzie Davies smiled sweetly despite the bile rising in her throat. She was nineteen and this old geezer must have been closer to her grandad's age but from the look in his bloodshot eyes she could sense he was keen to bridge the generation gap.

The Dover Castle was her family's local but it wasn't somewhere she would usually spend her Friday nights. She'd normally be dancing in a club, eyeing up boys her own age. Tonight was different. It was work and it felt like it. Without Kenny Knight's wad of cash sitting pretty in her purse she would certainly not be giving the time of day to a scruffy old git dressed like a navvy. Her skin started to crawl.

'What are you drinking?' demanded McVey, placing a sweaty palm on the back of her hand. His breath stank.

'Thanks. I'll have a small vodka and tonic, please.'

'Oi, barman,' he rasped. 'This lovely lady would like a large vodka and tonic with a slice of lemon.'

John, the barman, looked at Lizzie for confirmation but, before she could even nod, McVey interrupted.

'Hey, cunt, I said double vodka. And I'll have another bitter.'

'Oi, manners!' said Lizzie. 'Would you kiss your mother with a mouth that dirty?'

'My old dear Lord Mayors more than I do,' laughed Pat, who looked back at the barman and went on 'And this cunt, is still a cunt.'

Lizzie shook her head, pretending to be horrified. John's pride was bristling and he looked defiantly at McVey for a second before realising that he might be about to make the worst, or the last, decision of his young life. His eyes dropped downwards and he focused intently on getting the drinks.

'Make it a triple,' ordered McVey.

'You're not trying to get me drunk, are you?' said Lizzie as she worked hard to keep her false smile looking natural.

'I'm sure you can handle it, you look very...capable.'

McVey ground his arse down onto the bar stool as if he was trying to adjust his underpants without touching them. Up close Lizzie spotted that he had streaks of grease and a light smattering of what was hopefully Daddies Sauce on the thighs of his strides. She also noticed that his gaze was wandering purposefully from her ankles up to her chin like a butcher sizing up a fresh carcass for prime cuts.

He was shameless. Predatory.

The lecherous glint in Pat McVey's eyes made Lizzie feel nauseous, but gamely she breathed deeply and took a small sip from her drink.

'So what are you doing in here all on your own on a Friday night, Patrick?' she asked politely.

McVey's face darkened and he narrowed his eyes which knitted his eyebrows together like a thick, dark monobrow cloud across his forehead.

'I was waiting for some people...but now that you're here, fuck 'em. What about you, darling? All dressed up and nowhere to go?'

'I wouldn't be looking this good if I was spending my night in here, love,' Lizzie said with a smile. 'Just in for a quick one then I'm off to a party.' She laced 'quick one' with as much suggestiveness as she could muster as every one of her senses screamed to her to get the job done as quick as possible and get out of the way.

McVey took the bait like a fat, greedy trout.

'Oh yeah, where is this party then? I might tag along.' McVey's hand crept along the bar and rested on Lizzie's arm. She leapt up from her stool immediately and downed the triple vodka in one.

McVey raised his eyebrows. 'Fucking hell, you can put it away for such a skinny little thing.'

'I'm in the mood, Pat,' she said as she pulled her coat on. 'If you want a party let's go.'

'I'm game, my dear. But I must warn you, I might not be quick and I don't normally settle for one.'

His wink made the feeling of sickness come back, but she held it down, smiled and blinked at him coquettishly. McVey, who could scarcely believe his luck, finished his drink and they made their way out of the bar.

Lizzie felt a momentary sting of guilt. What type of fate was she leading this man to? He was a horrible piece of work, that much was obvious, but she abhorred the thought of being involved in any kind of violence. There was still time to call it off...

Just as she was having second thoughts, they walked under an underpass. McVey pushed her roughly against the brick wall and stuck his tongue down her throat. It felt revolting, like an oversized slug, and his mouth tasted of rotten eggs.

Fighting a strong impulse to knee him in the nuts, Lizzie submitted long enough for his heavy hands to slide down her back and start to roughly knead her backside. She shuddered as she felt his erection brush against her stomach.

It was only when he pushed his right hand up her skirt and tried to insert a thick finger inside her that Lizzie grabbed his wrist and pushed him away.

'Easy, tiger,' she said, forcing a weak smile. 'Leave something for later.'

That was it. That brief encounter washed all her concerns away.

***

Lizzie's job was done so quickly that she barely had time to register it. She had to put up with McVey's roaming hands and sleazy overtures all the way to Whitechapel but once they were inside the flat Pat stomped into the kitchen to search for booze.

From the hall she could hear a stereo pumping out the Underdogs' song "Love's Gone Bad". Love, she thought, had never even started. Through the partially open door she could see a small gathering of young, good-looking men and women deep in conversation. Lizzie started to take off her coat but before she realised what was happening, a dark-haired fellow in his twenties wearing a tight-fitting green polo neck sweater ushered her quietly back onto the flat landing.

Before he closed the door on her, the handsome stranger grabbed a bottle of champagne from a small telephone table in the hall and placed it in her hands.

'Kenny and Steve send their regards and their thanks,' he murmured almost inaudibly. 'Be lucky, Lizzie.'

Then he was inside and she was outside, all dressed up with nowhere to go. Lizzie walked down the stairs and into the street clutching the heavy bottle wondering what would happen next.

As she hit the street the initial thrill of pulling off the job gave way to a mixture of emotions – fear, rage, regret.

Was that all she was to the Knights? *Live bait?*

Suddenly she felt like a cheap tart. Lizzy felt the nausea rise again and this time she didn't fight it. She puked up right there on the streets, which at least got the taste of McVey's tongue out of her mouth. Then she looked at the bottle in her hand and hurled it with all her might. The champagne exploded onto the pavement, showering the slabs in splinters of glass and French fizzy glory, and Lizzie Davies stomped off into the night.

***

Diana Ross was singing '*Love is here, and oh my darling, now you're gone,*' as McVey swaggered from the kitchen into the front room. Ever the charmer, he barged a few female dancers out of the way before flopping himself down in a strangely shaped chair.

Pat cast an unimpressed glare around the room, sneering at the four different coloured walls and cutting edge furniture. What a palaver. Why did everything have to be "new" these days? Things were moving too fast and all the old ways were being swept aside. Even the fucking telly in this joint was egg-shaped. Maybe he'd crack it open in a bit.

The geezers at the party looked like a right bunch of queers as well – all bright shirts and trousers so tight you could tell whether or not they'd been circumcised. The birds were all right though, plenty of flesh on offer. McVey's mouth watered and he shouted over to the young bloke who had let him into the flat.

'Hey, mush, where's that tart I came in with?'

'She's just powdering her nose, mate, she'll be back soon.'

The guy moved off into the hall. McVey glugged his glass of whisky and carried on ogling for a while before the opening notes of Pink Floyd's "Candy and a Currant Bun" distracted him. What the fuck was this shit?

In his drunken haze Pat failed to notice that gradually the other party guests were moving out of the room. It was only when he looked for a light for his fag that he realised he was alone apart from one suited figure who stood in the doorway.

'Give us a light for my snout, mate,' McVey ordered.

'It's lights out for you, cunt,' said the figure as he moved forward across the small room and slammed a pickaxe handle against the side of McVey's head.

McVey dropped clumsily over the side of the chair but as he hit the ground and rolled, he registered that his attacker was Roy Storer and fumbled for his Luger.

'He's got a gun,' shouted Arthur as the rest of the Knights inner firm piled into the room. 'And it ain't his fucking old flintlock.'

The pistol cracked. Roy spun backwards clutching the top of his right arm as blood pumped through the gaps in his fingers. Another wild shot lodged in the woodwork around the doorframe. Then one zipped past Steve's ear and made a crater in the wall.

The Knights dived for cover.

McVey looked wobbly. He still seemed stunned by the blow he had received, but with the alcohol working as anaesthetic he managed to pull himself to his feet and stumble forward towards the hallway.

Just as he left the room, Butch sprang out from behind the settee and slashed at the back of McVey's head with his machete. The blade cut deep into his neck but McVey staggered onwards towards the front door.

'Don't let him get out,' yelled Steve.

Before McVey could get a blood-soaked hand on the front door bolt he turned and fired another two shots at the front room door to repel any pursuers.

'Five shots,' said Steve.

'He's still got a round left,' hissed Kenny. 'Hang back.'

'Oh, for fuck's sake. This gets worse,' grumbled Arthur.

After a few moments, Steve finally poked his head into the hallway. The front door was wide open and there was a generous dollop of McVey blood on the doorstep.

The Knight firm went running after him in pursuit. In the distance they heard an angry altercation and another sharp crack from McVey's revolver. Six shots. All spent. Unless he reloaded. Or had a second gun.

They ran towards it cautiously, with Arthur taking the lead. About 75 yards down the road, he held up his left arm and called out.

'Woah, look.'

An elderly man was lying on the pavement next to a phone box, his briefcase a couple of yards away from him.

At first it looked like just some old soak but as they got closer they could see that the guy was quite well-dressed – black suit, white shirt, black tie with a splattering of fresh blood discolouring the shirt.

'Dressed like that he's either a mason or an undertaker,' mused Butch.

'Maybe he'll do a self-service funeral,' quipped Arthur.

'You're sick,' spat Roy.

He knelt down next to him. The old man's eyes were wide open and staring up at the night sky, but he was still making a low gurgling sound.

'We'd better call an ambulance.'

'Fuck that,' hissed Kenny. 'With McVey still on the loose? We need to finish this now.'

They scanned the deserted street for some trace of activity. It was quiet; too quiet. And the clouds made the darkness seem darker. Everything was magnified. The wind felt extra cold, the buildings looked starker, the tension was cranked up.

'All those gun shots...the filth will be here soon,' said Steve.

'Where the fuck is he?' growled Arthur. He turned towards Butch and nodded towards the machete. 'If you'd hit him right with that fucking thing we'd be digging his grave by now.'

'I fucking whacked him with it,' hissed Butch. 'It would have taken any normal geezer's canister off. He's like fucking Rasputin.'

Steve shouted to them all and pointed to a smear of blood at the entrance to an alleyway. He looked around the corner of the building and gestured for the others to follow him. They crept up the alley as quickly and as quietly as they could but it was littered with garbage, beer cans and bottles, that clattered under their feet.

Suddenly McVey emerged from a doorway with his gun aiming straight at them. They leapt for cover but the impotent click of Pat's pistol proved that he was spent.

He staggered forward with his head hanging awkwardly to one side and with the light from a small back door bulb illuminating his blood-soaked bomber jacket and shirt.

'Come on, you fuckers,' he growled deliriously. 'Let's have it. On the cobbles, one at a time. That's how it's done.'

'Fair enough,' growled Arthur who stepped forward ready and threw a solid right-hander.

Despite his bedraggled state, McVey managed to dodge Arthur's swinging punch and then, lurching forward, he lashed out with the same dagger that he had dispatched Billy with. The blade sliced across the top of Arthur's chest and he fell backwards clutching the wound.

'For fuck's sake, finish him off,' yelled Kenny. He picked up an empty beer crate and threw it at Pat. The heavy wooden object glanced off McVey's head and he fell forward onto his knees. They surrounded him in an instant and kicked him to the ground savagely.

Roy seemed to be in competition with Arthur, whose wounds were still aching wildly, to see who could hurt their slag prey fastest. Steve eventually yelled at them to stop and he rolled the beaten McVey over onto his back. McVey was still alive and breathing in short, heavy gasps.

Steve picked up the discarded dagger that was still wet with Arthur's blood.

'Kill me then, you cunt,' McVey demanded gruffly. He squinted as he struggled to get Steve and the others into focus. 'I'm fucking done anyway. You young bastards think you know it all.' His voice lowered to a semi-coherent mumble. 'The old ways...best ways...yesterdays...all fading away...'

'It's our way now, Pat,' said Steve quietly as he put McVey out of his misery with a single stab to the chest.

Then he pulled the blade out and hurled it with all the strength he could muster towards Regent's Canal.

***

Roy Storer's new Singer Gazelle was parked close to a vandalised phone box that stood next to a lay-by on a deserted country road. The engine was still running and the headlights were illuminating the light drops of misty rain. Steve Knight finished his call and got into the passenger seat. Roy clunked the vehicle into first gear and resumed their journey.

'What's the word?' said Roy. 'Is he OK?'

Arthur's blood was still wet on the back seat.

'It looks like we got him to our bloke in time,' said Steve quietly. 'He's stitched him up and he's out of danger. Never mind that, what about you?'

Roy had an old jumper on but the lump of bandage wrapped around his arm was clearly visible.

'I'm all right, just a scratch. He might have got himself a better gun but his aim weren't no better. What about the flat?'

'Kenny's got someone on it now, cleaning things up. The neighbours have all been spoken to, but the area is lit up with coppers. I don't think the old fella at the phone box made it.'

Roy snorted. 'That's just like McVey, killing a civilian for no fucking reason. The dirty bastard. I reckon we've done the world a favour.'

'It certainly clears the way,' said Steve almost to himself.

'Clears the way for what?'

'Things are going well for us on the business front but this small time bullshit is like quicksand, Roy, it's dragging us down. We are just fighting like fucking rats in a barrel with all these two-bob firms that are going nowhere. We don't need it. We need to break free, we need to progress.'

Roy said nothing. He was drained, both mentally and physically, and he knew that he and Steve still had to dispose of the body deep in the densest part of Epping Forest.

Maybe once McVey's festering corpse was out of his boot and six foot under he could start to pull himself together, although Billy's funeral was still on the horizon. At least his cousin would receive a respectful send-off. McVey's final resting place would be far more anonymous. But who would want to remember that piece of shit?

***

Steve and Roy had taken turns driving, with the headlight beam providing an almost hypnotic tunnel of light through the complete darkness of country lanes. There were no street lights in this uncivilised backwater and the roads were claustrophobically narrow. When they reached their destination, they felt drained. Neither man was expecting the further trauma that came from the boot.

The worst thing about transporting a fresh corpse is the stink. It releases gasses, it releases fluids, and it releases waste. Ideally a dead body should be slotted into a zipped-up sleeping bag before transportation. Or at least wrapped in plastic sheets; otherwise your boot ends up decorated in blood, piss, shit and dribble and stinking like the trunk of Roy Storer's Singer did now...

'Shit. Don't he pen and ink?' Roy moaned.

'Always did. Alive as well as dead.'

'I know but fuckin' hell...'

'You're gonna have to torch this now to get rid of this stench.'

'No, Steve. You and Kenny are going to have to cough up for a deaf and dumb cleaner and then break the bastard's fingers to make sure he don't tell no one nothing.'

They dragged Pat McVey's corpse up a hill, him between them like some old drunk they were helping home. When they were five minutes from the road they turned into a small clearing and then began.

***

It had taken two long exhausting hours of digging to bury the bastard and their muddy, sweat-soaked clothes now clung to them damply as Roy drove back to the Smoke.

The two men sat in silence, lost in their own thoughts until Steve suddenly reached across to the steering wheel and gave it a hard tug to the left. The vehicle veered sharply towards a grass verge.

'Watch it, what the fuck are you doing?' yelled Roy as he regained control of the car and brought it back quickly into the centre of the lane.

'There was a rabbit sitting there transfixed on the road...'

'We nearly ended up in fuckin' ditch – for a poxy rabbit? For Christ's sake,, Steve. I've only had this jam-jar for a couple of months.'

'No need for senseless killing, Roy,' said Steve calmly as if nothing had happened.

'What? You nearly done in me motor to save Bugs Bunny. You didn't seem to have much of a problem putting McVey out of his misery.'

'That's different. He deserved it. What's the worst a rabbit can do? Chew yer carrots? Leave a patch of them little round shit raisins in your garden?'

'Shit raisins? That's a shit reason, Steve. Besides I don't have a fucking garden. I live in a high-rise flat, as well you know.'

He shrugged. 'That's just an example, Roy. An illustration.'

'A piss poor example. I don't get it.'

Steve sighed, and then adopted the kind of tone that a harassed teacher might use when addressing an unruly young pupil.

'McVey was a virus. He was poison. He was cancer. He was a mental cow-son who would have continued to spread misery for the rest of his no-good life. Killing him was business for us and a mercy for the world, but that little rabbit weren't hurting no one.'

Roy looked grim. 'There's a lot more bastards like McVey around though and they seem to be multiplying like fucking rabbits.' His voice was soft; his tone grudging.

A slight smile played around Steve's lips in the darkness.

'One thing at a time, Royston,' he said. 'One thing at a time...'

Chapter Eight: A Taste Of Honey

Lizzie Davies stretched up to the shelf above the cleaning section and pushed a box load of bleach bottles into place with a grunt. Even with a small set of steps it was hard for her to reach and she grunted with exertion as she felt the nylon of her pinafore stretch tightly across her backside. To say her uniform was close-fitting was an understatement. She suspected that Tariq Bucak, the store manager, gave all the young shop-girls an outfit at least a size smaller than they required, the better to ogle them as they went about their duties. He was a lecherous old bastard and no mistake. Buttocks seemed to be his thing...

Templeton's on the Hackney Road called itself a supermarket, but it was more of a glorified corner shop than the Co-op. Still it fulfilled the contemporary demand for "self-service" for people who couldn't be arsed to make their way to a proper store like Sainsbury's or Tesco's.

Lizzie had more or less fallen into a job there when she had left school and through a combination of laziness and lack of ambition she had remained there. The wages were crap but as long as she avoided the creeping hands of Mr Bucak, it suited her fine. If she needed more money she could always take in some ironing.

She stretched once more to slot the box neatly into place.

'Don't jump,' said a rich, velvety voice behind her. Even before she turned around the electric tingle that shot up her spine told her it was Steve Knight.

Lizzie's face reddened as she turned to face him. Steve offered an outstretched hand to help her down from the steps.

'If you'd stretched another inch your pinny would have split, Lizzie,' he smiled. 'That would have made old Bucak's day.'

'Steve,' she said, not needing to feign her surprise. 'Are you in for some shopping? I didn't think that was your thing.'

Lizzie realised she was still holding his hand so she let her fingers drop from his grip.

'It most certainly is not my thing,' he grinned warmly. 'I'm here to see you of course. Just to say...thank you for the other night. I'm sorry Kenny got you involved. I would never have asked you to do something like that but I, I mean we, all appreciate what you did.'

Lizzie felt a little cheap and her eyes dropped to the floor. Doing dirty deeds for the Knights was not something she had ever considered before. It had seemed a good idea at the time and the money helped pay off her mum's catalogue debts, but she'd already heard whispers that Pat McVey had gone on a permanent holiday – of the kind Billy Butlin didn't supply.

Pangs of doubt, worry and guilt were keeping her awake at night.

Steve sensed her regret. It embarrassed him slightly.

'Anyway,' he continued, 'I'd like to give you a little something by way of my gratitude.'

'That's alright, Steve,' she mumbled. 'Kenny sorted me out.'

Steve's laughter boomed across the shop floor. 'I don't mean a few ten bob notes peeled from my brother's sweaty grip. I'm talking about a trip up West. Carnaby Street, Oxford Street, the King's Road. A little expedition into our bold consumer society with the opportunity to purchase a little piece of sartorial splendour just for you.'

'Oh, Steve, I can't...' stuttered Lizzie as her face reddened once again. The idea of taking any further payment for her dirty deed still lingered in her mind but a shopping trip...with Steve Knight. It seemed too good to miss.

'I won't take no for an answer,' Steve said firmly but with a smile. 'You are coming with me, get your coat.'

'But I'm still working...' Lizzie protested.

'I'll sort that. Where's old Tariq lurking?'

Lizzie pointed to the manager's office at the back of the store. Steve nodded and strode off purposefully in that direction. She watched him go. He was immaculately dressed in carefully tailored slacks, a sports jacket and a bold red turtleneck sweater. Her mind wandered into scenarios that made her blush. The uneasy sense of regret that had troubled her was gently warming into something far more agreeable, and erotic.

Whatever Steve said to the store manager did the trick. Tariq shuffled out of the office alongside Steve and not only willingly gave Lizzie the rest of the day off but the rest of the week as well.

His downtrodden demeanour gave her the distinct impression that his wandering hands would wander no more during those long, boring stocktaking sessions in the back shop.

They stepped out of the supermarket and she saw Steve's Jaguar sitting there, gleaming in the sunlight.

Lizzie slid down onto the thick leather of the passenger seat and Steve bent down slightly into the car and handed her the end of the seat belt. She could smell his aftershave. His lips were almost touching her ear.

'Right Liz darlin',' he said warmly. 'You're in with the in-crowd, so let's go where the in-crowd go.'

Her smile was as broad as Canning Town flyover.

***

Carnaby Street was buzzing with activity, a noisy mass of brightly coloured patterns, hip young guns and cynical traders. Lizzie felt glorious as she strolled from shop to shop with Steve by her side. They walked together almost like lovers, she decided, keeping the thought to herself, with her handsome escort carrying a growing number of bags from the boutiques they had visited – Lady Jane, Irvine Sellars, His & Hers, Take Six...she'd take six if he asked her, she thought.

Lizzie felt slightly light-headed. The afternoon was like a magic carpet ride away from a morning spent pulling on her Templeton's uniform and pricing cans of baked beans. This was another world.

Steve had mentioned her job during the journey; he reckoned she could do a lot better than stacking cereal boxes. He chatted about how things were changing and now he was talking about how Twiggy, who was just a young sort from Neasden, had the world at her feet and was wowing the Yanks, the Frogs and even the Japs.

'Her dad was a chippie, her mum worked in a factory...and the *New Yorker*, a posh septic magazine, just devoted almost a hundred pages to her,' he said. 'The world is changing, Liz. The working class are on the up and the old guard ain't gonna put us back in a box anytime soon. A girl like you could have anything you want – if you put your mind to it.'

Steve dropped the bags and steered her towards the glass-front window of Kleptomania.

'Look at yourself. You are gorgeous! You look a million dollars! With the right photographer you'd be a model.'

She blushed and started to protest.

'Nah, think about it. Come on, let's find somewhere to get a coffee.' They found a small coffee bar a few streets away and sat together in a small booth with red leather seating. Lizzie sipped a cappuccino while Steve had a mug of tea. The noises coming out of the gleaming Gaggia espresso machine made her laugh. It wheezed, it spluttered and it made a great burbling racket that would wake the dead.

'It sounds like a horror film,' she giggled.

'Have you never been to a coffee house before?'

She shook her head.

'You should have said! I'd have taken you to Heaven & Hell in Old Compton Street, or the 2i's...'

'I like this place. It's classy.'

She took a sip out of her drink. Some of the whipped cream on top of it stayed on her upper lip.

'Very classy,' Steve grinned as he gave her a serviette to wipe it off. 'It's more like a bleedin' pudding than a drink.'

'It's Italian...'

'Italian my arse! The bloke that runs this place is from Bermondsey.'

Lizzie giggled. 'Ha, a definite wrong'un. Wrong side of the drink.'

Steve smiled. Then they both sat silently. She glanced at him as he systematically stirred his tea; then watched him go through the same routine three times more. That was odd enough, she thought, but his expression was more puzzling. Steve looked as if he was building up to something, and this surprised her. He didn't seem the type of man who had to summon up courage before he spoke. She had felt a frisson of chemistry between them several times and allowed herself to wonder if he felt the same.

'I've really enjoyed today, Lizzie,' Steve said finally. 'You know this ain't a pay-off, don't you? That's not what I intended. I just thought it would be...nice to spend a little time together.'

'It has been nice,' said Lizzie, but her eyes dropped down towards the tabletop. 'Maybe we could do it again sometime?'

Her words were so quiet they almost drifted into the hubbub of the cafe.

'That would be nice,' he said, 'But at the moment things are...well, complicated.'

Lizzie looked almost visibly deflated. 'I understand.'

Steve reached out and placed a heavy palm on the back of her slim hand to comfort her. She was beautiful, inside and out, but the world that he was submerged in at the moment was a volatile and violent place. And she was such a sweet, young thing that he just could not bring himself to let her get involved any further. Besides she wasn't the sort of bird he'd use just to make another notch on the bedpost. "In it and bin it, rump and dump it, fuck it and chuck it" as Kenny often said expecting the listener to smile, no matter how many times they'd heard it.

No. Not that. Lizzie was one of your own. She was the kind of woman you'd marry, the kind you'd protect and have kids with.

Steve was still furious with his brother for getting her involved with the murder of Mad Pat McVey and decided to address it.

'What you did the other night, Liz, was something I would never have asked you to do,' he said quietly.

'He forced me up against a wall, Steve.' Lizzie said, her voice faltering. 'Under the old walkway. Pat...he stuck his tongue down my throat... I can still taste it.'

She started to sob. Steve put his arm around her and drew her closer.

'He pawed me. He touched me. I thought... I thought he was going to rape me...'

He hugged her tighter.

'I am so sorry, Lizzie. You shouldn't have been involved at all. I hate to think of you frightened and alone and vulnerable... But...' He hesitated. 'What you did for us does mean a lot to us... It means a lot to me. I know we could have handled things a bit better but just remember, you'll never have to deal with that bastard again. He won't be bothering you. Not now, nor tomorrow. Not ever.'

He gave her another hug, kissed her forehead gently and released her. Lizzie wanted to ask why but thought better of it.

'I'm not a brass you know,' she said solemnly. 'Your family has always helped out in our area. Keeping the undesirables in check. That's why I done what Kenny asked me to do.'

Steve nodded and drained the remainder of his mug.

'I know, Lizzie. You're a good friend. If you ever need anything from me, anything at all, just ask... I really mean that.'

She could think of a couple of things she needed from him but it would not have been ladylike to say...

'Let's just enjoy the rest of today,' Steve said, closing down the conversation. He stood up and pulled his jacket from the back of the chair.

'Now come on, drink the rest of that fancy concoction and let's keep shopping. We ain't even had a sniff of the King's Road yet.'

Lizzie smiled broadly and took a final sip of her coffee.

As she stood up, Steve leaned over and wiped a tiny spot of whipped cream from her nose. The brief contact sent a shiver down her spine.

***

It didn't take long for the whispers about Patrick McVey to reach Little Pig's big ears and, as a consequence, the ears of Rodney Huggins. The two men sat in one of the small upstairs rooms in the Angel in St Giles High Street. Huggins nursed a pint of Guinness, Morgan – sulking about missing out on a Wimpy – sipped at a Scotch & Dry.

'So he's definitely a goner,' said Huggins.

'Brown bread, Mr H.'

'And the Knights...?'

'Steve did it.'

'And where have they disposed of the body.'

'That, Mr 'Uggins, I do not know. But I do know where and when it happened...'

***

When Bernie Sternschuss rang Aphrodite's Palace, Steve took his call with hesitation. Bernie was an old friend of his fathers and an old lag with serious, if elderly, underworld connections. But that one phone call in March 1968 would turn out to be a life changer.

Steve agreed to meet him in the top bar of the Tipperary pub in Fleet Street, known to those who frequented it as the "Top of the Tip". It was a small, quiet room with no danger of anyone overhearing your conversation. And way off the manor.

Bernie was old East End and as Jewish as a bar mitzvah. He had worked in the diamond trade as a youth but fell out of favour with Hatton Garden's master jewellers because of his tendency to befriend the sort of men who robbed them.

'So, Steve,' said Bernie when the younger man arrived. 'I hear you've been doing very good business these days.'

'Can't complain, Mr Sternschuss. Ducking and diving, you know how it is.'

'Oi yoy yoy! What's with the Mr Sternschuss! I knew you when you thought your *schvantz* was just for pissing out of. Bernie. Call me Bernie.'

'Sorry, Bernie. Just a bit of respect kicking in.'

'I heard about your little, um, experiment a couple of months ago...' He paused. Steve looked blank. 'In East Ham...'

'What Phillips's?'

Steve looked shocked. In his haste to move up to bigger jobs, he had talked the firm into robbing W. Phillips & Co in High Street North while the owners were in Majorca. Unfortunately, no one had done too much groundwork.

'Yes. A fucking disaster I heard. A shoddily organised smash and grab raid using scooters as getaway vehicles...am I right?'

Steve nodded.

'A big police presence in Wordsworth Avenue for the Communist Party rally in Plashet Park, arise ye dockers and all that palaver. You gained nothing more than bruises and battered egos...except for Kenneth who copped a face full of fire extinguisher from the schmuck in the shop. Bad planning, or more likely no planning? Am I right?'

'How do you...?'

'Please. I hear about most things. I also hear Kenneth is still mad at you. So, this is what I figure happened. You got rid of the monkey on your back, that klutz – that fuckin' thick *kelev!* – Patrick McVey, and you thought you could move up a division.'

Without waiting for answer, Bernie went on: 'So here's my question – are you still interested in promotion?'

'Very.'

'Then listen...'

Bernie Sternschuss sketched out his scheme in the vaguest of details. A big Hatton Garden jeweller was opening a second store in Surbiton. On a certain day in the not too distant, a serious amount of "tom" would be travelling west in an armoured van.

'If you're interested, if you have the chutzpah, I will give you all I know about the move and all I ask in return is 30 per cent of the takings.'

'20!'

'25 and I'm robbing my children for you.'

'You don't have any kids, Bernie.'

'You're like a son to me. I look at you and I'm kvelling. I can't help myself. Now, are we in business, Steven Knight, or do I have to go to those schmucks south of the river?'

'We're in business.'

'Good. I trust the Turk about as far as I could throw one of his rotten gut-rotting horse meat kebabs.'

They shook hands.

'Brandy?'

'Best make it a double.'

This was perfect, thought Steve. Except for one small thing. He still had to convince Kenny.

***

The Knight brothers were counting their takings in the office at Aphrodite's Palace when Steve broached the subject.

'You've got to be fucking kidding me?' roared Kenny scornfully. 'I thought we'd put all this to bed after the last fuck-up! Things are going fine the way they are. Why would we want to try something else when it was such a dog's dinner the last time?'

'We can't stand still, bruv,' said Steve in a calm tone that only served to infuriate Kenny more. 'Bigger risks bring bigger rewards.'

His brother's jaw wobbled in disbelief like a stranded tiger fish gasping for air.

'Piss off, Steve, we ain't running British Leyland.'

The younger man persisted. 'The brasses, the pills and the collections can all take care of themselves if we set them up properly. Okay, so we might pick up a little more work here and there but we need a big score to really get us going. I don't want to be doing two-bob work all my fucking days.'

'Where is all this coming from? From all your new poncey mates? What's wrong with what we are doing? That's your bird talking, that is.'

'It's got fuck all to do with her!'

Steve wore the exasperated expression of an exhausted parent dealing with a boisterous toddler. 'The scooter job didn't work because we fucked up the planning, not because there's no value in turning over jewellers! There's got to be a better way.'

'Didn't work? It was a fucking catastrophe,' yelled Kenny. 'We nearly got collared. And what did we come away with? That's right, the square root of fuck all! I can still taste that fucking fire extinguisher. We'd have been better off pushing a few pills to those fucking hippies at that festival up at Parliament Hill. The only good thing about that caper was it taught us a valuable lesson – stick to what you know.'

'No!' yelled Steve as he slammed the safe door shut and spun the combination lock completely round three times. 'That's not the point. We're now one step closer to finding the way to get a better result. Hatton Garden is the source of what we want but this time we have to get to the gear before it's locked away. That's the place for a big job and that's what we should focus on. We can fuck about for a few bob here and there for years, so why not go for it all at once?'

'It's hardly a few bob. This is the family business. Our old man gave his life for this and we've been close to it a few times. Is it not good enough for you any more? There are thousands of punters on our manor who wish they had what we have and you're not satisfied?'

'I don't give a fuck about any of that! It's bullshit. There's a whole world out there beyond our "manor"...a whole city on our doorstep and we are pissing about fighting for the scraps with every mug within a ten mile radius. I don't want to be doing this forever, bruv. We can pay people to do the dirty work. We have to expand, think bigger. Get out of the gutter and away from cunts like McVey and the McCaffertys.'

'I get it,' said Kenny quietly, as he waved a finger at his brother. 'Now you've got that high-class brass it's not good enough round here for the likes of you. Yeah, now it all makes sense.'

'Don't talk shit. Anthea's got fuck all to do with this. I just want a brighter future for all of us.'

'Oh, yeah, sunshine and rainbows with all your freaky friends. Get a grip on yourself, you soft cunt.'

An ominous silence filled the room as the brothers stood glaring at each other. Just like they had been in the old days, stubborn with neither giving an inch but eventually Kenny breathed out heavily.

'You ain't going to let this go, are you?'

Steve seized his chance. 'There's a world of opportunities out there, Kenny. They are all open to us...we just need to grab them. All it takes is the bollocks to do it.'

Kenny plonked himself heavily onto a chair. 'So this is going to propel us into the big time is it? Blagging a load of tom from a security van. I dunno... Look, bruv, if you're looking for something different I've had an offer you might be interested in...'

Steve grunted and walked to the small bar at the back of the room where he poured out two glasses of Glen Grant whisky.

'You do this job with me and then we can look at your idea for a blag,' Kenny said with a smile. 'If you're looking for a new opportunity that's a nice little earner then this is it.'

Steve passed him a glass and sat down close to him. 'Go on then, what's the big plan? Doing over a gas meter? Pinching knickers off a washing line?'

'Cheeky cunt. A face I know in Custom House has a pal in Glasgow who wants someone out the picture permanently and it has to be done by someone from out of town.'

Steve snorted incredulously. 'What? A hit? Up in Jockland? We are hardly going to be inconspicuous, are we?'

'If we keep our traps shut and do the business double lively we'll be back on the John Wayne home before the ambulance arrives for the target. The geezer even drinks in a boozer near the station. If we get in and out quick he won't know what hit him.'

'And what about his mob? I'm assuming he ain't just some mug punter off the street? Surely they're going to have something to say if we knock off their guv'nor bang in the middle of their manor. We'll have to fight our way back to the station. Just the two of us? It'll be like the fucking Alamo.'

'That's the beauty of it,' said Kenny. 'We do it on a Saturday afternoon. In, boom, put the geezer down, few shots in the ceiling and tell the rest of them if they pop their head out of the door they will fucking lose it. We slip into the crowds of football groggles and shoppers and we are in and out like Eric Flynn. If we time it right we can get to the station and the train will be waiting and then it's bang on to Stephenson's jockey Rocket and 'ome to the good old Smoke.'

'What about the filth? Gun shots in the city centre in broad daylight aren't commonplace even in Glasgow. There's going to be mobs of the old boys in *MacBlue* out on the street.'

'I've got hold of a Walther PPK with a silencer, a real fucking James Bond shooter. No one will hear a fucking thing. Besides this geezer is a proper face. No one in that pub is going to have anything to do with the Old Bill.'

Steve sipped his whisky and looked out of the window. He was concentrating heavily while not really focusing on anything in particular, just hoping that a solution might magic itself out of thin air.

'I mean, I could do it with Arthur,' Kenny said slyly. 'But you and me, we know each other 100 per cent. In a situation like that we're virtually telepathic.'

'And if we do this thing together then you'll go for the Hatton Garden job?'

'I'll consider it,' said Kenny with a broad grin.

Steve turned his back to the window then drained the remainder of his Scotch in a single gulp.

'All right, bruv, get your fucking long johns on, we're heading for the Frozen North.'

'Yes!' Kenny punched the air.

'I'll leave it to you to get the phrase book.'

***

Rodney Huggins had met a wall of silence over the murder of Mad Pat McVey. People who had been at the party told him, hand on heart, that there had never ever been one, that they had never met the Knights and that they had certainly never heard of any Patrick McVey. They didn't even recognise his picture. But fully briefed by Eddie Morgan, the detective had managed to trace the victim's steps from the party that never happened to the alley where no one saw or heard a thing.

Huggins stood by Regents Canal in the half-light, lit up a Silk Cut and pondered. It was only when he flicked the butt away that he noticed the tip of a blood-stained blade poking out from the bramble. As he gingerly collected Pat McVey's dagger in his handkerchief, one word came from Rod Huggins's lips.

'Gotcha.'

***

'We should have got the fuckin' sleeper.'

'Stop moaning. This was your daft idea to start with.'

'At least it gets us out of London, I spose... So how's it goin' with old snooty drawers?'

'If you mean Anthea, I ain't seen her for a while. She's got...' Steve looked out of the train window as he searched for the right word. 'Problems. Any'ow, what's this I hear about you and a certain blonde dancer?'

'Yeah. She's about me.'

'Who's she dance with?'

'The Go-Jos.'

'What, as in the sorts on *Top Of The Pops*?'

'Yeah.'

'Fit. And you're keen on her?'

'Fuck me, who am I sitting with, Ironside? Yes I'm keen. Yes we're together. Yes she wants us to get a place. But you'd know all this if you hadn't been fucking off with a fucking toff who's fucking off her nut...'

'Bruv, that was almost poetry.'

'Fuck off. How much longer?'

Steve looked at his watch. 'About three hours.'

Kenny sighed. 'Got any new jokes?'

Steve smiled.

'Yeah, bird gets on a bus in Whitechapel with her baby. The bus driver takes one look at it and says "Christ, that's the ugliest fuckin' baby I've ever seen". Well the woman goes garrity. She goes straight up to the conductor and says, "Excuse me, your driver just insulted me." The conductor says, well that ain't right madam. You shouldn't have to take that. You go back and give him a proper mouthful. I'll hold your monkey for you...'

***

Steve and Kenny were almost anonymous as they walked towards the exit at Glasgow Central station. The whole concourse was teeming with life...soldiers and sailors either coming from or going to somewhere, young dolly birds out for a day's shopping, hatchet-faced women dragging wheeled baskets about and crimson-cheeked old codgers in worn suits who looked half-pissed despite it only being midday.

'Where's all the geezers in skirts?' rasped Kenny.

'That's only on shortbread tins, you dozy git,' grinned Steve. 'It's not fucking Brigadoon up here; they've got electric lights and everything now.'

He paused, smiled and added. 'Aberdeen, now that's a different story.'

'Jock cunts,' Kenny sneered. He straightened out his suit jacket a little as the loaded Walther was hanging heavily in his inside pocket. 'They've got electric but no decent football teams, eh? And it's still fucking freezing. Let's get this done.'

He stopped and looked back at the huge wall of train times that loomed down on the platforms.

'The London train is still on course for one o' clock, that gives us forty-five minutes to get the job done and get out of this shithole.'

'What?' Steve said sarcastically. 'No opportunity for sightseeing in the Athens of the North? That's a crying shame, bruv.'

'Fuck off.'

They turned out the station and walked straight into two greasy looking rockers in studded leather jackets pushing a teenage boy about. The young kid had a French crop, a Fred Perry polo shirt and a pair of matching black eyes.

'Oi, leave him be,' said Steve.

'Do you want some instead?' said the bigger of the two. But when he turned and saw the look of let's-have-it steel in Steve Knight's eyes, his bottle completely went.

'Ah, sorry man, misunderstanding,' he mumbled.

He pushed the kid away.

'Twat. You're thirty and the kid's, what, seventeen?'

Kenny pulled a face. 'You know Rome wasn't built in a day,' he said, looking around. 'But...this...*shithole* town could have been.'

The rockers bristled but said nothing.

***

The Admiral Bar had a grand name that bore no resemblance to its dull low-rent interior. In business terms, the pub was a sinking ship. The small windows were grey with dust and grime from the street outside and were mostly obscured with painted slogans advertising the few brands of beer that were behind the bar.

Whatever the fuck "Heavy" was, it seemed to be popular in this godforsaken watering hole.

If there had been a piano player present he would have abruptly stopped tinkling but as it was, Kenny and Steve had every pair of eyes on them as soon as they entered the pub. The bird behind the bar looked half-fit and also half-alive, thought Steve. She was pale skinned with a mass of red hair and so skinny you could almost see through her. The boozer was mostly populated with old Jocks. There were a bunch of them at the tables under the front window, huddled over their half-pint glasses, card hands, and cribbage boards. They looked as if they were waiting for the grim reaper to come and collect them.

At the very back of the main bar, four younger men were lounging about. They were well-dressed in a style that had been popular in London half a decade earlier. Three of them had Tony Curtis haircuts and thick sideburns like aging rockers, but the oldest of the group looked plusher and paunchier. He was more like a scar-faced bank manager.

He was Arnold Murray. Their target.

Steve clocked him immediately. He glanced at Kenny, raised his eyebrows slightly and nodded to make sure he got the message.

Three sidekicks. That was just about what they had expected. The seven rounds nestled in Kenny's PPK were more than enough to finish off their victim and either disable or dispatch his firm if they had the bottle to try and follow the brothers out of the bar.

Kenny had an extra clip and Steve's long coat concealed a large machete and a police truncheon. Just in case things got out of hand.

'Two pints of mild, please, love,' said Kenny.

If their entrance had not fully attracted the attention of everyone in the bar then his accent did.

'We dinnae have mild,' the skinny ginger barmaid replied in an accent so heavy it should have had subtitles. 'We've got these.' She waved her hand at three bar taps which all said McEwan's.

'Two pints of Export then, love, that sounds exotic,' said Kenny with a smile. Her low neck-line revealed the tops of her snowy white bosoms, which looked surprisingly ample for her build.

The Caledonian enigma grunted and started to pour the drinks. Steve glanced around casually. Most of the bar's other residents appeared to have lost interest in these exotic strangers. The old boys had gone back to the low rumbling conversations about the good old, bad old days of yesteryear when Caruso was king. Murray and his mob still kept glancing over at them but obviously did not seem to see the brothers as an immediate threat.

The barmaid plonked the pints on the bar. Kenny gave her a five pound note. She grunted, and held it up to the light, before begrudgingly accepting it as legal currency.

'Fuckin' Sassenach money', she moaned, but with a promising twinkle in her eye.

'It's being so cheerful that keeps you going,' laughed Kenny.

The woman smiled and then walked over to the far corner to assemble a roll-up using the sports section of the *Daily Record* for the debris.

Steve took a sip from his beer and pulled a face.

'Fuck me, this is rough,' he said quietly. 'Like camel's piss.'

'Well don't fucking drink it, son' murmured Kenny.

He glanced at an old nicotine stained clock behind the bar.

'It's gone half past. Let's just get this done. Ready?'

Steve nodded and they both span around and launched their pint pots over at Murray and his sidekicks. The pints shattered on the table, soaking the Jock firm and covering them with wet splinters of glass.

Kenny Knight whipped out his Walther, levelled the silenced barrel at Arnold Murray and pulled the trigger.

All he heard was a dull click.

Murray immediately pushed the table over and dived behind it for cover. His mob all sprang into action, producing cut-throat razors and making straight for the Knights.

Kenny did not panic. He gave the base of the gun's handle a firm slap. It did the trick. He pressed the trigger again firing four quick shots into the Jocks' legs. They fell to the ground screaming. Murray used the chaos to make for a door at the side of the bar.

Steve instinctively made a dash for him but the burly villain hit him hard with a forearm smash that propelled the Londoner back against the bar. As Steve staggered, the translucent barmaid took her chance to try to strangle him with a beer-soaked tea towel.

Her quick-thinking took him by surprise. Steve's hands shot up immediately and he started to pull the tight material away from around his windpipe. Kenny fired a single shot that smashed straight through the woman's thin white shoulder and the tea towel tourniquet fell away. She shrieked in pain as a vivid splash of her blood decorated the pub's limited array of optics.

'Get after the cunt,' screamed Kenny.

Steve dived through the back entrance but was surprised to find himself in a large, dark stockroom with no exit. A whisky bottle span from a corner of the room and caught him just under his throat, forcing all of the air from his lungs. He collapsed onto a pile of wooden crates. The Glaswegian hoodlum played his advantage. He leapt forward and slashed at Steve with an open razor. But the gleaming blade only managed to slice through the thick fabric of his Dunn & Co Crombie.

As Kenny followed them in, turning on the light, Steve lashed out with a solid kick to Murray's shins. The target stepped back just enough for Kenny to deliver two muted shots to his chest.

Arnold Murray fell back hard, like a pole-axed moose, and his skull cracked heavily against a metal storage cabinet before he rolled onto the stone floor, never to rise again.

'Job done,' said Kenny in a matter-of-fact manner. 'Now let's get fucking out of here.'

Back in the bar, the old men had sounded the retreat leaving their cards, their cribbage boards and more surprisingly their unfinished halves on the tables. Only the barmaid and Murray's gang were still around, most of them rolling on the floor groaning.

One powerfully built guy with dark eyes made a lunge for Kenny's ankle and was quickly dispatched with a kick to the jaw.

The Knights stopped just before the pub door to compose themselves and conceal their weapons. The cut in Steve's jacket was decorated with some blood but on the dark fabric it only looked like a damp patch. They'd do.

The brothers stepped out of the pub door. It took a few seconds for them to register how different things looked from when they had arrived a few minutes before. Then the street was fairly deserted; now it was full of boisterous young Jocks, most of whom were merrily tearing lumps out of each other.

Kenny stumbled forward and disappeared from sight among a mass of furiously scrapping youths. Steve was disorientated for a moment. *What the fuck?* Then he registered the scarves the young men were wearing, a mixture of green and white clashing with a similar amount of red, white and blue.

Ah fuck. Celtic v Rangers! It must be derby day, it must...

Just as Steve Knight realised that he was in the heart of another bout of legendary old firm football violence, a half-empty bottle of Sweetheart Stout sailed through the air and glanced off his head. The bottle only broke when it shattered on the ground but its impact sent Steve crumpling onto the pavement among a sea of kicking and scuffling boots.

'Fucking hell. KENNY! *KENNY!*'

Steve Knight tried to make himself heard over the ruckus but couldn't. So he lashed out with his boots, knocking the nearest hooligans off their feet. It took a moment for his head to clear enough for him to drag himself up, only to have a strapping freckle-faced Jock shove him straight back down again.

The Celtic fan laughed loudly and threw his head back displaying a set of rotten teeth that would have given a dentist nightmares and an American comedian half an hour of material.

Steve sprang up and delivered a solid punch to his ginger attacker's solar plexus. The big man went down like the *Lusitania.* He stepped over him and began fighting his way out of the crowd.

It took him maybe ninety seconds to reach the opposite side of the road from the Admiral Bar. People were starting to gather outside the pub just to watch the unfolding chaos. *Where was Kenny?* Panic gripped his chest tightly until he saw his brother a few yards down the road trying to punch his way through a rear-guard battalion of Celtic fans.

Steve pulled out the truncheon from his coat and began swinging it wildly at anyone between him and his brother. He felt a good punch glance off his ribs and immediately whacked his attacker twice as hard.

Steve's relentless skull-cracking eventually cleared a path to Kenny and they managed to get off the main road and into a side street. Safe!

'You fucking Cockney cunt!'

Kenny was astonished to see Barry McCafferty coming straight at him from the left flank of the Celtic mob. He looked mean as hell and bloodied from battle, but there was no mistaking the chiv in his hand.

Unfortunately for the Jock, he hadn't seen Steve, who blindsided the angry Scot, taking him down like Dave Mackay.

The sound of police cars ringing out in the distance dissipated the brothers' smiles.

'Down here,' said Kenny breathlessly. 'If we make our way round the back of the station we can still make it.'

At the end of the alley, just before they emerged back onto a main road, they dusted themselves down and tucked their tools back out of sight. Just two well-dressed but dishevelled business men in a city centre that was being torn apart by an age old football rivalry – no one even gave them a second look all the way to the station.

'What about that barmaid?' said Steve.

'She could toss my caber any day.'

Steve slapped his brother's back. 'Ha. We left her writhing on the floor of that pub but not quite in the way I'd pictured it.'

'Blimey. So you are capable of thinking outside of Anthea's box, bruv. Who'd have thought it?'

***

Kenny poured a whisky miniature into a plastic glass and pushed it in Steve's direction.

'We done it, bruv, we fucking done it,' said Kenny in a whisper, barely disturbing the decorum of the First Class carriage. Their cuts and bruises already raised a few eyebrows. He smiled and went on: 'That's a monkey in our bins.'

Steve looked astounded.

'500 quid?' he spat through gritted teeth. 'We've put our lives on the line for a poxy 500 knicker? You told me it was a big earner!'

'It's not bad for ten minutes graft is it?'

'Ten fucking minutes? We've wasted the whole bleedin' day on the *Flying Scotsman*. We could be banged up for life...for peanuts! Fucking peanuts!'

'Shush. We don't need any more attention.'

'You soppy cunt. The whole firm could have gone down the Suwannee for half a grand! You are off your fucking nut.'

'You have to admit it was a buzz though,' laughed Kenny who drained his glass and poured another.

Steve looked out of the window, shaking his head half in despair and half in shock. How could his brother be so dim? So reckless?

Then a half-smile began to play around the corners of his mouth. Kenny's stupidity had played right into his hands.

He leaned forward, grinning like a shark. 'Right Kenneth,' he said. 'Here is what is going to happen. As soon as we get home I am putting my plan into action. If we're going to throw caution to the wind, we might as well go down for half a mill...'

'Shit me. Are you still banging on about this security van blag?'

'If we don't try then we'll never know. And I ain't talking about a few trays of tom. I'm talking enough gear to set us up for life. Bernie gave me a solid tip. It's a job he would have done himself if he wasn't older than Methuselah.'

'Bernie Sternschuss is a flash old kosher cunt,' growled Kenny. 'I don't trust him further than I could throw him.'

'We don't have to trust him and you don't have to throw him. This job will be done right. Planning, preparation, all the boxes ticked before we even pull on a balaclava.'

'What do we know about armed robbery? Fuck all.'

Kenny Knight's voice was an angry whisper. Steve matched it.

'We know fuck all about contract killing and we still muddled through that today. We might need some experience on board though and I know just the geezer who can help us.'

Kenny shrugged his shoulders and said nothing. His brother was relentless when he wanted something. Like a dog with a fucking bone. It had been the same since they were nippers. The only thing to do was grunt in agreement. The alternative – suffering months of ag – didn't bear thinking about. Besides Steve was right. Coming to Jockland for peanuts was bananas. As the train rolled onwards to the border both brothers drifted into thoughtful silence. But not for long.

'You got any new jokes, bruv?'

Steve thought for a moment and said 'Sharon's having a bit of fanny trouble so she goes to the specialist. She's quite shy and she's never had a man look at her Jack and Danny let alone stick his finger in. She's got her feet up in the stirrups and he says "You're nervous aren't you, my dear? Would you like me to numb you down there?" "Oh yes please," she says. So he sticks his nose up her Jack and Danny and goes "Num, num, num, num...".'

Chapter Nine: Gardeners' Question Time

The Manor Garden allotments had evolved into a kind of shanty town of old sheds. Populated almost entirely by old men, it was sealed off at the front from the road by a wall of abandoned doors that had been liberated from bomb sites and demolition jobs all across the post-war East End. A rail track ran along the back with trees on either end making it a self-contained kingdom. Known locally as The Garden, the small piece of Hackney Wick was home to a warren of carefully carved out plots. From a distance it looked like a dump but on closer inspection it was an oasis of calm among the grime and noise of inner London.

Steve stood at the entrance to the plots and wished that he had left his Chelsea Cobbler lizard skin shoes at home. The criss-crossing paths ahead of him were all thick with mud. He looked around to see if there was anyone he could send in on his behalf but despite the late morning sun that was heating up the horticultural haven there were no passers-by.

Steve decided to take the plunge, literally, and he strode into the squelching sludge looking for his target. Fuck it, if things went well here then coughing up for a new pair of rhythm and blues would be the least of his worries.

Steve wandered through the maze of vegetable patches. He surprised himself by actually feeling a little empathy for the ageing geezers who spent their time toiling here – a platoon of stooped pensioners with grey hair and braces and creaky smiles that lit up faces that had seen way too much.

The place had a strange serenity about it, despite the fact that it was only a goal kick away from the endless activity of the world's greatest metropolis.

'You looking for someone, son?' A cackling voice broke Steve out of his daydream.

Steve looked at the old codger who was standing next to a wheelbarrow full of horse shit. It was so fresh it was still steaming. He was a small but stocky old fella with a shock of unkempt white hair sticking up from the top of his head like a wizened teddy boy. His rough serge trousers looked as if they had seen action at Passchendaele. Even his collarless white shirt was splattered with dried mud.

'I think I've found him,' said Steve, flashing a smile.

The old man returned it, revealing a mouth full of yellowing stumps. They were the kind of teeth you'd expect to see on an exhumed corpse.

Ronnie Harper had seemed to have been an old fella back when Steve and Kenny were boys; at least a generation older than their old man. Older than Methuselah. Older even than Bernie Sternschuss.

Ronnie and Mickey had never been bosom buddies but they had worked together on occasion and had always appeared to get on well. It was only when the brothers took a more active part in their father's business that they learned exactly who Ronnie was, and more importantly of his reputation as London's finest "peterman".

Harper was the safecracker's safecracker. In the immediate post-war years he cracked open more safes – known colloquially as "peters" – than Slack Eddie Chapman.

If truth be told, he was at it throughout the war too.

In the semi-darkness of the musty old shed, standing stooped in front of its concertinas of cobwebs, and straining tea into two enamel mugs next to a tiny wood burning stove, Ronnie looked a pale shadow of the legendary rogue he had once been.

Steve sat on an old kitchen chair and watched the old man. He had already half convinced himself that he had made a wasted journey.

'If I'd known you were going to turn up in your Sunday best I'd have put a dustsheet or something down,' said Ronnie with a dry cackle. Steve laughed as he realised just how much his King's Road casual wear clashed with the surroundings.

'You've done well, young Steve. I've been following your fortunes from afar, piecing together news and information of your antics from the usual busy bodies, y'know, pub blabbermouths, wannabes and loose-lipped ex-lags...as I'm sure the Old Bill have been doin' too.'

He thrust a steaming mug towards Steve and settled himself down onto a camping stool with a grunt.

'Have you heard about the twins?'

'Of course, Ron. The whole world knows about them now.'

'I didn't much care for them...'

'Bullies,' both men said as one.

'And noncing about with bent Lords weren't much help to that, Ronnie. Talk about drawing attention to yourself...'

'That's how it can go, son. The more you get away with, and the more you flaunt it, the bigger that target gets on your back.'

Steve pointed over at an ancient transistor radio in the corner.

'I'm surprised you've heard a dicky bird if you're getting your news from that. It looks as if it still picks up Lord Haw-Haw.'

'I get my news straight from the street,' Ronnie said grandly, adding 'And *The Sun* newspaper of course. It's a sad state of affairs, what with them and that lot from Camberwell all banged up. It don't look like any of them will be out any time soon. You've got to be careful, boy.''I don't let these things just float by, Ronnie,' Steve said quietly. 'I think about it all the time. Fuck knows I have to, because Kenny never thinks beyond his next pay day or whatever tart he's trying to poke. What the twins achieved is fucking legendary but all I can do is try not to make the same mistakes as them. Maybe try and find another way forward.'

'So what's this visit about, son? You thinking of growing some marrows or what?'

Steve grinned broadly.

'Nothing like that. I was in the area and just thought I'd look you up.'

'Bollocks, you were. Double bollocks. I might be old but I'm not fucking senile. What you got in mind?'

'I'm a bad liar, ain't I?'

'The worst! You're a straight talker Steve and I don't think you have to sugarcoat anything you want to say very often, that's why you're so shit at it. You know you don't have to dance around the houses with me. What's on your mind?'

Steve paused for a moment and subtly tapped the toe of his shoe on the dusty floor four times. *1-2-3-4.*

'I'm thinking of something big, Ronnie. Bags of sparklers and plenty of them.'

Ronnie let out a long, wheezing breath and raised his eyebrows in disbelief.

'For fuck's sake, Steve, have you been talking to Bernie Sternschuss? We'll never hear the end of his "golden opportunity". Every fucking Tom, Dick and Harry will be looking to pull off a job like that. Take my advice, son, cunts will be tripping over each other to get at some bullion or diamonds and they'll all end up wanking their nights away in a cold cell, believe me. Just because the Crokers got away with something big, now everyone thinks it's a good idea but they are too fucking lazy to go abroad to do it. From what I've heard you are doing alright, son, stick with what you know.'

'That's what everyone says, Ronnie, and I'm fucking sick of it,' snapped Steve. The outburst surprised even him.

'Nobody's got any vision...stay where you are, stick with what you're good at. Things are changing across the whole country and everyone in the East End just wants to plod on like it's still 1950. It does my fuckin' nut in.'

'All right, son, take it easy. I understand. It's just...well, sometimes it is the best decision to stick at what you're good at. I tried a few different things when I was a lad but when I jemmied the back off my first safe then that was it for me. I knew right there that that was it for me. Until I finally hung up my tools I stuck with that and it always put steam on the table. Suited my old girl as well, always money for clobber, a week in Southend every year and I only did about three years porridge in all that time.'

Steve sipped his tea thoughtfully. He'd enjoyed listening to Ronnie talk for as long as he could remember. The old man's steady, husky tone was the aural equivalent of warm honey; he always had a worthwhile opinion and never sounded as if he was giving a lecture.

'That's sort of what I came here for,' said Steve.

Ronnie laughed quietly. 'Whoa, you'd better just be thinking about getting advice, Stevie boy. These old hands ain't good for nothing other than pulling spuds out the ground these days.'

'I don't believe that, Ronnie,' said Steve with a smile. 'There's life in the old dog yet.'

He waved his hand around the dusty shed. 'Surely this is just a place where you spend a bit of free time, not a fucking tomb.'

'I do all right,' said Ronnie, his words sautéed lightly in indignation. 'I still get my whistle on twice a week and visit a young lady up West for some how's-yer-father. It costs a few bob granted but she reckons me old hampton is still as firm as a toffee hammer. My old girl just ain't interested any more. I think her old growler has healed up.'

Steve shook with laughter.

'You've still got it, Ron,' he said with a broad smile. 'You can't just hide yourself away in here until the grim reaper comes knocking. I know you still want that buzz, tell me I'm wrong?'

Ronnie, who had suddenly found the tea leaves swilling around at the bottom of his cup entrancing, said nothing.

'What if I was to tell you that we weren't looking at a bank job but getting at some gear from the back of a security van?'

The old man looked up from his cup but remained silent.

Steve went on: 'What if I told you we can get to the gear before it's locked away?'

'Those vans are pretty solid, Steve. You've got the back doors to get through, then the inner cage, radio controlled alarms, guards and a driver doing everything he can to turn your best laid plans to dust...it wouldn't be easy, son.'

'You're not wrong. But it wouldn't be impossible.'

'Not if you had the bottle and the proper planning...'

'And the right people...'

Ronnie laughed and banged his cup down on a shelf loaded with plant pots and lemonade bottles loaded with brown liquids of unknown origins. 'You can't mean me, Steve?' he said with a dusty giggle.

'Who better? We need someone to get us access to the goods as quick as possible. We can bang away at those doors and fuck about with explosives until the Old Bill drag us away kicking and screaming, but with someone like you onboard we can be in and out and on our way to the South of France before they know what's fucking hit them.'

Ronnie peered out of the shed's small dirty window and scanned his eye across the allotment. The boy was right. It did look like a fucking graveyard.

'You think I can still do it, do you, Steve?' he said without turning around.

Steve got up from his chair and placed his hand reassuringly on the old man's shoulder. 'I know you can, Ron.'

***

It was a Saturday afternoon in Central London. The sun had already started to descend from its zenith. Steve and Roy sat together in Steve's Jag as they watched a security van drive past them towards Fenchurch Street.

'That's the one,' said Steve quietly. 'Ten minutes later than last week but same time as the week before. They must think if they alternate every fortnight then that will bamboozle any would-be blaggers. Fucking mugs.'

Roy watched the vehicle disappear in the distance and shook his head in a slightly despairing manner.

'I don't know, Steve. It looks like a fucking tank. How we going to get in to that in the middle of the day? It's madness, shouldn't that be something we work up to after a few other jobs.'

'You know that's not my style, Roy,' said Steve. 'If we are going to do a job then it might as well be a big one.'

'I figured that,' said Roy. His tone was sarcastic.

Steve sighed. 'We're not stealing buns out of the back of a bread van any more, mate. Have a bit of vision, Roy.'

'We never went hungry though, did we? Even though we never had two fucking pennies to rub together.'

Steve smiled but said nothing. The two old pals sat together in silence for a moment before Roy piped up.

'You don't think our last visit to Hatton was an omen, do you?'

'That's in the past, Roy. No scooters or dodgy tips this time, I guarantee that. If there's one thing I've picked up, it's the need to plan things properly. That last time we were like virgin schoolboys, we went in unprepared but we have to learn from that. I'm not coming away with fuck all other than a face full of fire extinguisher ever again. Those days are long behind us but at least we have successfully identified one way that was fucking useless. Now we just have to make sure that doesn't happen again and it won't if we put the graft in.'

'And you think this old geezer is going to help us get the job done?'

'Of course he is! I know my old man wasn't always the best judge of character but with Ronnie he was bang on. He might be knocking on a bit but skills like his don't fade away. He can get into anything! He'd have your old dear's drawers off if he met her down the Darby & Joan.'

Roy laughed quietly. Steve continued: 'He'll get the doors off that van and into the safe inside as quick as a flash. We just need some other distraction to give him time to do it.'

Roy had nothing to add to the conversation so for a few minutes they both sat quietly again and watched the traffic go by. They were aware of a strange noise that was building up in the distance. Eventually the source of the racket was clear.

'Look at those dirty bastards,' Roy piped up as he pointed to a group of long-haired student types that had appeared behind them. The hippies were waving placards that bore a myriad of slogans mostly relating to peace and CND. They were slowing the traffic on Aldgate to almost walking pace. 'What the fuck are they complaining about now? A generation ago kids their age would have been getting ready to face the Luftwaffe and now look at these long-haired soap-dodging cunts out on the streets moaning about anything that doesn't go their way at the drop of a fucking hat. Fucking no-good scruff-bucket layabouts! I've never seen so many soddin' beards and specs in the one place before. They want to try marching down our manor and see what happens. It would be fucking bedlam.'

Steve slapped both his hands against the steering wheel, made a whooping sound and shouted 'Yes!'. It was as if he had reversed 3 and 5 through the card at Walthamstow dogs and just watched them all win. Roy almost jumped out of his seat with shock.

'What the fuck are you so happy about?'

'You might be a miserable bastard most of the time, Roy Storer,' said Steve with a broad smile. 'But sometimes you can be a fucking genius.'

He started the car engine and pulled away from the side of the road sharply as Roy looked on in bemusement.

***

The Shacklewell skins held court in a pub called the White Hart down Stoke Newington Road. It was an old-fashioned boozer with a pool table, a dartboard and a jukebox filled with boss reggae 45s from labels like Studio One, Blue Beat and Trojan. That's where the facilities began and ended and any passer-by that expected a warm welcome and an inside toilet were in for a rude awakening.

The owner, Colin "Fat Col" Gannon, had long since given up hope of attracting a wider clientele since Harry Prince and his unruly gang of "peanuts" had first colonised the pub. He knew he should have barred the lot of them on their first visit. He should definitely have banned them over the graffiti in the khazi and the way they liberally decorated his Formica tabletops with fag burns. But he had not and now they had attached themselves like bleeding barnacles to the place.

Tonight was no different, they were the only punters in the bar and they were fucking around, dancing and shouting as usual. Col knew that some of them were topping up their drinks from cheap bottles of booze they had brought in inside an old sports bag. The only upside was the gaggle of young sorts that hung around them, hard but smartly turned out little birds who occasionally bestowed favours upon him in return for a few free drinks. He just prayed he'd never get an offer like that from Big Brenda.

Eventually the gang calmed down and sat together conspiratorially, obviously planning their next bout of bovver or some other dirty deed.

When Steve Knight and Roy Storer walked into the saloon bar the atmosphere curdled immediately. The two men headed straight over towards the row of small tables that the skinheads were gathered around.

The gang all knew who these unexpected visitors were and they knew that they were real hounds to whom respect was due. Yet their body language told a different story. They looked defiant, crossing their arms as if to say 'This is our manor and we would never just roll over and accept an intrusion without putting up some front...even if the fucking SS waltzed in.'

Twenty pairs of young defiant eyes drilled into the outsiders. But nobody made a move except Harry Prince who stepped forward, inadvertently puffing out his chest until the buttons on his Brutus shirt strained against the checked fabric.

'Mr Knight. This is a rare honour. What can we do for you?' said Harry brightly, even though the words almost stuck in his throat.

Roy and Steve were only a few years older than he was but with their rep and their family connections he knew that he had to know his place...without losing face. After all Steve's father was the famous Mickey Knight, a proper face. Harry's old man worked in the sausage factory.

'Please, please, it's Steve, Harry. We're all friends here.'

'Okay,' said Harry in a measured tone. 'What can we do for you, Steve?'

Steve took off his jacket to make it clear that he was in no hurry to leave despite the frosty reception.

Nice whistle, thought Harry.

'I wonder if you'd be interested in assisting us with something. We have certain needs that I think you might be able to help us with.'

'What is it you are after, Steve? Pills? Fencing? Muscle?'

'Just one thing, Harry,' said Steve with a friendly grin. *'Chaos.'*

***

On a quiet Tuesday evening at Aphrodite's Palace, Steve and Kenny called the firm into the office for a meeting about "The Job". Everyone knew something big was in the offing, but none of them knew the details. Still they were taken aback to see an old man with dirty finger nails and a slight stoop standing behind the brothers.

'Gentlemen, this is Mr Ronald Harper, an old friend of our father's,' said Steve. 'He will be joining us for this enterprise.'

Puzzled glances were exchanged.

'*Old* is the fucking word,' Butch whispered to Arthur. 'He makes Methuselah look trendy.'

'Sshh,' said Roy.

Steve shot Butch a look and tapped the map of London that was spread across the desk.

'So, gentlemen, you know why we are here, let's run through this. To start off Kenny will have a van waiting at Holborn Circus with Arthur, Butch and Ronnie, while myself and Roy will follow the security van from their pick-up at Fenchurch Street to make sure the poor souls don't get lost along the way.'

'So why is he here?' interrupted Arthur abruptly, pointing towards Ronnie.

Steve sighed slightly. 'Mr Harper...Ronnie is going to make sure we get in that van easily and out with the goods as quickly as Errol Flynn getting in and out of a Hollywood starlet.'

'Why are you planning to hit them on a Saturday though?' said Arthur. 'Surely that's the main trading day for shops. Wouldn't they want their stock before then?'

'This shipment ain't full of cheap engagement rings and tacky tom, Arthur,' said Steve evenly. 'This is uncut gear, rough stones heading straight for a dealer who is only open by appointment only. The security firm obviously think that when the streets are busy there's less chance of someone having the balls to do something in front of so many witnesses.'

'But we do?' said Butch quizzically.

'I think you've answered your own question, mate,' smiled Steve. 'We'll be masked up of course but if everything goes to plan there will be so much aggro on the street that no one will be hanging about to clock number plates and give descriptions to the filth.'

'Aggro?'

'Yeah, it's all in hand.'

'What if one of those Joe Public have-a-go heroes want to do their civic duty?' said Butch.

'We're not fucking about here,' snarled Kenny. 'If any civilians want to "have a go" then they need to be put out of the picture sharpish. Me, Steve and Arthur will all have shotguns and the rest of you will be tooled up. Obviously it's all for show but if we need to use them then so be it. If anyone's squeamish about that then now is the time to say.'

No one said a word. The only sound was that of Steve turning his lighter over on the table four times.

Kenny tensed up slightly but he kept his mouth shut, even though his brother's obsessive behaviour was starting to get worse and it worried him, especially with such a major job on the cards.

'Hopefully though, have-a-go heroes are not going to be much of a problem,' said Steve. 'We have a crate of M18 smoke grenades that we intend to decorate the street with and a planned peace march heading down on Charterhouse Street is going to meet up with our distinctively unpeaceful short-haired friends from Shacklewell at the same time.'

'Those fucking peanuts,' spat Arthur, 'Are you sure they can be trusted?'

'Who said anything about trusting them?' asked Roy. 'We're weighing them out for doing something they would usually do for fuck all – kick the fuck out of some hairy students. I don't think they will disappoint us.'

'So you reckon the hippies, the skinheads and that security van are all going to meet at the same point at the same time?' said Butch. 'That's a bit of a stretch ain't it?'

'Steve and Roy have done all the timings, Butch,' said Kenny. 'If it all works out it will be perfect, if it don't work we just drive away.'

Steve looked over to Butch and smiled. 'Kenny's right,' he said. 'We ain't dragging you all into something half-cocked. Either everything goes to plan or we forget the whole thing and try again another day.'

He looked around the room waiting for any further questions. Butch and Arthur looked undecided but they still nodded their heads in agreement. 'So,' Steve continued. 'Kenny jumps out the van, puts the same type of strip of nails that we used on the whisky truck into the security van's path then as it grinds to a halt, I drop a smoke grenade and that will set the Shacklewell boys on their way into the peace march. Ronnie opens the van and we're in.'

'How easy is that going to be, old-timer?' asked Butch.

Ronnie ignored the implied slight and spoke up for the first time in front of the group.

'These Austin J2 vans have a pretty basic security system. The cab up front is isolated from the back with steel plates but we don't need to worry about them. There is only one sliding door on the driver's side, if we can get the geezers in the front out or away from their radio then that is a bonus but there are metal grills on all the windows and if we've put all of their tyres out of action then they ain't going nowhere anyway. What we're interested in is getting that single back door open sharpish, then getting the two geezers in the back out of the way so we can have a crack at the safe that's behind a caged area.'

'How do you know all this?' said Butch, a note of suspicion in his voice.

'It's my job to know, son,' replied Ronnie as if he were talking to a trappy schoolboy. 'Besides, these vans have been in use since 1956 so I've seen the insides of a few of them before. I've cracked these tanks more than once before, that's why I'm fucking here.'

Everyone in the room laughed apart from Butch whose cheeks were tinged with crimson.

'We've got good info straight from the security depot boys,' said Steve. 'We know what to expect inside these vans, we just have to deal with it.'

'An old squaddie friend of mine left me some C3 in his will,' continued Ronnie. 'That will help us get to what we need but there's no guarantee what nick the geezers in the back will be in when the door opens. Getting to the safe will be a little longer so that's why I need you gentleman to buy me a little time.'

'Hold up,' said Arthur, 'So we have to stand in the middle of the street on a Saturday with a smouldering security van and a couple of sparked out guards while "Old Father Time" here fiddles about with a safe?'

Steve had mulled the plan over and over in his mind and he knew that this was the weak spot. He did not doubt that Ronnie could blow the peter but if anything went wrong then they would be leaving empty-handed...if they were leaving at all.

'Ninety seconds is all we need,' he said with as much authority as he could muster. 'It will be chaos all around us; I guarantee it, more than enough to cover us. We just need to hold our nerve. You've all got the bottle, I know that, but we just need to put it to the test for one big job. Believe me, with this haul we'll all be set for life. I know that sounds like bullshit but it is the truth.'

After a slight pause everyone nodded. They weren't 100 per cent convinced, he could tell, but that was the best agreement they were going to get.

Steve prodded the map again, this time around the Kings Cross area, 'Once the job is done, we all head back in Kenny's van back to here, leaving the motor me and Roy will be using slap bang in the middle of the road to add to the congestion. We have acquired access to a small warehouse in Wharfdale Road and inside there are two motors that have been freshly half-inched by Mr Kelly who seems to have an uncanny knack of picking up jam-jars that still have the keys in the ignition.'

'He'd have the fucking sugar out of your tea,' laughed Arthur as he slapped Butch approvingly on the back.

Steve smiled but kept talking. 'Then we torch the van and get the fuck out of Dodge City before the sheriff and his posse come calling. You all know where the safe houses are, so get to where you are going and lie low for a couple of days until you hear from either me or Kenny. After that then it's business as usual as far as anyone is concerned. I'm sure we might get a pull from the law but as long as we keep our mouths shut and they don't find any gear we'll have our briefs on the case before any of youse need to pick up the soap for some big ugly bastard in the shower block.'

'When you put it like that it sounds easy,' grumbled Arthur, 'Too fucking easy.'

Steve breathed in deeply as if the speech he was about to deliver was Henry V before Agincourt.

'You're right, Arthur,' he said. 'It ain't easy but the best things never are. Things like this take nerve, they take balls of steel, and they take a cast-iron plan.'

He pointed towards his brother. 'Me and Kenny, we've put a lot of graft into this and we believe it will work or we wouldn't have even brought it to you. I know the scooter job at Hatton Garden was a fucking disaster but we learnt from that and I know it ain't ancient history but think of everything we have done since then. We're a better firm now and this is the next step. This moves us up a league.'

He wasn't expecting VE Day but his spontaneous oratory was worth more than the batch of grunts and brief nods that it received. Still, he'd show these doubting Thomases that he and Kenny were right with action not words...but not before he'd run the plan through at least twice more.

***

Half an hour later, just after they followed the rest of the firm downstairs to the bar, Kenny gripped Steve's arm to hold him back.

'What do you think?' he said quietly.

'Not exactly the explosion of enthusiasm I was expecting, bruv. But they are all still on board.'

Kenny looked around the empty office for a moment while he chose his words carefully.

'It's a gamble, Steve.'

'Life's a gamble, Kenny. That's what it's all about.'

***

Steve sat outside of Anthea's flat, aware that he had just removed and inserted the ignition key four times. *1-2-3-4*. He cursed himself. He kept trying to rein the funny business in but it seemed to be getting worse.

He thought initially that the worry with Pat might have exacerbated it but McVey was in the ground. Okay, the security van job had been weighing heavily on his mind but he knew that wasn't what was eating away at him now. It was Anthea.

Whenever he was near her, his compulsive habits became worse. She was the cause. She was the catalyst. The woman was amazing on many levels – smart, strikingly beautiful and as sexy as hell. But her own drug-fuelled behaviour had become so erratic of late that he could not accurately remember the last time he had paid her a visit. Her head was all over the shop. Even if in her case the shop was Fortnum & Mason.

Anthea was seldom seen without a joint gripped beneath those full sensual lips and he knew that cannabis was the tip of a trippy iceberg. Despite her denials, he was fully aware that she experimented with LSD more than once, and her flirtation with opium was an open secret. When he walked in now what were the odds he would find her with a needle in her arm? She wasn't the woman he met at Aphrodite's Palace any more. And she certainly wasn't the perfect mod bird he'd dreamed about after that first chance sighting.

What was it his mum had always said? That's it, 'be careful what you wish for'...

His thoughts turned to lovely Lizzie and how uncomplicated life could be with her. She was a good-looking girl and more importantly she was proper – down to earth and one of your own. Lizzie had a clear idea of what his life was really all about, and what the boundaries were.

Anthea's understanding of modern villainy had been gleaned from cheap pulp fiction and the Jimmy Cagney films she watched on TV through a haze of hash smoke.

He got out of the car and walked to the door, standing there for a minute or two while his reluctance wrestled with his libido. The libido won. He rapped his knuckles briskly against the woodwork.

Anthea's voice cut through the quietness of the mews. 'Come in for fuck's sake, you know it's open.'

Steve pushed the front door open and stepped into the flat. She looked at him grumpily. 'What is it with you and fucking door knocking?' she snapped.

'I didn't want to barge in,' said Steve. He resisted the temptation to fire back into her. Instead he forced a smile, even though he could feel the muscles across his shoulders tighten with tension.

'Oh why, Steve?' she shouted in a melodramatic drawl. 'In case I'm getting fucked on the floor by some hairy-arsed stud. You're such a square, man.'

Anthea he noticed was wearing black nylons under her dressing gown. It was as if she had started to get dressed at some point and then got distracted...just as he got distracted by the sight of her legs.

When she crossed them the stockings seemed to almost audibly whisper to him. 'Fuck me' they said, 'and then fuck me again.'

Anthea stood up snapping him out of his thoughts, lit up a large joint and strolled over to a drinks trolley where she poured herself a whisky large enough to tranquillise a shire horse. 'I might as well have a lover for all I've seen of you recently.'

'I've been busy, you know that.'

'Busy...'

Her tone put the seductive stockings out of his mind in an instant.

Steve felt a strong compulsion to slap the silly bitch into the middle of next week. Instead, he exercised extreme restraint and lowered himself carefully on her silly inflatable chair. He even managed a smile.

She gulped at the whisky then absent-mindedly fiddled with a small pile of pills that were sitting on the mantelpiece.

'Oh yes, busy, busy, busy... Mr Captain of Fucking Industry 1968, plying your sleazy wares...'

She sounded like she was on the outskirts of drunk. Not fully gone, but gone enough for the occasional 's' to slur.

'Talking of dirty cash, while you're here I need a little loan.'

'Since when have you had money worries?'

Anthea gave an exaggerated sigh as if even answering him was a sizable imposition.

'It's just that the gentleman who provides my party treats has allowed me a little more credit than I expected and now my account needs to be settled.'

'You mean you owe money to a fucking drug dealer?' said Steve. He rose to his feet quickly. 'Tell me who he is and I'll sort it.'

'That's not the way things are done here, Steve. This is not some backstreet peddler. He comes from a good family. He needs to be paid and I am temporarily indisposed.'

'Has Daddy's money not come through this month? Maybe he has skipped town with his Swedish maid?'

Steve strode across the room and stopped directly in front of her. She stared at him defiantly.

'Don't be such a peasant, Steve, I've only asked for a little loan. God knows you've got enough. Call it an allowance if you like? Surely you can afford it? For me? You help me out with an extension and I'll help you out with yours.'

She reached down and grabbed him through his trousers. Steve pushed her hand away. Then he leant forward and spoke in a quiet tone that came loaded with a side order of threat.

'You don't know the value of money because you've never had to work for it. Women round my way know what it is to put in a shift just to pay the rent and have a little bit left over for themselves.'

'What? Horrible little pig-faced shop-girls with their uptight small-minded ways? Working all week for a pittance and celebrating with a few gins at the weekend. Dropping their knickers in the dark and bringing another generation of oiks into the world because they are too afraid of what the neighbours might say if they take the pill...'

That was when Steve lost it. With a roar, he pushed his hand over Anthea's mouth and pressed her against the wall.

'You silly fuckin' patronising stuck-up bitch.'

A framed poster of *La Dolce Vita* dropped to the floor under the impact and its glass tinkled impotently on the thickly carpeted floor.

'That's it, hit me, you fucking brute, hit me,' she sneered through his fingers. 'That's how you get things done isn't it...violence! That's your answer to everything, you fucking caveman. You ignorant, pig-thick barrow boy.'

Steve drew back his other fist and then stopped himself. Never hit a woman, his dad had drummed that into him and he never would. Instead he turned around abruptly and headed out of the door, ignoring her expletive-heavy tirade of insults.

He walked on past his own car until he reached the phone box at the end of the road. This was unfortunate for the geezer using it who Steve yanked out and slung to the floor.

Moments later he had taken a piece of paper out of his pocket and was dialling the number written under the name "Charlotte".

***

Twenty minutes later Steve Knight was standing in Charlotte Clifton's front room in Knightsbridge. The whole of one wall was covered in books. She could have opened her own library. There were hardbacks, paperbacks, thick academic books, encyclopaedias. He looked at the names of the authors – Steinbeck, Émile Zola, Robert Tressell, Upton Sinclair, Márquez, Trumbo, Ursula Le Guin, and more familiar names like Jack London, George Orwell, Marx, Engels and Lenin.

Charlotte came in from the kitchen with two mugs of black coffee.

'Are you sure this is all you want? I have got beer somewhere.'

He took the mug.

'Ta. This'll do fine.' He nodded his head towards the bookcase. 'I see you're a bit of a Tory then.'

She laughed. 'I'm a Marxist, Steve. As I think you've guessed. New Left of course.'

'So no time for Stalin and his groupies.'

'That's right.' She picked up a leaflet from the table advertising a peace demo. 'We're doing this on Saturday if you're interested...'

Steve studied the leaflet and nodded. 'Yeah, I heard about this. A few of us might go along...'

Charlotte smiled.

'How many do you think there will be?

'Maybe four or five hundred. The hardcore. The ones who won't back down.'

'Good. Tell me, what do you do for a living, Charlotte?'

'I'm a lecturer. Social history at the LSE. And I dabble a bit in art, which is why I was invited to that party.'

She was short, 5-foot-one or thereabouts, and there was a faint echo of a northern accent – Middlesbrough maybe, or Darlington – suggesting humble roots. She picked a book by Richard Llewellyn off of the coffee table and stretched up to put it back on the correct shelf. As she did so, he noticed how heavy her breasts looked. She didn't dress well, but the boat race reminded him of someone. Yeah. Sophie Loren! Or a kind of sawn-off hippy version of her at least.

'Who were you there with?' she asked.

'Anthea Sellers. She's a model. Into art and that.'

'I know her. She hates me. Snooty cow. Sorry if she's a friend.'

He paused. 'An acquaintance,' he said. 'Friend is stronging it.'

He smiled and his grin turned her legs to jelly.

'All these spoilt brats swanning around thinking the world owes them something...they just shouldn't be in our scene. They're parasites. I can't stand them. And I think the feeling is mutual.'

'What exactly is your scene?'

She waved towards the magazines and papers on the table. There were copies of *International Times*, *Oz*, and *Black Dwarf* with the headline: "We shall fight, we shall win – Paris, London, Rome, Berlin".

He nodded. 'Why did you give me your number? I was intrigued.'

She shrugged. 'I fancied you, Steve. You're drop-dead gorgeous. If a man can pursue a woman, why can't a woman pursue a man?'

'Why not indeed?'

'So you're not one of these male chauvinist pigs then? You don't mind if a woman makes the first move?'

Their eyes locked.

'Mind? Not a bit. I'd welcome it.'

She put her coffee cup on the table, came closer and kissed him.

***

Half an hour later Steve Knight and Charlotte climaxed at the exact same moment. He rolled over and sunk his head into her pillow. She snuggled up closely and ran her fingers over his bicep. So hard. So strong.

'Beer now?'

'That would be great.'

She left the bedroom and returned three or four minutes later carrying two Whitbread Tankards and a bottle of red wine. Now unleashed, her breasts were magnificent. Each nipple stood out like the proverbial blind cobbler's thumb.

'Put them down.'

'Very bossy. Why?'

'I want to see you.'

She laid the bottles on the bottom of the bed and stood at the end, naked and unashamed.

'Do you think you could manage it again?'

Just the thought of it made his cock twitch.

'Five minutes?'

'Good. I want to ride you this time.'

***

Steve woke up at dawn, his throat dry and his mind groping to remember details of the previous night's fun. Charlotte lay beside him fast asleep, with a small smile playing around her lips. Good. He lifted the covers and gazed at her delicious nakedness.

He had rung her bell like a circus strongman last night. He'd come five, maybe six times; she'd managed more. And in-between they'd talked a lot. About everything about music, films, TV, clubs...and inevitably politics. She'd asked about the unions in East London and he was able to embellish his relationship with docks convenor Fred Prevost with a few tall tales. He had told her everything he knew about the London docks, the massive quantities of goods that came in – 61 million tonnes in 1964 – the militancy of the men and their cavalier attitude to private property which delighted her. And as memories of the conversation flooded back, another thought occurred, an extra idea to throw into the pot for the coming event, an extra twist...

He sat bolt upright. It was perfect. He had better get moving. He now had two meetings to get to today.

On second thoughts make that three.

Steve dressed quickly, carefully avoiding the empty bottles on the bedroom floor, and left Charlotte a note with the club phone number. He was home, showered, shaved and out of the door again by 9.30am.

***

Fred Prevost had retired but he was happy to arrange for Steve to meet his son Rick at Poplar.

The three men sat around the kitchen table sipping dark rum from a cargo that arrived from the Caribbean at the weekend. Fred may be out of the game, but Rick was now a shop steward at the West Indian docks and the family business carried on as normal. Half of the things in the little terraced house had come off the back of a freight ship, the larger items with the help of "approachable" members of the Port of London Authority police who were happy to turn a blind eye for a "nice drink".

'How's work?'

'Ticking over', Rick replied without much enthusiasm. 'You heard about St Katherine's and London Docks closing?'

'A crying shame,' said Fred.

Rick shrugged. 'Things change. We just have to stay on top of things. I hear Tilbury is the place to be. Or it will be at least.'

'East London will be fucked without the docks,' Fred protested. 'Think how many jobs they bring to the area.'

'So you'll fight?' Steve said rhetorically.

'Tooth and nail,' said Rick.

'Your lads still enjoy a good picket.'

'Beats working.'

'So how hard would it be to mobilise them on a Saturday morning?'

'What's the cause?'

Steve smiled. 'I've been thinking about that. Your lot still hate Franco don't they?'

***

Steve strolled down to the phone box and made a call, setting up another meeting for the evening.

Then he drove into town and parked up just off Charlotte Street. Two minutes later he was standing at the doctor's reception desk getting eyed up by the little blonde sort behind the jump. He flashed her a smile. Any other day and he'd have followed through with some chat but he didn't think his cock could take any more fanny for at least a day or two.

"Blondie" took him through to the waiting room and went off to get him some tea. The inside of it was like a modern art installation. Steve sat uncomfortably on a bulbous white leather couch and stared up at one of the bizarre paintings that decorated the light yellow walls. It was a frameless chunk of canvas featuring some random blocks of colour and thick black lines.

Steve was no stranger to fashionable art. Anthea had dragged him to a few gallery openings where he'd watched many a toffee-nosed cow-son *ooh* and *ahh* over work by Beuys, Bridget Riley, Paolozzi, Hamilton and Blake. All of it was pony. Three-dimensional triangles, metal hoops, random lumps of wood piled up, and paintings like this monstrosity – which looked like a fucking multicoloured migraine – was no better. Shit on a fucking stick. The only thing that made it interesting was the dough these chinless saps were ready to splash out on it, because that made it worth nicking.

Maurie Goldberg had put him on to this place, without knowing it. Maurie was a Labour councillor from Stepney and a first-class fence. His cousin was a psychiatrist, and by the look of his Harley Street surgery a very rich one.

The young dolly bird from reception stepped into the room, holding a cup of tea. The sharp contrast between her jet black miniskirt and her well tanned thigh snapped Steve out of his thoughts.

'Doctor Hoffman will see you now, Mr Monk,' she said sweetly and gestured towards a door opposite her. 'I'll take your tea through.'

'Thank you, darling,' said Steve with a twinkling smile. The "Monk" had been a precaution. It wouldn't do for his real name to turn up on any bits of paper related to a head-shrink.

In contrast to the waiting room's arty minimalism, Hoffman's office was warm and welcoming in an old-time way – all brown leather, polished wood and thick velvet curtains. There was even a roaring fire on the go. Steve half expected to find Sherlock Holmes puffing his pipe by the hearth. Hoffman was smoking a pipe but that is where the connection ended. Unsurprisingly he had a large, but carefully trimmed, beard and his clobber was part country gent, part hobo – up to and including the waistcoat with its attendant pocket watch.

But if the look was Old English, the voice still had a tinge of Vienna.

'Please, Mr Monk, ve vill take a seat, yes?' He sat down and gestured to another well-upholstered easy chair that was facing him.

'No couch?'

'No straitjackets either. Not yet at any rate. Now, Harold...you don't mind if I call you Harold do you? I'm Leo.'

'Not at all. I'm Harry to my friends but whatever suits you, Doc.' Steve smiled inwardly. The soppy cunt wouldn't have a clue what Harry Monk was, although his receptionist might be partial to some.

'That's a good start. Now tell me...Harry, vot exactly are your concerns? The notes my assistant took over the telephone say that you are suffering from some sort of anxiety, a strong desire to complete tasks in groups of four?'

Steve squirmed slightly. 'I wouldn't say anxiety; it's more of a kind of tic...just something I occasionally feel compelled to do. Once it's done then I'm all right.'

'But you do feel anxious until this action has been performed?'

'Not anxious exactly... It's more of a pain in the arse than anything.'

Hoffman rubbed his beard for a moment and then tapped the left leg of his round spectacles.

'Would I be correct in suggesting that you have come to me to perhaps ease this pain?'

'At these prices I would hope so, Doc.'

Hoffman offered no more than a half-smile.

They talked for an hour all told. To his surprise after that initial awkwardness Steve began to open up. Maybe it was the warmth of the fire or Hoffman's soft, deep tone but the guy seemed easy to trust.

Seeing a shrink was just not something that was done on his manor. In popular imagination, anything to do with mental health was framed with images of rubber rooms and Bedlam. If you had something on your mind you blocked it out with booze, or battered someone until it went away. Yet here he was telling a stranger everything about his tic and his life. Well to a point. He didn't divulge anything about the firm. As far as Hoffman knew his patient was something big in insurance, which had an element of truth. With the Knights, you coughed up and you were fully insured. Fail to pay and unfortunate accidents tended to happen. Windows do break...and so do legs.

Precisely sixty minutes after he'd entered the room, Hoffman brought their session to a close.

'Look, Mr Monk, I am not going to say that because some barbarian teacher caned you four times ven you vere young that we have reached the root of your problem. It is far more likely to be much deeper underlying than that. But I can say with certainty that you have some form of what we call obsessive-compulsive disorder. It is brought on by stress and, I know you don't like the vurd anxiety, so shall we say uneasiness or apprehension? It seems at this stage that you are managing the distress caused by this condition and yet it is problematic because it is so noticeable. Removing this behaviour completely vill, I think, be a complex procedure and something that vill need a lot of vork.'

'You mean a lot of visits to you?' said Steve with just a touch of sarcasm.

Hoffman removed his glasses and rubbed the bridge of his nose as he closed his eyes for a moment.

'I'm not some kind of mind mechanic, Mr Monk. I can't simply knock off the switch marked compulsive behaviour and send you on your vay. And besides, if this is not something you are truly interested in addressing then any amount of visits here will have little effect.'

'Look, Doc, all I want to know is how to stop all this and get on with my business. I'm not here to find out if I was a jolly Jack tar or a flamin' unicorn in some past life.'

'I understand your scepticism, Harry, and whether you return here or not for further consultations is entirely up to you. But can I suggest one thing, and this is free of charge as technically our hour is up, just find out the one thing...the one social interaction that triggers this behaviour the most and stop putting yourself in that situation. Do you know what that is?'

Steve sighed deeply then took a long deep breath through his nose. 'I think I do,' he said slowly.

***

Instead of driving to the club, he went straight to Anthea's – which was of course the opposite of what the shrink advised.

He had to finish it. He had to tell her it was over face to face like a man.

He stood outside Anthea's flat and took a moment to look up and down the cobbled mews street. The place almost stank of money. But not his kind of money – not the kind you fought and grafted for, no. This was money that had been handed down. Easy money. Privileged money. *Snob* money.

The kids who lived around here had come straight out of public school into cushy jobs set up by Papa or idled their useless parasitical lives away feather-bedded by generous allowances.

What he could smell was entitlement hand in hand with over-privileged excess. Steve pulled a face as if he had just walked through a London sewer. Most of the residents only ever met someone working class when they were slumming it or having someone change their tyre or unblock their khazi.

The bourgeoi-fuckin'-sie. If the pompous braggarts, arty-farty creeps and braying slack-jawed elitists that he had met with Anthea were anything to go by then they could all go and fuck themselves sideways. Steve Knight knew where he was from and who his people were, and they weren't here. Anthea was his only link to this world and that link was about to be severed.

He paused outside her door and stopped himself from knocking. Instead he barged straight into her gaff like a proper toff only to be confronted by a startled looking Christian.

'Steve, I...'

'You – fuck off!'

Christian left immediately.

'You can't talk to my friends like that,' said Anthea, her voice tinged with anger, and alcohol. She was wearing nothing except a bath towel.

'I think you'll find I can say what the fuck I want to who the fuck I like, darling.'

She screamed and ran at him, her right hand curling out to scratch his face. He caught her wrist and held it tightly. She tried to claw at him with her left hand but he caught that too.

'You're hurting me.'

'I'm really not.'

'Why are you even here?'

He stepped closer to her. 'I'm here to say goodbye, Anthea. I'm here to say we're over. Thank you for the good times, but it's got to stop. You're not for me and you're doing my head in.'

'You bastard!'

She spat. The gob hit him smack in the middle of his forehead and dribbled down his nose.

He let go of her wrists and wiped his face with his handkerchief.

'Thank you for proving my point.'

Anthea lashed out and caught him on the shoulder. He picked her up, put her over his shoulder and marched her into the bedroom, dropping her on to the bed gently. She lay on her back and undid the towel exposing her nakedness.

'This is what you want, isn't it? Come on, Steven. Take me, I'm yours.'

He turned around and walked out of the bedroom. Anthea ran behind him.

'That's it, keep going, you fucking headcase,' she screamed. 'Steve Knight, the big boss of fucking nowhere.'

Steve walked out of the front door and shut it behind him. Before he had even let go of the handle a heavy whisky decanter came smashing through the window to shatter into a hundred pieces on the cobblestone street.

Steve could hear a deep, heavy sobbing noise through the newly created gap in the glazing but he kept on walking towards his car without even a pause for thought.

Chapter Ten: Diamonds Are Forever

Steve Knight parked up in a side street near Aphrodite's Palace and walked towards it in a reflective mood. He wondered if putting a match to the place would help him mentally as every time he visited the building it reminded him of the Knights' greatest failure and the ghost of Mad Pat McVey. He wanted somewhere stylish, somewhere smart. And here he was stepping over a used condom lying at the corner of the doorway... *They didn't show that on* Land of the Giants *on the telly, dishy Deanna Lund as the miniature Valerie Scott coming face to face with a six foot johnny and a puddle of spunk... The thought made him smile, almost as much as the memory of Hoffman calling him Harry Monk did.*

Steve wasn't expecting anyone to be in his office and was pleasantly surprised to see Kenny behind the desk.

'Ken...'

He noticed his brother had the palms of his hands pressing down firmly on the leather-topped surface. His eyes bulged and his mouth drooped open. A layer of sweat covered his face. Heart attack?

'Fucking hell,' screamed Kenny as thick veins stood out across his forehead and a layer of sweat covered his face.

'You okay?'

'YES!' he shouted. 'Yes, yes, yes....'

Kenny's head sank with a gasp and a moment later a young woman with peroxide hair came out from under the desk casually wiping fluid from around her mouth. She smiled flirtatiously at Steve, spat Kenny's Harry Monk into a small waste bin then left the room quickly.

Kenny remained seated while he wrestled his spent member back into his trousers.

'For fuck's sake, Kenny, do you need to do that here?'

'Where else am I going to do it? I ain't going into any of their rooms, they're the size of fucking coffins. I ain't sitting on a bed that has had a hundred other men's hairy bollocks resting on it. Besides, I was bored. Where have you been? Shafting Anthea?'

'I had a prior engagement.'

'A prior engagement? Very la de fucking da. Who was it with this time? The Queen Mother?'

Steve pondered. Should he come clean? His brother was really the only person he could truly trust.

'I've been to the quack.'

'Why, what's up with you?' asked Kenny as he walked over to the small bar and reached for a bottle of whisky and two glasses. 'You got crabs again? I told you that those posh strumpets don't give a Donald Duck who they open their legs for.'

Steve paused again. 'I thought I would see someone about my...problem,' he said finally.

'You what? You've been to a fucking shrink?' yelled Kenny.

'Keep your voice down, bruv. It's nobody else's business.'

'It will be our business...our business right down the khazi if the word gets out that you are mental.'

'Mental!'

'Can you imagine one of the fucking New York mafia going to a shrink? It'd never fucking happen.'

'Look, you know everyone in the firm is aware of my...thing. I've heard all the whispers and the snide comments but fuck 'em. Fuck the lot of them. Do you think I don't try to keep a lid on it? Do you think my nerves don't grind together like broken glass under an army boot every time I have to do something? I think you've done well enough so far with a "mental" brother and I ain't fucking stopping. If anyone don't like the things I do they can tell me to my face and if they do they had better be prepared to get carved up like a fucking turkey. I know I'm fucked but I'm going to keep going and I'm going to grind this disorder into the ground too, and I won't ever fucking give up. So you can either get used to it or fuck right off.'

Kenny looked stunned at the outburst. He said nothing for a while and finished pouring both drinks. Then he stared out the window, sipping his own thoughtfully.

Eventually he spoke, 'Do you think I don't understand what you are going through, Steve? I know better than anyone what we went through as nippers because I was there. Do you think I like seeing you like this? Do think I like hearing the sniggers and the sly digs? I'll tell you something, if I could stick my fist right in the face of everyone who dared say a fucking word about what you go through then I would but I can't hit them all.'

He laughed and handed Steve his drink. 'I'm working on it though, bruv. We'll get through this, we're the Knights. We're on the verge of something really big here and it's all down to you, Steve.'

He raised his glass in a gesture of respect. 'We're moving up, Steve, and I will be beside you every step of the way.'

'That's a nice speech, Kenny,' said Steve solemnly, and then his face cracked into a wide grin. 'It would have been even nicer if you had done your fucking fly up though and I didn't have to look at that wrinkly old winkle.'

The brothers laughed. Steve took a bottle of Scotch and two glasses from his desk draw and poured them both a double.

He then sat with Kenny and talked him through the extras he had thought of for the big day.

When he finished Kenny Knight shook his head.

'Can I be the second person today to say that you're mental, bruv? That's either pure genius or it's borderline insane.'

'I think it's probably a bit of both...'

***

Four hours later the brothers arrived at the White Hart in Stoke Newington Road. It was still early so the pub was deserted except for Fat Col behind the bar, and Harry Prince sitting in a booth drinking a glass of Barley Wine. Toots and the Maytals were playing on the jukebox. Kenny bought him another bottle, and the three men sat around a table quietly going through the plan for Saturday. When Steve was satisfied that the younger man knew exactly what was expected of him, he walked up to the jukebox and put on Aretha's cover of "I Say A Little Prayer". He would be tonight for sure.

'Here, Harry,' said Steve. 'Who was that geezer bird who was in here the other night.'

'Brenda, my sister.'

'Careful, Steve,' said Kenny.

'No offence meant.'

'None taken. All of us call her "The Tank".'

'Because of her size? She's a big old girl.'

'No, because when it kicks off she goes into battle like a fuckin' Panzer.'

Kenny and Steve laughed.

Harry went on: 'I tell ya what, you wouldn't wanna get on the wrong side of her. She bit half of her last boyfriend's ear off in a row and spat it on the floor. He's going "Why did you do that?" and she's told him it was his fault "cos you never fuckin' listen"...'

***

The next day Steve thought he'd have one more go to end it well with Anthea. Big mistake. Donovan's "Hurdy Gurdy Man" was playing on the dinky Dansette but it was hard to hear it over the shouting.

'Who the fuckin' fuck do you think you are?' screamed Anthea almost as soon as Steve entered the flat and the foul-mouthed tirade continues.

The empty bottles – one gin, two of wine – that lay scattered across the room along with the heaving ashtrays and a small mirror flecked with traces of white powder explained why she was already off her trolley.

She was sitting on a once gleaming white chair that was now stained with booze and ash. Her eyes were rimmed with red and her hair hung down over her shoulder, lank and greasy. The room stank of booze, sweat and something else. Quite possibly desperation.

'Look, please. I didn't come here for an argument.'

'No, you came to fuck me and leave, the same as you always do. If it wasn't for the wet patches on the bed sheets I'd never know you'd been here at all.'

Steve's patience snapped. 'That's because you are either stoned, pissed or flying off to fucking Venus on a purple cloud or something. That's why I leave, Anthea. I'm not even sure if you know who I am some nights. How many other cocks do you take when you're tripping out of your skull?'

'Oh you fucking pleb,' screamed Anthea as she launched a thick ashtray towards him. He ducked deftly and it smashed against a poster on the wall, tearing Alain Delon's handsome mug into shreds. 'It's only your cock that I take, darling. Yours and only yours, that's why I'm in this fucking mess.'

She slumped back onto the armchair as soon as the words slipped from her mouth.

'What mess? I've given you everything that you've asked for. You don't want for nothing, people around my way brought up whole families on a fraction of the money that you piss away every week.'

'Oh please, spare me the kitchen sink dramas. I'm fucking sick of hearing about the Blitz spirit of the old East End. The proud but hardy Cockneys? You're all a bunch of fucking thieves and liars.'

Steve stepped forward angrily but stopped himself from grabbing her wrists. She knew just exactly what to say to wind him up. It worked every time.

'Oh, did I forget to say wife-beaters?' she hissed. 'Go on big man, take a swipe. Hit me right in the stomach. You'd be doing me a favour. I don't want this bastard anyway.'

'What bastard? What are you talking about?'

'Your baby you fucking imbecile, what do you think I mean?'

Steve's mind raced as he struggled to take on board the enormity of Anthea's words. As he wrestled to form a coherent reply he said exactly the wrong thing.

'Are you sure it's mine?'

Anthea leapt to her feet, screamed and hurled a glass tumbler directly at him. The glass went wide but the whisky inside it splashed across his shoes. 'Get out, get out you fucking animal.'

Steve couldn't take any more. He strode over and squeezed his hands around her throat. The speed of his movement caught her by surprise and she was struggling for breath before she could even reach for his wrists. Steve's eyes went blank as his grip on her windpipe tightened. Anthea tried and failed to loosen his steely grip. She started to gurgle, and her eyes began to bulge.

Suddenly he realised what he was doing and let her drop to the ground gasping. Anthea lay wheezing on the floor. She didn't notice the father of her unborn child open her front door and close it gently four times.

By the time he'd shut it a fifth time Steve Knight was back on the street and walking towards his car. There was only one thing on his mind. He had blocked out all other thoughts. All he could think about was the job.

***

Steve and Roy were parked up in a long row of cars in Fenchurch Street. Butch had stolen the bland Vauxhall Cresta they were sitting in the early hours somewhere north of Hoxton way, and now it was tucked in perfectly with all the other anonymous looking vehicles at the edge of the road. On the opposite side of the street a towering but nondescript building stood. The only thing that made it stand out was the ornate segmental arch above the archway that cut through it.

Steve looked into the rear-view mirror intently, focusing on the traffic coming up the road towards them.

'Are you all right?' asked Roy.

'Of course, mate,' answered Steve from the passenger seat but the tone of his voice told another story.

Roy chose his words carefully.

'You feeling okay about this job, Steve? Y'know, it's a step up from our usual antics. I mean, no one would blame you if you pulled it...'

Steve looked directly at him.

'I have never been more sure about anything in my life, mate. This...this is what I live for. This is what we do...it's all the other shit that gets in the way.'

'Like that bird?'

A flash of anger registered on Steve's face.

'Facing a fifteen stretch is all in a day's work, Royston, dealing with Anthea...well, that's uncharted territory.'

'I know she's a bit of a looker mate but there's plenty of spare around,' Roy said carefully. He suspected he was prodding an open wound. 'Why don't you give her the old Spanish Archer?'

The car went quiet again.

'If only it was that easy...'

Steve stared absent-mindedly into the distance, adding 'If only she weren't up...'

'What? Up the fuckin' duff?'

Steve nodded. 'Though the amount of gear she gets through I dunno if the poor little sod will be born or just float out 'er Jack and Danny on a big green cloud of puff...'

'Does Kenny...?'

A sudden low rumble in the road beside them snapped both men back to attention. It was the Austin J2 van they had been waiting for and it was slowing down as it approached the archway.

'991 RPH' said Steve under his breath as he scanned the vehicle's number plate and double-checked the small scrap of paper in his hand. 'That's the one, Roy, that's the baby! We're fucking on. Get ready.'

Steve glanced at his watch. The van was bang on schedule.

For the next five minutes they sat in silence with their car engine running, although it felt a lot longer. Both men did what they could to deal with the adrenalin that surged up inside them.

Eventually the van reappeared through the archway and out onto the road. Same licence plate. No messing. As quickly but smoothly as he could, Roy pulled out and got behind the van as it headed towards the A40. The Knights' grand plan was literally in motion.

***

Kenny's voice cut across the tense silence in the van as it sat at the side of Holborn Circus.

'You dirty bastard,' he hissed as he scrunched up his nose. 'That smells like fucking death.'

Once the odour that was drifting throughout the vehicle had been brought to everyone's attention the howls of protest began.

'That's an old man fart for sure,' exclaimed Butch.

'Cheeky bastard,' said Ronnie, as he rolled his new balaclava through his fingers. 'Nothing wrong with my guts, son. I was brought up on straight, healthy British nosh. Boiled beef and carrots.'

'Somebody's fucking pants must be boiling,' gasped Arthur. 'What a stench.'

Ronnie smiled and sang to himself quietly: *'Boiled beef and carrots, boiled beef and carrots. That's the stuff for your darbykell, makes you fat and it keeps you well! Don't live like vegetarians, on the stuff they give to parrots, from morn till night, blow out your kite on boiled beef and carrots.'*

'We sung that different in the Kate Karney,' laughed Butch, who sang loudly '*That's the stuff for your darby kell, makes you fart and fuck like hell...*'

'Keep it down for fuck's sake,' said Kenny as he peered down at his watch. 'They should be with that van now. Ten minutes chaps, no more, sit tight.'

Arthur was peering out of the van's back window. 'I can see those fucking peanuts heading up the street. There's fucking loads of them, I think they've brought all their mates for a day out.'

'Good stuff,' said Kenny as he looked ahead for any potential obstacles. 'Nearly there, lads.'

***

Steve and Roy were less than half a mile from the rest of the firm when a police car joined the flow of traffic and slipped onto the road just in front of the security van.

'Jesus Christ,' exclaimed Roy. 'Is that an escort?'

'Nah, mate, definitely an Austin. Don't panic "Captain Mainwaring". Just keep behind them, nice and easy. They've never had company on any of the other runs we've observed. It's just a coincidence.'

'A bit like the coincidence of my fuckin' pants just going a shade browner. Fucking coincidence...'

Roy kept their car moving evenly behind the target. Suddenly the police car screeched off to the left without indicating and drove off at speed. Roy and Steve breathed a collective sigh of relief. Sweet. As they approached the end of Newgate Street they pulled down their balaclavas. As soon as their car rolled into Holborn Circus, Steve rolled down the passenger window and hurled a smoke grenade over the car roof straight into the path of a group of protesters. The timing could not have been more exquisite. 'Ho, Ho, Ho Chi Min,' they chanted. 'We shall fight, we shall win!'

***

Harry Prince stood in front of his mob and sneered at the crowd that was walking down Charterhouse Street repeating their silly little slogans, waving placards and trying to ignore the burning glares from him and his mates. God he hated hippies. Scruffy, stuck-up, mummy's boy snobs and do-gooders...this marching rabble was full of them. He didn't even know what they were banging on about. Their signs and banners seemed to advertise an unconnected message of peace, socialism, CND and shit about the Vietnam war. "Make love, not war" read one placard held aloft by a fit student bird.

'The fuckin' women's movement,' he muttered.

'I wouldn't mind checking out that woman's movement,' said his pal Mickey Mohan.

'Yeah but you'd have to hose her down first'.

'And find her a bra to burn.'

'Probably get it to gobble you off just for a bit of peace and quiet.'

'There are fucking loads of them though, H. Look, they've filled the road and seeped onto the sodding pavements.'

'Not scared are you, Mick?'

'Not one bit. As soon as we start putting the boot in then most of them will disappear like shit off a hot, shiny shovel. Great idea this, Harry, beats the hell out of a barney with Millwall.'

'Yeah, great ideas... I'm full of 'em,' laughed Harry who patted the pocket of his Sta-Prest trousers just to feel the wad of cash that the Knights had given him as an advance for today's job.

It was easy money and he would share some of it out with his mob when the deed was done. Some of the hangers-on that he had roped in to swell their numbers might even get a taste if they put a good shift in. The rest of the dough would keep him in reggae records until Christmas.

Harry reached into his Harrington jacket for the reassuring item that nestled in the deep inside pocket. His weapon of choice was a footlong length of thick rubber hose filled with lead shot and sealed at both ends with heavy-duty waterproof tape – custom made for aggro.

***

A few hundred yards away another demo started to assemble near Ludgate Circus. Militant London dockers had decided to stage an unofficial protest against a firm called Carmen Franco Imports that had recently opened up at the southern end of Hatton Garden. The firm had made no attempt to hide its clear and outrageous links to General Franco's despised fascist regime in Spain. It was opened in his daughter's name for God's sake.

Or so it appeared...

In fact the building had been standing empty for some time. Steve Knight had paid the Spicer brothers to erect a false shop name, stick a freshly engraved brass plaque by the front door and hang heavy drapes behind the windows.

There was nothing more guaranteed to piss off a Communist docker than fascist Spain, and Rick Prevost had rightly earned himself a couple of hundred quid for the small matter of getting the lads mobilised. Not only did their wildcat action add to the chaos. It also shut off police access to Hatton Garden from Holborn entirely. This was the final piece of his recipe for inner city chaos. "Arise ye workers" indeed.

***

The Shacklewell skins had been well drilled for today's blood sport and as soon as Harry Prince saw the thick plume of white smoke begin rising at the front of the demo, he shouted his command and they moved forward as one.

Harry struck out at every geezer he could reach but in his wild frenzy, a few soppy birds got in his way. Soon his cosh was soaked in Commie claret, but he kept on swinging. He barely heard the sound of loud bangs and screeching tyres further down the road.

***

As the security van sped forward to avoid the bedlam of the peace march, the driver, Dan Hancock, took his eyes off the road for a second to peer in his wing mirror at the growing conflict behind him. He failed to see the figure in a boiler suit and balaclava who materialised from between two parked cars and rolled a black strip on the road in front of him. By the time Hancock noticed the myriad of sharp metal points on the ground, it was too late to do anything except run straight over them.

Instinctively he put his foot on the brake and the vehicle shuddered to a halt. Butch darted out in front of the stationery vehicle and aimed a thin iron rod directly at the windscreen grill. It pierced through the metal mesh and shattered the glass behind it before slicing across the driver's arm and coming to rest in the thick upholstery of the front seat.

Butch leapt onto the front bumper and jammed the barrel of a pistol through the grill.

'Touch that radio and you are fucking dead,' he screamed.

The driver held up his hands in meek surrender.

Meanwhile, Steve had spun his stolen car round in a furious handbrake turn and it was now resting across both lanes of the road. He dropped two more smoke grenades then moved swiftly out of the car to help Ronnie remove his explosive equipment from the back of the vehicle. Roy ran to the security van and punctured both back tyres with a metal spike. Kenny and Butch took their positions a few feet away from each side of the security van's back door and they scanned the area around them for likely troublemakers, brandishing their shotguns in plain view of any potential heroes.

With Butch still levelling his gun at the driver and Roy keeping watch on the road in front of them, Steve hovered over Ronnie as the old man attached the C3 to the van's back door and fiddled with the detonator switch.

'You all right there, pop?' Steve shouted down at the old man.

'Getting there, son,' answered Ronnie. He sounded surprisingly calm. 'Piece of piss, Steven. At least I ain't got no Jerries shooting at me arse.'

A few seconds later Ronnie stood up.

'I think we better step back a little.'

'Heads down,' Steve screamed.

The gang all moved away from the van swiftly and took shelter down behind the cars nearest to them. Ronnie was still jogging away as he clicked the switch and a massive explosion shook the street and threw him forward onto the pavement.

Many of the car windscreens in the immediate area were shattered, including the Knights' getaway van. A few shop windows also blew, adding the shrill ringing of their alarm systems to the general melee.

The detonation had been deafening and disorientating but the Knight firm shook it off just in time to see two guards emerge from smoke at the back of the van, both swinging truncheons blindly in front of them. Kenny and Arthur leapt forward and knocked them to the ground with the butts of their shotguns.

The guards lay unconscious on the ground but just through the dwindling smoke, Kenny spotted a bizarre city gent type running straight towards them. Tall and skinny, he looked like young Charles Hawtrey from the *Carry On* films. He was also brandishing his umbrella like a weapon. Kenny did not hesitate. He took aim and unloaded a single cartridge of shots straight at the would-be hero's legs.

The man fell forward onto the ground screaming as blood poured from his upper right thigh and soaked his pinstripe strides from the inside out. Butch put an end to his wailing with a heavy boot to his face.

Kenny's shotgun roared again as a warning and demolished the large plate glass window of the only nearby shop that had escaped the shockwave of the explosion.

'Let's get this done sharpish,' Kenny screamed, as Steve helped Ronnie move his equipment into the back of the van. There was a small bang as the inner cage door of the van was opened with a crowbar then the wait began.

***

Harry Prince and his skinhead mob were still striking out furiously at the protesters, most of whom had never been in a fight before, poor darlings. Certainly they had never felt the connecting crack of a knuckleduster or even witnessed violence this demented in real life.

Hundreds of the hairies had managed to flee past the brutal ruckus but after hearing a loud bang in the distance ahead of them, and what sounded like shotgun blasts, the escaping students had no choice except to turn back and retrace their steps towards the skins. It was like a herd of sheep running into an abattoir or a shoal of fish swimming towards a school of sharks.

The sheer size of the returning stampede split the Shacklewell mob apart and soon it became apparent that even though most of the hippies were fleeing in terror, a hard core of demonstrators – Trotskyists of the rival International Socialists and the International Marxist Group – were willing to fight using their placards and belts as weapons.

'Stand firm!' screamed Harry, taking out a man in a Gay Liberation Front T-shirt with a swift right-hander.

The Shacklewell skins regrouped. Two packs of Reds were coming at them, swinging their makeshift weaponry.

'Get these cunts!' yelled Harry as both sides clashed together in a violent melee oblivious to the robbery only yards in front of them.

His sister Brenda was the first into the fray. She grabbed a protestor by his long hair, jerked his placard out of his hand and brought it up sharply between his legs. Her mate Helen took hold of the other end of it and for a moment, before it broke, the women lifted him clean off the floor.

There he was, as Steve noted later, 'hoist by his own placard'.

When it snapped and the protestor fell to the floor, Brenda booted him in the head and left him unconscious.

'Sisters stop!' shouted a well-spoken female protestor. 'We're all on the same side here...'

'It's useless,' Charlotte Clifton told her fellow lecturer. 'They're in the grip of false consciousness...'

'Sisters,' cried her friend again. At which point Brenda headbutted her unconscious and Helen put her monkey boot into Charlotte's retreating backside.

It didn't all go the skinheads' way. The placard wood was light but when Mickey Mahon got whacked around the face with one it hurt like buggery. He hit back with a vicious steel-capped boot to his hippy attacker's knee which put him out of the action. But for the most part, the skins won the day.

The familiar sound of police sirens could be heard in the distance as more smoke bombs were scattered on the road behind the security van but no one in the battle seemed to care.

The Knight brothers were getting their money's worth from Harry Prince and his platoon of peanuts.

***

Two squad cars raced up New Fetter Lane to reach the reported carnage only to find the main road closed off by around 180 dockers who were staging a sit-down right across Holborn.

In the middle was a banner proclaiming "Royal Group Of Docks Shop Stewards Committee". In front of it, standing, was Ricky Prevost who was singing songs from the Spanish Civil War over a megaphone: *'There's a valley in Spain called Jamara, it's a valley we all know so well. It was there that we gave of our manhood, and most of our brave comrades fell...'*

Ahead of them PC Laurence Pryor saw an angry driver get out of his Singer Chamois and remonstrate with the protestors. He watched aghast as four burly dockers stood up without a word and turned the car upside down.

***

Kenny Knight looked over at Arthur who was nervously tickling the trigger of his shotgun. 'What the fuck's going on in there?' he screamed.

Steve's head popped out of the back of the van.

'Nearly there, just hold on.'

'For fuck's sake,' yelled Butch from his position at the front of the van. 'Tell the old cunt to get a move on, I can hear the Old Bill.'

'Just hold on,' screamed Steve, as he jumped back onto the street. 'Steady, just a few more seconds.'

Right on cue Ronnie tumbled from the van with surprising speed. He had the detonator in his hand.

'Right, chaps,' he said calmly, 'I think we'd better step back again.'

As soon as they were all a good distance away he pressed the button in his hand and a low thud shook the van almost onto just its left side wheels. The van rocked for a few moments more as white smoke poured out of the gap where the back door had been.

Steve waited ten seconds for the smoke to clear then he jumped back into the van. Seconds later there was a scream of delight then he emerged into the street carrying a smouldering, but still intact briefcase. Roy was already back in their getaway van, revving the engine as he cleared the remaining glass from the shattered windscreen with his leather gloved hand.

The first police car on the scene finally broke through the battling demo crowd. It came from the north end as the cops were still waiting for mounted officers to clear the dockers to the south.

The vehicle came to a halt at Steve's dumped vehicle. The police driver pushed his bumper against the abandoned motor and attempted to nudge it out of the way.

Kenny fired both barrels of his weapon in his direction, as a warning. The cops evacuated and retreated. Kenny's shot burst through the windows of Steve's dumped vehicle and peppered the bonnet of the cop car.

'If I'd have known we would be having this much fun I could have improvised a mortar and an RPG,' chuckled Ronnie.

Arthur hugged the old soldier like a lost relative.

As soon as Kenny Knight was in the van with the rest of them Roy threw off the handbrake and accelerated forward, but the van thudded to a halt before he was completely clear of the parking space they had been in.

The security van had come to rest just a few feet too close to them to allow clear access to the road.

'What the fuck's going on?' screamed Kenny as white specks of spittle flew from his mouth, forcing their way through the mouthpiece of his balaclava.

Three more police cars had pulled up behind the vehicle he had just shot at and the ringing tone of other emergency vehicles was coming from Hatton Garden.

'Get us out of here.'

'It's that fucking van,' yelled Roy. 'We'll have to move it.'

'For fuck's sake!'

'Fucking cunting thing.'

Foul oaths filled the air as all of the passengers except Ronnie leapt out of the back of the van back into the scene of the crime, and put their shoulders against the passenger side door of the security van. The heavy beast creaked and the steel rims of its punctured wheels screeched slowly across the tarmac.

Roy edged the getaway van forward until it finally slipped past the stricken Austin. The firm leapt back into the van. But the police had charged out of their cars, truncheons in hands, and were almost within touching distance.

Roy accelerated forward and the cold wind blew tiny particles of shattered windscreen into his face. The balaclava protected him and he squeezed his eyes tight to prevent bits of dusty glass getting into them.

'There's no one behind us,' yelled Kenny. 'Keep fucking moving, Roy.'

Kenny's words immediately came back to haunt him as a police car emerged from Furnival Street and locked into position to their rear. Roy moved forward relentlessly, ignoring red lights and pedestrian crossings but the cop car kept on his tail.

'What the fuck are we going to do?' screamed Roy as he pushed the van to its limits up Grays Inn Road. 'This geezer is right up my arse.'

Kenny clicked back both hammers on his shotgun and flicked his head towards the back door handle as he looked at Steve.

'We'll slow down, you open the door brother and I'll blast the bastard.'

'We could still lose him,' said Steve.

'In this old heap and all of us in the back?' hissed Kenny. 'Fuck that. Get ready.'

Steve moved into position at the back door. Whatever it took had to be done and he did not have a better idea. They had all come too far to fuck things up now. Kenny gripped his weapon and nodded to his brother.

'Slow down, Roy,' Steve shouted as he gripped the handle of the back door. 'Let's get rid of this tail.'

As Steve threw open the door and Kenny tensed up ready to shoot, the brothers were shocked to find that the police car was almost touching the back bumper of the van. Kenny took aim squarely at the driver. Suddenly a small car shot from a side street and hit the coppers' vehicle squarely on the passenger door.

The police car was forced violently into the path of a lamp post where its journey ended.

From the open back door Kenny could see that the pursuit vehicle's shattered windscreen was stained with two large patches of blood.

A dishevelled figure emerged from the car that had hit them and ran shakily back up to the side street which they had emerged from.

Kenny looked over to Steve and let out a loud whooping laugh. 'Did you see that? A Mini! A fucking Mini taking the Old Bill out of the picture! Is that one of your mates?'

'I have no fucking idea,' said Steve through gritted teeth as he pulled the back door closed. 'Notch that one up to dumb luck. Roy, what's happening out there, mate?'

Roy stared at the cracked wing mirror on his side. 'Nothing behind us, Stevie boy. Looks all clear.'

'Okay,' shouted Steve. 'The warehouse ain't far ahead. We get in, offload then get the fuck out of town. Are you all ready?'

A chorus of 'fuck yeah!'s filled the vehicle. Steve stared forward, willing the distance between the van and its destination to disappear. As another few hundred yards passed without even the distant sound of a siren, he started to smile slightly.

'I told you this would work, Kenny,' Steve said quietly, but with a maniacal grin on his face. 'I fucking told you.'

***

As they approached the warehouse Steve had split the contents of the briefcase into two sports bags and given one to Kenny. Steve opened one of the black velvet pouches. Inside it were four immaculately folded packs of crisp white paper. The first one he inspected contained a small pile of what looked like little grey stones.

Fuck yes. This package alone was enough to retire to Spain on. If all of the other packs were like this then they had a small fortune on their hands...

Inside the warehouse, they swapped vehicles. Kenny gripped his bag firmly and got in the passenger seat of one of the stolen cars alongside Arthur. Butch set light to their getaway van inside the factory then jumped in the car with Kenny and Arthur.

Steve clutched his bag tightly, as Roy accelerated to get him and Ronnie away before the van's petrol tank caught light and set the whole building ablaze. As the smoke rose in the distance behind them, both cars split off in different directions.

***

Three months later.

Steve Knight stood on the front step of his Old Street flat and waited patiently in the crisp winter air. His deep tanned skin clashed sharply with his black suit, immaculate white shirt and black tie. In the grey, cold light of morning his healthy complexion stood out as a few pasty-faced pedestrians shuffled past in thick scarves guarding against the frosty atmosphere. Steve felt the chill himself and was pondering whether to return to his penthouse and retrieve an overcoat when an Aston Martin DB6 skidded to a halt on the pavement in front of him. The electric window on its passenger side slid down with a hum and a voice from inside the car boomed out into the street.

'"El Presidente", nice to have you back in Blighty. You look like a fucking Arab, get in or you'll scare the neighbours.'

Steve got into the car and Kenny shot off into the street before he had the door fully closed.

'Good to see you, bruv,' said Kenny with a grin as he powered his car through the Sunday morning streets. 'We thought some Spanish sort must have kidnapped you and kept you as a sex slave in her villa. When did you get back?'

'I flew into Heathrow late last night.'

'Well I'm sure Ronnie's family will appreciate the gesture. Poor old bastard. Still, he went out with a bang though, eh?'

'What happened?'

'Heart attack. Died in his armchair at home while listening to the football results. He'd been pushing the boat out over the past few months though,' Kenny laughed quietly. 'Since he got his share of the job he was over at Aphrodite's every bleedin' day working his way through the girls. He was "stiff as a poker" they were saying. Dirty old bastard.'

Steve tapped the rich, polished mahogany of the dashboard. 'I see you've been splashing out as well. Very tasty.'

'Well, I had to treat myself, Steven, and we can't all spend our cut lying on a beach noshing fucking paella all day.'

There was silence between the brothers for a moment as Steve struggled to find the right words.

'I had to get away, Kenny, you know that don't you? What with...' his words drifted off into the atmosphere.

'I know, mate, you don't need to explain anything to me. But you're back now, we'll sort things out. You've got unexpected responsibilities. It's just a pity we have to deal with that twisted bitch.'

Steve ignored the mention of Anthea. Even in his current relaxed state the mere thought of her was liable to bring back enough memories to kick-start all his own anxieties. He would get Roy to find out when the baby was due and weigh her out the necessary...all in good time...

'There was another one and all. Bird called Charlotte? Kept ringing up the club. I told her you'd fucked off to the States doing security for the Kinks.'

Steve laughed. 'That would've been a blast but Spain worked for me, bruv. It's beautiful over there, Kenny, beautiful. I could stay over there in Marbella for good, mate, no problem.'

'Well you ain't emigrating yet, mate. We need you here, the business is fucking booming. That money we invested in those clubs up West is paying off big time and Butch and Arthur have set up that little team you suggested to collect all of our old protection payments. The cash is fucking flooding in and we are barely breaking a sweat. Arthur was complaining that he hasn't had to break anyone's nose in over two months.'

Steve smiled and felt a pang of guilt that he had not seen any of the firm for twelve long weeks. He was looking forward to seeing them all even though it had taken Ronnie's funeral to bring them all together.

'Has there been any more trouble from the Old Bill?' he asked.

'Nah!' Kenny roared dismissively. 'They've got fuck all on us. After that first shakedown they never bothered us. Stupid bastards. What did they expect? Did they think we'd be sitting around our gaffs with a pile of uncut sparklers sitting on top of the TV?'

'You don't think you driving about in this thing is going to raise any suspicions?' said Steve carefully.

Kenny snorted with derision. 'I'm a businessman ain't I? We're moving into a new decade soon. Like you always say, the working class are on the up. We're Knight Brothers Incorporated now mate, so fuck the lot of them.'

Steve smiled as Kenny sped through the gates of the crematorium.

***

The Dover Castle was packed out, mostly with old folk who had suddenly remembered what close friends of Ronnie's they had been when the chance of a free drink and a poke at a pukka fuck-off buffet was on the cards. The only missing regular was Eddie Morgan who had excused himself an hour before, complaining of stomach cramp.

At the very back of the bar the Knight firm sat at a table around a large bottle of 12-year-old Islay Single Malt.

'To Ronnie,' said Kenny as they all raised a glass into the air.

'Poor old sod,' said Butch, 'But at least it gave Arthur another opportunity to drag his undertaker's suit out of moth balls.'

'Cheeky cunt,' mumbled Arthur. 'I'm not blowing all my dough on fancy gear that's in fashion one week and out of it the next. I've got...classic style.'

'Yeah, classic for 1948, you miserable bastard,' laughed Roy.

Some of the guests at the wake looked over to the noisy table at the back but quickly remembered who was footing the bill for the booze and food so they kept their disdain to themselves.

A barmaid approached the table.

'Mr Knight,' she said to Steve.

'Yes, love?'

'There's a gentleman who needs to see you in the back yard. He says you know him. Name of Rodney Huggins.'

'Filth!' hollered Kenny. 'Here? On a day like this? Have they no respect?'

'He says to say it's unofficial but of definite interest, Mr Knight. And that he'll be brief.'

Steve shrugged. 'What have I got to lose?'

Huggins sat alone in the yard, sipping a pint of milk stout. He was wearing a grey Gannex mac.

'Very Harold Wilson,' quipped Steve. 'All you need is a pipe and you'd proper look the part, Rodney.'

'Ah, Steven...long time...beautiful tan.' Huggins started to rise.

'Don't get up.'

'I won't keep you.' The detective looked around furtively. 'I just wanted to have a word with you about Patrick McVey.'

'Oh yes?'

'And the night you stabbed him to death.'

Steve waited a beat and replied slowly 'I have no idea what you're on about, officer. If you've paid your snout for that little nugget they've had you over, my son.'

'I'm afraid I'm not dealing in gossip, Steve. I have a number of local eye-witnesses who can place you at a party where a fight took place. I have another local eye-witness who says that he saw the street fight that ended Patrick McVey's life and saw you plunging him. But better than that, Steve, I have the murder weapon, a dagger which I personally found on the banks of the canal where you chucked it that night, but not quite hard enough as it happens. You won't be surprised to hear that the fingerprints on the weapon have been perfectly preserved. And you and I know that they are also a perfect match with your own.'

Steve said nothing. His face was impassive but his mind was doing somersaults.

'Please don't think about scarpering, Steve. I have uniform front and back. You won't get as far as the Co-Op let alone the Costa. We have enough on you to send you down for a 15-stretch. And I can throw that little shop-girl, Elizabeth Davis, into the frame as an accessory, if you play up. You like her don't you, Steve? So much nicer than that West End bint.'

'So you've been doing your homework, Mr Huggins. Well done. But don't forget, I'm a very wealthy man.'

'Ah yes. I hear you're partial to a bit of Bassey. "Diamonds Are Forever" and all that.'

Steve refused to bite. 'My books will show that I've made my dough the hard way through honest business enterprises, and I have enough of it to pay for the best brief money can buy.'

'Yeah, Steve, but you're bang to rights on this one, son. Why waste your life behind bars when...'

'When?'

'I can be a very accommodating man...'

'Yeah I've heard. How much?'

'A monkey, Steve. One a week, in cash, in my bin. That's not much to pay to keep your liberty is it?'

'Two large a month?'

'Precisely that. Deal?'

Steve hesitated, but only for a moment. 'Deal,' he said solemnly.

'And don't go thinking about having Arthur or Butch get shot of me for a lot less, Steve, because the blade with your dabs is tucked away in a nice safety deposit which my brief has instructions to open in the event of my imminent death either by design or misadventure.'

'I said deal.'

'Shake?'

'I'd rather not.'

Steve walked back into the pub furious at his own stupidity. Someone close to the firm, maybe someone there today, knew enough to point bent plod in the right direction. The grass would be found and dealt with. But if he had disposed of the knife properly, Rodney Huggins wouldn't have a case. He'd saddled himself with a monkey on his back; and a monkey a week out of his skyrocket. *Fuck it.*

It was a problem, but not, he was sure, an insoluble one.

At the back table, the lads were still laughing and drinking.

'What was that about?' asked Kenny.

'Tell you later, bruv. Nothing to fret about.'

Steve picked up his pint and looked around the bar. It was a fairly uniform collection of rough-looking old-timers but there was little Lizzie Davies sitting in the corner looking as fresh as a daisy in her dark, turquoise mini-dress.

He nodded towards her and raised his glass. Lizzie's face lit up like a Christmas tree. God she was beautiful when she smiled. He winked and she looked away in embarrassment. Steve felt a warm glow inside as he remembered the day they had spent together shopping. How long ago had that been? Too long that was for sure.

Roy's fist bumped against his arm playfully and snapped him out of his daydream.

'Oi, Omar Sharif,' he quipped. 'How about a few words for the lads now that you are back in God's own country?'

Steve grinned and turned his attention back to his mates around the table.

'What do you want me to say?' he asked with a smile.

'Say what you feel, bruv,' said Kenny with a surprising tenderness. 'It's been a rough old couple of years but it's all paid off now.'

Steve took the opportunity to refill everyone's shot glass with malt whisky while he pondered on his toast. No one spoke. He cleared his throat.

'I'd just like to say on behalf of my brother and I, how much we value...' he began.

'Blah, blah,' interrupted Roy. 'It's not a fucking wedding. Just say what you really mean you boring cunt.'

Steve laughed then paused again before he spoke. 'Okay, you shower of shitty-arsed bastards, here it is, straight from the 'eart. This is for all of us. Things are changing in this great city of ours every day and we are right at the forefront of it all. We are the vanguard and we're Londoners, real Londoners, born and bred. And so it's only right that we are the ones who benefit from those changes.'

He raised his glass high into the air. 'This is to our way – and fuck everyone else.'

'To our way!' four voices answered as one.

'And fuck everyone else!' shouted Kenny. 'Fuck 'em all.'

'All or nothing!' Steve added.

'ALL OR NOTHING!' came the heart-felt reply.

***

The lock-in lasted until daybreak when one by one the Knights' firm staggered bleary-eyed into the unwelcome sunshine. Not a single one of them noticed the photographer taking their mug shots from an old Ford Anglia thirty yards or so up the road. Metin Demirer usually did wedding snaps but he was happy to do his brother's friend, Kemal, this small favour even if it meant staying up all night. He always tipped so well.

To be continued.

END